Though Mountains
FALL

Though Mountains FALL

DALE CRAMER

BETHANY HOUSE PUBLISHERS
a division of Baker Publishing Group
Minneapolis, Minnesota

© 2013 by Dale Cramer

Published by Bethany House Publishers
11400 Hampshire Avenue South
Bloomington, Minnesota 55438
www.bethanyhouse.com

Bethany House Publishers is a division of
Baker Publishing Group, Grand Rapids, Michigan

Printed in the United States of America

Library of Congress Cataloging-in-Publication Data
Cramer, W. Dale.
    Though mountains fall / Dale Cramer.
        p.   cm. — (The daughters of Caleb Bender ; 3)
    Summary: "This epic trilogy concludes with the Amish community's pacifism
sorely tested by attacking bandits and the equally cruel Mexican troops sent to
defend the Amish"—Provided by publisher.
    ISBN 978-0-7642-0840-9 (pbk.)
    1. Amish—Fiction. 2. Christian fiction. I. Title.
PS3603.R37T48 2013
813'.6—dc23   2012034483

Scripture quotations are from the King James Version of the Bible.

Cover design by Lookout Design, Inc.
Cover photography by Mike Habermann Photography, LLC

Author is represented by Books & Such Literary Agency

13   14   15   16   17   18   19   7 6 5 4 3 2 1

For Ma and Pa

Books by Dale Cramer

Sutter's Cross
Bad Ground
Levi's Will
Summer of Light

THE DAUGHTERS OF CALEB BENDER

Paradise Valley
The Captive Heart
Though Mountains Fall

THE FAMILY OF CALEB AND MARTHA BENDER
SPRING, 1925

ADA, 30   *Unmarried; mentally challenged*

MARY, 27   *Husband, Ezra Raber (children: Samuel, 8;*
Paul, 7; twins Amanda & Amos, 2)

LIZZIE, 26   *In Ohio with husband, Andy Shetler (5 children)*

AMOS &   *Twins, deceased*
AARON

EMMA, 23   *Husband, Levi Mullet (children: Mose, 3;*
Clara, 2; Will, 1)

MIRIAM, 22

HARVEY, 21

RACHEL, 19

LEAH, 17

BARBARA, 15

Chapter 1

Caleb Bender spent the day riding a mule-drawn planter, putting down row after row of seeds, and there was nothing in the world he loved quite the same way. Like any Amish farmer Caleb was deeply attuned to the seasons and found a unique joy in each of them, but springtime was his favorite. It was a time of awakening, a time when he could feel the promise of *Gott* in the earth and a sense of divine purpose in the sinews of his callused hands. A time of hope. Planting a field was a prayer, an act of purest faith.

Stopping at the end of a row Caleb took off his wide-brimmed hat, wiped his bald head with a shirtsleeve and took a moment to survey his valley, a five-thousand-acre oval of prime pasture high up in the Sierra Madres of northeast Mexico. The valley wasn't entirely his, but he took a kind of proprietary pride in it because he and his family had been the first to come here three years ago, in the spring of 1922.

It was the kind of spectacular day that only happened a few times each spring, a sky so deep blue it was almost painful, a light breeze blowing, a little chilly in the morning yet warming in the afternoon. The shadow of a hawk passed over him, cruising on the wind, drawing Caleb's gaze to the western mountains where he'd been standing when he first set eyes on Paradise Valley. He felt it even now, the thrill of hope in that first vision. It really did look like paradise, lush green bottomland bracketed by long, low ridges on the north and south. Caleb and his family were pioneers of sorts—advance scouts for a new settlement. They had dug themselves into the valley, shaping earth and straw into bricks and building houses with their bare hands. Even their barns and buggy sheds were finished by the time the Hershbergers and Shrocks came the following year.

The main group arrived last summer, and a big industrious colony of Amish all pitched in, making adobe, cutting timber, erecting houses and barns. More families arrived, and now there were ten homes scattered along the base of the ridges on both sides of the valley, new tin roofs gleaming in the afternoon sun, smoke trailing peacefully from chimneys as wives and daughters cooked dinner. There were new barns and fences to corral the livestock, and everywhere he looked Caleb saw bearded men in flat-brimmed hats and suspenders working teams of sturdy horses, plowing and planting fields. In the coming weeks the industry of ten Amish families would turn Paradise Valley into a quilt of bright green from one end to the other.

Across his lane, in the field down nearest the main road, his son Harvey and a team of four huge Belgian draft horses pulled a wide harrow, the long row of steel disks shiny from use, smoothing fresh-plowed earth. At nineteen, Harvey was his only son now. There had once been two boys older than Harvey, twins, but Amos fell victim to the flu epidemic of 1918, and Aaron died last August on the road back from Agua Nueva at the hands of the bandit El Pantera. His death was a crippling blow to Caleb, and a pall hung over the entire family still.

Along the far edge of the same field where Harvey was plowing, Domingo Zapara rode behind another corn planter just like the one Caleb was driving. A Mexican native, half mestizo and half Nahua, Domingo was a striking figure, tall and proud. He wore his black hair long and loose, hanging past his shoulders under a wide-brimmed Amish hat that once belonged to Caleb. Even the hat had a heroic story behind it.

More than just a trusted hired hand, Domingo had become almost like a son to him. Reared by his father to be a Nahua warrior, Domingo wouldn't hesitate to put his own life in danger to protect Caleb's family from bandits. Late last summer, after the confrontation in which Aaron was killed, it was Domingo who, along with Jake Weaver, tracked El Pantera north to his stronghold at Diablo Canyon and rescued Rachel, Caleb's nineteen-year-old daughter. It was a debt Caleb knew he could never repay.

Domingo's planter stopped halfway down a row and he craned his neck. He appeared to be watching something in the road behind Caleb, and when he climbed off the seat of the planter and started trotting across the field toward the driveway Caleb looked over his shoulder to see what was happening.

A solitary rider approached from the west on a painted pony, cantering along in no particular hurry and not looking like much of a threat. His sombrero hung behind his neck and there was a bandolier of bullets bouncing against his chest. A bandit.

As the rider slowed and turned in, Caleb climbed off his planter and met Domingo at the lane. The two of them stood shoulder to shoulder, watching, waiting.

"I know this one," Domingo said. "Alvarez. He rides with El Pantera, but my father trusted him."

"I know him, too," Caleb said. "He has been here before."

The bandit stopped his horse in front of them and dismounted. He was a dark, leather-faced man with a huge mustache and a thick head of coal black hair. The butts of two cross-draw pistols peeked out the front of his jacket.

"*Hola*, Domingo!" he said, thumping Domingo's chest like an old friend. "You have become a *man* since I saw you last! It has been a long time, my young friend."

"*Sí*, Alvarez." Domingo nodded. "The last time we met was before my father fell at Zacatecas." His hand drew the sign of the cross on his chest as he said this, and Caleb made a mental note of it. It was the first time he had ever seen his young friend use any kind of Christian gesture.

"A good man," the bandit said solemnly. He then looked at Caleb and added, "Perhaps you do not remember, *señor*, but I have been here before."

"*Sí*, I thought you looked familiar. You are welcome to water your horse, and if you're hungry—"

"*Gracias*, but no. I will let the horse drink, and then I must be on my way."

As the three of them walked up toward the trough by the windmill the bandit said, "It is no accident that I stopped here today. I bring news, and it concerns both of you."

Domingo eyed him cautiously. "News of El Pantera?" It seemed to Caleb that Domingo always knew what was coming.

Alvarez nodded. "Two days ago I stopped for the night in Diablo Canyon. The men in the bunkhouse were full of talk about a young whelp who turned back El Pantera and five of his best men in the pass at El Ojo." He grinned at Domingo, and his fingers curled into a fist as he added, "It seems the blood of Ehekatl flows *strong* in his son's veins."

Domingo shrugged. "It was a narrow pass. A child could have held it."

"But a child would not have broken half the bones in El Pantera's body, would he?"

12

"So El Pantera is still alive?" Locked in a fight to the death, Domingo and the bandit leader had fallen together from a cliff. The fall had nearly killed Domingo, but the fate of El Pantera remained a mystery. Until now.

"Sí, he lives," the bandit said, "but he is not the same man. His left arm was so badly shattered he has lost the use of the hand, and he has only recently begun to ride a horse again. They say he is half crazy with rage, and he swears revenge."

"Against me?"

Alvarez glanced at Caleb. "Sí. And against your friends, too. There are already twenty men in his camp, and more are coming. He wanted me to stay, but I told him I had to go to San Luis Potosi for my brother's wedding." A casual shrug. "I don't have a brother. I only came here to warn you."

Caleb couldn't resist asking. "Why?"

The bandit's eyes smiled, though his mouth was completely hidden behind his mustache. "Because Domingo's father was my friend, and because you treated me and my men with respect, señor. You gave us bread, watered our horses and talked to us like men, so I wanted to warn you of the storm that is brewing. If I were you I would flee. And say nothing of this meeting. . . . If El Pantera learns I was here, he will kill my whole family."

"This is bad news indeed," Caleb said. "When do you think he will come?"

"I'm not sure. It will be a little while before he is strong enough to ride so far, but he *will* come. Three weeks, maybe four—that would be my guess."

"Well, there's not much left for him to steal. With all the newcomers, our winter stores are almost gone."

The bandit shook his head grimly. "You misunderstand me, Señor Bender. El Pantera is not coming here to steal. He is coming to burn and to kill."

Before sundown Miriam went to the barn to do her chores. With her dark complexion and raven hair, Caleb's daughter could have passed for a Mexican if it weren't for the Amish dress and prayer *kapp*. As she dipped a bucket into the feed bin she saw the shadow of someone behind her and spun around, surprised.

Domingo drew her against him and kissed her. Miriam let herself melt into him and kissed him back.

Holding her in his strong arms, he brushed aside a wisp of hair that had escaped her starched white prayer kapp and gazed into her eyes.

"Your mother is doing much better these days," he said softly.

To anyone else it might have seemed an odd thing to say under the circumstances, but Miriam knew what he meant. Mamm had been thrown into a state of mental confusion and despair by Aaron's murder last summer, along with the kidnapping of Rachel and a diphtheria outbreak that claimed the lives of four children in the Paradise Valley colony. And then Miriam disappeared for ten days while she and Kyra tended Domingo's wounds at the abandoned silver mine in Parrot Pass. It was there, alone in a veritable Eden, that Domingo asked Miriam to be his wife. After long deliberation she accepted, on two conditions: he would have to wait, and their betrothal would have to remain secret, for it would have broken her mother. For the last six months Mamm's fragile mental state was the only thing preventing them from being married.

"*Jah*, it has been more than half a year," Miriam answered, meeting his eyes. "Christmas was hard for her with Aaron gone, but since then she has grown stronger, more like her old self. Just this morning she was helping me gather eggs when she slipped and fell. Now, you know what the floor of the chicken coop is like. She soiled her dress, her hands, her kapp, but, Domingo, she was *laughing*. While I was helping her up she laughed like a schoolgirl. It did my heart good." Laying her head against his chest, hearing his strong heartbeat, she said softly, "Perhaps it is time for us to be married."

He nodded. "I must talk to your father first. I have too much respect for Señor Bender to do this behind his back. Everything will change for you now, *Cualnezqui*. Are you sure you want to go ahead?"

Tightening her arms about his waist, she said, "I've never been more sure of anything in my life. I am *yours*, Domingo. I am forever yours."

There was a faint crunching of straw behind Domingo and the shadows deepened. Miriam stepped back hastily and looked around him.

Her sister Rachel stood in the big barn door, the westering sun slanting through, backlighting the red hair along her neck, at the base of her kapp. Rachel's hands covered her mouth and tears welled in her eyes.

"How long have you been standing there?" Miriam asked.

"Long enough." Rachel's eyes flitted back and forth between them. "Miriam . . . you and Domingo are going to *marry?*"

Miriam nodded slowly, moving toward her younger sister, reaching to her.

But Rachel stepped back, keeping her distance.

"How could you not tell me this, Miriam? How could you keep a secret like this? From *me!*"

Miriam shrugged an apology, shaking her head. "Rachel, among the Amish, wedding plans are *always* secret."

"But this is not an Amish wedding!" Rachel cried, glancing at Domingo. "If you marry an outsider it will break our mother's heart! You will be banned, an outcast in your own family. I know

15

how you feel about Domingo, but Miriam, have you considered the consequences?"

"Of course I have—carefully, and with great sorrow," Miriam answered softly. "I know what lies before me if I take this path, but I am twenty-two years old and I know my own heart, my own mind." She put a palm against Domingo's chest and smiled confidently into his eyes. "Gott has brought us together, and though I know our path will be filled with trials, it is *our* path, and together we can face anything."

Rachel was silent for a second. The words that spilled out of her next came quietly but with an unmistakable undercurrent of threat.

"What would Dat say if he knew?"

Miriam was stunned into silence. Before she could find her tongue, Domingo said, "Your father will not know until I choose to tell him." He didn't return Miriam's puzzled glance. His black eyes were locked on Rachel. "Everyone has secrets. Now that you know ours, I think you would do well to keep it."

Rachel stared at him a moment longer, then nodded meekly as her eyes dropped away from him. Without another word, she turned and walked softly out of the barn.

Baffled, Miriam asked, "What was *that* about?"

Domingo shook his head, still staring after Rachel. "You will have to ask your sister. I cannot say."

She knew that tone of voice. There was a point of honor here, somewhere. "Cannot? Or *will* not?"

He shrugged. "For me, one is the same as the other."

Domingo saddled his horse and went home for the day, and a few minutes later Rachel came back into the barn. No matter what else happened, the cows still had to be milked.

Sitting on a three-legged stool Miriam glanced around at her

16

younger sister, wondering what was going through Rachel's mind. She refused to speak, wouldn't even look at Miriam, and yet her eyes betrayed more sorrow than anger. It was puzzling. They were completely alone; why didn't Rachel just speak her mind? They had always been so close, slept in the same bed together all their lives and shared secrets. Now it seemed an impenetrable barrier stood between them, and it broke Miriam's heart.

"Rachel."

No answer. Not even a look.

"Rachel, I'm sorry."

Still no answer, just the steady *rip rip rip* of milk in the pail.

"Rachel, I'm so sorry about keeping this a secret from you. It was just . . . this was a decision I had to make alone, out of my own heart and no one else's. I found a pearl of great price, and I had to decide whether to sacrifice everything for it. The burden was mine alone. There was nothing you could do, and I didn't want to be swayed. Can you understand that?"

Rachel was silent for a long time, but then she took a deep breath and said, "Jah. I know what it is to carry a burden you can't share."

She still wouldn't look at Miriam, but the lines of pain and sorrow etched themselves even deeper in her face and the anger left her entirely. Could it be that something *else* was bothering her? Was it possible Rachel bore a secret of her own—something as earth-shattering as Miriam's secret? Domingo's words came back to her now.

"You will have to ask your sister."

"Rachel, if you have something you want to tell me, you know it is safe with me. You can tell me anything. It couldn't possibly be any worse than—"

"Oh, it can be worse," Rachel said. "A *lot* worse. You have no idea."

17

Miriam's hands stopped milking and she looked around at Rachel. The cow shuffled its feet and let out a soft *moo*. Worse than marrying an outsider? Only one thing sprang to her mind.

"Rachel, you and Jake aren't . . . in *trouble*, are you?" Jake was *the one*, the love of Rachel's life.

"No," Rachel said, instantly and firmly. "*I'm* not, anyway."

"So . . . Jake has done something?"

Rachel was silent for so long Miriam wasn't sure she'd heard the question, but at last she spoke, very quietly.

"He killed a man."

Miriam recoiled, nearly falling backward from her stool. "He did *what?*"

Rachel came and knelt beside her, gripping her arm with both hands, her eyes full of tears. Words spilled out of her, mingled with a great long sob.

"Remember I told you about the bandit who came to me in the middle of the night when I was chained in El Pantera's barn, and Jake pulled him off of me before he could do anything?"

Miriam's head backed away, her eyes wide. "Jah?"

"Jake strangled him with his handcuff chain. The bandit was *dead*, Miriam."

Miriam's hand covered her mouth, shaking. "Oh, my stars! Poor Jake! What must he be going through?"

But Rachel shook her head and pulled away, dabbing at her eyes with a handkerchief.

"He doesn't know. We lied to him, Domingo and me. We both knew the guard was dead, but we told Jake he lived. Jake doesn't know."

"Rachel, you must tell him. His *soul* is in danger."

Rachel's face contorted as she looked up at Miriam and cried, "I can't! They'll send him to Ohio to face the bishop, and then his father will never let him come back. *I'll never see him again!*"

Rachel's future husband, or his soul. An unthinkable choice, perhaps even more difficult than the one Miriam had made. There was nothing she could say. She could understand why Rachel might keep such a burden to herself. It was her choice to make, alone.

Just like her own.

As the sun kissed the western hills Miriam wrapped her arms around Rachel's shoulders. In the dim twilight of an adobe barn in the mountains of Mexico two sisters huddled together against the world, and wept.

Chapter 2

Sitting among a hundred Amish on the second level of her father's barn for church services that Sunday, Miriam felt the kinship of her people more acutely than ever, for she felt the nearness of its loss. Despite a cool morning breeze they flung the doors wide to let in the sunlight while they sang songs from the *Ausbund*, the ancient traditional hymns that welded them together. Caleb gave a short devotional and then read a prayer of thanks from the prayer book. Miriam knew why he chose that particular prayer. Despite grievous losses, her father was indeed grateful for good weather, good neighbors, and for the calm that had reigned over the last six months. There had been no more outbreaks of diphtheria, and the bandits had stayed away. But before he closed the prayer he added his own plea for Gott to send a bishop to Paradise Valley.

This, too, Miriam understood. Everyone knew that without leadership their blossoming community would wither and die. She had already witnessed little differences of opinion over length of hair and width of hat brim, not to mention that the Yutzys, who came from a more liberal district in Geauga County, wore buttons on their clothes. A bishop would work with the men to resolve such differences and restore unity—to a point. Experience had taught her that perfect unity among so many human beings, each with his own needs and wants and fears and opinions, was elusive.

She bowed her head and uttered a prayer of her own for peace and patience. Soon now she would marry Domingo, and the ban would follow as surely as night follows day. She could already envision the hurt in her mother's eyes, feel the pain of separation from her sisters. From that day forward she would never be allowed to eat at her family's table, nor would any of them accept a gift from her hand. The ban was no illusion. It was a concrete reality she would have to endure for the rest of her life.

After her father's long prayer everyone stood while John Hershberger read a chapter from the Heilige Schrift, and then sat through a brief message delivered by Roman Miller. Roman was no preacher, but in the absence of a minister the men often shared the duty and did the best they could. This was followed by the testimonies of men who had brought their families to Mexico to be free.

Through it all, Miriam stole glances at the men sitting across from her. Micah Shrock, the strapping son of Ira and Esther, sat on the back row with the other boys, behind the married men, and when she glanced at him he didn't look back. Micah avoided eye contact with her these days, and never spoke to her at all if he could help it. They'd been engaged to be married, until Miriam put on the clothes of a Mexican peasant and went with Kyra into the mountains to look for Domingo. Micah had put his foot down, given her an ultimatum.

She went anyway. Micah wasn't the only one who wouldn't forgive her for that.

Next to Micah sat Jake Weaver, the love of Rachel's life, always smiling, good-natured and affable, completely unaware that he was a murderer in danger of hell's fires. Directly in front of Jake was the self-righteous Levi Mullet, Miriam's brother-in-law. He and Emma had rushed into a marriage just before leaving for Mexico to hide the fact that their first child was already on the way. They'd gotten away with it, or so they thought, but there was always a hint of fear in his eyes, for he had been raised to believe that no sin would ever go unpunished in this world. He lived in constant fear of Gott's reprisal.

Atlee Hostetler, the wiry little newcomer, sat ramrod straight on the backless bench trying to stay awake, bleary-eyed from staying up too late drinking hard cider. He'd come to Mexico to escape the whispers about his binges, but the rumors had followed him.

Miriam didn't know them all, though she suspected that every single person present harbored secret desires and secret fears they held closer than kin—secrets that would always keep them at arms' length from each other.

The service ended as it began, with a song. The richly timbered chorus of voices melding in her father's barn moved Miriam more than anything that went before it, for in the comfort of that moment she discovered a small but profound truth: her people were never more purely and perfectly united than when they sang together, as one.

❧

Paradise Valley enjoyed mild temperatures year-round, and a fair amount of rain during the growing season. Surrounded by ridges and mountains on three sides, they were sheltered from all but the worst of storms and wind. But Caleb Bender knew, perhaps better than anyone, that the worst storms didn't come from the western skies.

They came on horseback.

After lunch Caleb strolled down his lane to join a group of men who were already there, waiting. He had spread the word earlier that he wanted to talk to the men in private, away from the women and children, about a matter of great concern. Only the married men were there, the heads of households. The women and unmarried boys had no say.

Atlee Hostetler had a coal black beard that came to a point, and he stroked it as he looked up and down Caleb's driveway at the row of saplings just starting to bud.

"You planted a lot of trees here, Caleb."

It was Levi who answered him. "Jah, my Emma did that. She loves trees. Planted them all over. There's even maples up on that ridge. Don't know as they'll thrive in this climate, though."

Caleb chuckled. "They'll thrive if they know what's good for them. That daughter of mine won't have a shirker. If all her trees live, in twenty years they'll change the face of this valley, that's for sure. Won't be the same place." Then his smile disappeared as he kicked at the dirt, dreading what he had to say next. "I'm not real sure we'll be here in twenty years yet. That's why I wanted to talk to you men—" he glanced over his shoulder toward the house, where a clutch of younger girls were tending the babies while the women cleaned up from lunch—"out here where the women can't hear. We got a decision to make. You all remember what happened last summer."

Mahlon Yutzy's face darkened. "The diphtheria?" Mahlon's twelve-year-old son, William, had died of the disease. Three of the five new families had lost a child in the epidemic within weeks of their arrival.

"Well, that too," Caleb said, "but I'm thinking the threat of disease is behind us. Mainly I was talking about the bandits—the ones who took Rachel . . . and killed Aaron."

Even now it was hard to make himself say the words. The wound was still too fresh. Caleb chewed on his lip for a moment, staring at the horizon, composing himself, and the other men exchanged worried glances.

He felt a hand on his shoulder, and his old friend John Hershberger said softly, "What *about* the bandits, Caleb? Is there news?"

Before he could answer Caleb heard hoofbeats in the drive behind him. Domingo trotted up to the group and swung down from the saddle with a wince. After six months he still limped a little from the broken leg he suffered at El Ojo. He led his horse up to the group.

"*Guten tag*," the young native said, reaching out to shake hands. One by one they shook his hand and switched from Dutch to High German.

"I still can't get used to hearing German from a Mexican!" Atlee Hostetler said, the dialect causing him to struggle a bit himself. It was different from Pennsylvania Dutch, but they all understood it because it was the language of their Bible.

Domingo shrugged, smiled. "My German was a gift from a former employer," he said. "It's not perfect, but I figured it was better than your Spanish."

Their hats all tilted down, hiding their faces as they laughed quietly at themselves. "You figured right," Yutzy chuckled, then pointed at Domingo's Amish hat. "If not for the poncho I would have took you for Dutch—riding a standard-bred horse and wearing an Amish hat."

Domingo nodded toward Caleb. "The horse and the hat were both gifts from my *current* employer."

"There *is* news," Caleb said, answering John's question and steering the conversation back toward his original purpose. "That's why I asked Domingo to come. He knows some of the bandits, and sometimes his friends tell him things."

The whole group ambled slowly down the driveway toward the middle of the valley while Domingo told them what he and Caleb already knew: El Pantera was still alive, and looking for revenge.

"He will come soon," Domingo said. "And he will bring an army. Thirty, maybe forty men, with guns. This time he will come for blood."

"It's just not right," Levi said. "We have done nothing to this man."

"We have done plenty," Domingo answered. "El Pantera is a proud man. Jake Weaver embarrassed him in front of his men, then we escaped from his barn and took Rachel with us. In the bandit's mind Rachel was his property—he had stolen her fair and square. Worst of all, El Pantera was badly injured in the fight at El Ojo, and that was *after* I shot his prize Appaloosa and two of his men. Mark my words, he will come for his revenge."

Mahlon Yutzy shook his head. "There is nothing we can do against an army. They will slaughter us like chickens."

"That's why we needed to talk," Caleb said. "Our lives might be in danger, and the lives of our wives and children. Maybe the Coblentzes did the right thing, going home." He didn't want to be the one to suggest it, but he would not withhold the truth.

They all knew the story. Freeman and Hannah Coblentz had packed up and gone back to Ohio, leaving behind a half-built house after their little girl died of diphtheria. Cora, their eldest daughter, was being courted by Aaron and was devastated by his loss. All of it together was more than Hannah could bear.

"There are still things you can do to protect yourselves," Domingo said. "Don Louis Alejandro Hidalgo, the owner of

Hacienda El Prado, keeps a cadre of armed guards at the *hacienda*, three miles from here. He has said that if you can get your families behind his walls you will be protected. Anyway, there is time to prepare. My friend said it might be a month before El Pantera is well enough to ride this far, let alone fight."

"But what if we're in the fields working when they come?" Levi said. "They would be on us before we could get our families out."

"If you post sentries in the high places they can see the bandits coming ten miles away," Domingo said. "That would buy you a little time."

"Jah, and then what? He could still burn our houses and barns, and what will stop him from coming again and again? Will we live our whole lives at the mercy of this animal? The Coblentzes were smart, if you ask me. Maybe we should *all* go back—to a more civilized country."

Caleb nodded gravely. "We are faced with a hard choice. We must decide whether to go or stay. If we stay, we must find a way to keep our families safe."

"But we can't leave now!" Noah Byler said. "We sold everything we have to come to this place, and my son is buried in this earth. Caleb, all we want to do is live in peace. Is there no law in this country? Does no one protect the innocent?"

Caleb looked him in the eye. "Only Gott," he said quietly.

They walked a ways in silence, each of them weighing the question in his own mind, but in the end Caleb knew they would all look to him for an answer. He was the oldest and had been here the longest. He was also the only one whose child had died at the hands of the bandits.

It was John Hershberger who finally asked, "What do you think, Caleb? Should we give up and go back to Ohio?"

Caleb shook his head slowly. "I won't tell another man

what he should do, but as for me, I don't want to leave. From the beginning I felt Gott led us here, and that has not changed. Whatever befalls me—and I have already paid a great price—I still think it is Gott's will that I should stay. And if Gott wants us here, then Gott will deliver us. Somehow."

Ira Shrock's face, always red, grew redder as Caleb spoke, until at last he could not keep silent.

"We need to find a way to get troops to come," he said. "These bandits should pay for their crimes. It's not right to let them feast on the innocent. They should *pay!*"

Caleb cleared his throat. "We already tried to get them to send troops, Ira. I practically begged the government official in Monterrey, but he wanted money—a lot of money. More money than we have."

"Hidalgo is rich," Domingo said. "Perhaps you can persuade him to pay for the troops."

They talked at great length, walking the fields of Paradise Valley, but in the end they could see no other choice. They would not take up arms against the bandits themselves, and none of them had the money to bribe the official to send troops to the valley. Most of them had spent their last dime to buy the land. Domingo was right. Their only option was to appeal to Don Hidalgo. After all, he was the one who sold them the land in the first place.

One by one they grudgingly assented, nodding and mumbling among themselves until John Hershberger summed it up for them. "We don't have much choice. If we leave now we lose everything we have. There is no one to buy our farms."

"Then it is decided," Caleb said. "Tomorrow morning I will go talk to Hidalgo and ask him if he will pay the bribe. In the meantime we will trust Gott." With a glance back toward his home he added, "I'll thank you men not to talk about this to the women. My Martha doesn't need something else to worry about just now."

Domingo raised an eyebrow. "Will you at least put sentries on the heights?"

"Jah," Caleb answered, with a wry smile. "We will trust Gott, and post lookouts."

Chapter 3

After breakfast on Monday morning Caleb hitched a horse to the buggy and took Domingo with him to Hacienda El Prado. The village at the feet of the hacienda was buzzing with activity, as usual whenever the *haciendado* was present on his estate. Don Hidalgo only visited El Prado for a few weeks at planting time and harvest, dividing the rest of his year between New York and Paris, so the peons and merchants who lived at his beck and call kept themselves very busy whenever he was in attendance. Caleb drove through the village, past the beautiful stone church with its oak trees and graveyard, right up to the ivy-swathed gates of the hacienda itself. Two armed guards met him there and, after relieving Domingo of his gun belt, waved them through.

The main house sat on a hill well back from the gates, shadowed in the rear by a sprawling flower garden dotted with shade trees, marble benches, and shallow ponds where exotic fish meandered in the shade of weeping willows and arched-stone footbridges. Caleb left his buggy with a stableboy while he and Domingo went on up to the back entrance of the main house. Yet another armed guard frisked them before leading them through a maze of hallways to a waiting room crowded with a dozen barefoot Mexican peasants.

They didn't wait long. When Hidalgo's minion came out and saw an American face he ushered Caleb into Hidalgo's grand library ahead of everyone else, explaining that Caleb was, after all, a landowner. But when Domingo got up to come with him, the butler's eyebrows went up.

"Your peon can wait here," he said.

It took Caleb a second to get his meaning, but then he hung back, his eyes narrowing.

"Domingo Zapara is no peon," he said. "He is my *friend*, and he goes where I go."

Despite the fact that Domingo was a head taller the butler still managed to look down his nose at him for a second, then sniffed and said in a distinctly condescending tone, "*Muy bien.* Follow me."

Hidalgo's cavernous library, with its high frescoed ceiling, exquisitely crafted mahogany woodwork, and Persian carpets was without a doubt the most opulent room Caleb had ever seen, and it was only one small part of a house large enough to contain twenty such rooms.

"Señor Bender!" Hidalgo rose from behind a massive, ornately carved desk, greeted Caleb with a warm handshake, and ushered him to a leather chair in front of his desk. He ignored Domingo, who remained standing quietly behind Caleb, hat in hand.

Hidalgo seated himself behind the desk and folded his hands on the blotter. His hands were soft, the nails neatly manicured. Ten years younger than Caleb, the haciendado carried himself like royalty and he was dressed like a politician. His smile faded as he spoke.

"Fuentes wrote to me about the bandit attack last summer, Señor Bender. We were all deeply saddened to hear of the loss of your son. A terrible tragedy. It must have been a very difficult time for your family."

Caleb nodded gravely. "Sí, we miss him badly, especially now, with spring planting to do. He was a good son, and an able worker."

"I was also informed that one of your daughters was taken, but she was later restored to you. Is this true?"

"Sí. Rachel was kidnapped, but this young man"—Caleb glanced over his shoulder at Domingo—"and another were able to rescue her."

"Sí, that is the story I heard. You are lucky, Señor Bender. This El Pantera is a very bad man."

Caleb nodded. Pictures of his son's last moments flashed across his mind's eye. A bad man indeed.

"This is what I came to talk to you about, Don Hidalgo. El Pantera. Even now he makes plans to attack us. They say he is full of rage and he seeks revenge."

Hidalgo's head turned, just a notch, so that the stare he fastened on Caleb seemed slightly wary. "And what will you do?"

Caleb looked down at the hat in his lap, already sensing resistance in the haciendado's language. *What will you do?*

"We were hoping you might help us."

Hidalgo nodded. "Sí, I will be happy to help. I have told you before, Señor Bender, you and your people are welcome behind the walls of the hacienda when bandits attack. You will be safe here."

Caleb sighed. "Gracias, Don Hidalgo. We are grateful for your protection, but you must understand that we are farmers. Even if we run to the hacienda, our livestock will be slaughtered, our houses and barns burned. We would lose everything."

Hidalgo squinted at him, puzzled. "Then perhaps you should band together and defend your farms from these men. There are ten families in your valley now, are there not?"

"Sí, but we cannot fight. It is against the laws of our Gott to take up arms against our fellow man."

"Bandits—vermin, rabid dogs," Hidalgo said with a shrug.

"Men, still," Caleb answered evenly. "Made by the hand of Gott. I talked it over with the others, and it seems to all of us that the only solution to our problems is to bring *federales* to the valley. If there are troops here, the bandits will stay away. But Señor Montoya—the official in Monterrey you recommended to us—he wanted money. Señor Hidalgo, we have given you nearly all the money we have to buy the land."

Hidalgo leaned back in his chair and a leery smile came into his eyes. He nodded slowly. "I see. You have come to ask me to pay Señor Montoya's bribe so he will send troops here to protect you."

Caleb nodded thinly. "Sí, though I still don't understand why a bribe must be paid at all. Montoya is a government official. Don't they pay him a salary?"

Hidalgo chuckled. "This is Mexico, Señor Bender. Montoya's salary as a civil servant is a token. Anyway, why would any man aspire to such an office if there were no way to profit from it?"

Caleb's hopes were fading. The tone of Hidalgo's voice had already told him what his answer would be.

Hidalgo leaned forward, once again clasping his hands on his desk.

"Señor Bender, I have the deepest respect for you and your people. You have worked very hard to build a homestead here in our mountains, and you have gained the trust of all those around you. But if you will not defend your own farms how can you expect someone else to defend them for you?"

"In America there were policemen to protect the innocent."

Hidalgo's eyes narrowed. He took a deep breath and exhaled through his nose like a little hiss of steam. "America is a *rich* country with plenty of policemen to go around. But Mexico is a poor country, and we have just been through a bitter revolution. In Mexico these days there is never enough of *anything* to go around."

As he was speaking a paneled door opened behind him and a woman in the full regalia of a Mexican baroness glided silently into the room. Her face, her bearing, matched a regal portrait in a gilded frame hanging on the wall directly behind Hidalgo's desk. His wife. Caleb glanced up at her, and Hidalgo, following his glance, turned and saw her. He held up a finger and said, "I will be with you in a moment, *mi amor*."

She nodded, and remained.

Hidalgo stared at Caleb a minute longer as if waiting for a rebuttal, but Caleb could think of nothing more to say.

"My offer stands," Hidalgo said, and there was an air of finality in his tone, like the banging of a gavel. "You may bring your people here, behind the walls of the hacienda, and I will guarantee their safety. But with all due respect, Señor Bender, it makes no sense for me to pay a king's ransom for troops when I have no need of them myself."

Caleb nodded, his jaw working, his eyes downcast. The irony of Hidalgo's words seemed lost on Hidalgo himself. But Caleb, with a farmer's common sense, saw quite clearly the hypocrisy of an aristocrat, sitting in the grand library of his palatial estate with his fine clothes and manicured nails, complaining that there was not enough to go around. Caleb braced his palms on the arms of the chair to rise, but Domingo's hand pressed firmly on his shoulder. Domingo came around him then and leaned his fists on the edge of Hidalgo's desk, glaring at the haciendado.

Hidalgo bristled, staring up at him. There was only indignation in his eyes. The man was too powerful to fear any peasant.

"Don Hidalgo," Domingo said softly, with a little bow of the head to show at least the pretense of respect, "I think in his haste my American *amigo* has failed to mention one or two things that may interest you. First, everyone knows Hacienda El Prado enjoyed the favor of Pancho Villa, and while he lived none of his men would dare lift a hand against you. But Pancho Villa is dead." Again, Caleb noticed Domingo making the sign of the cross on his chest as he said this. "You no longer have him to protect you, my haciendado, and if El Pantera comes all this way with a hundred armed men, do you really think he will be satisfied with the spoils of a few poor *gringo campesinos?*"

Caleb glanced up at Hidalgo's wife. Her eyes widened perceptibly.

Domingo leaned a little closer to Hidalgo and said very calmly, "El Pantera will never stop with the outlying farms, Don Hidalgo, and you know it. His men are fierce and well-trained. They learned how to storm a hacienda during the Revolution. You and your family can sail away to Europe if you wish, but when you return your fancy furniture and your beautiful paintings will be gone, and your grand hacienda will be a smoking pile of rubble."

Caleb caught a glimpse of outright fear in Hidalgo's wife's face, and the involuntary opening of her mouth before she raised a black-lace fan to hide it.

There was fire in Hidalgo's eyes, and his chair slid back roughly as he rose to his full height, jerking stiffly at the hem of his tunic.

"Your audience is at an end, Señor Bender. I will not be intimidated in my own house. My servant will show you out."

With a hard glare at Domingo he added, "And take your insolent peon with you!"

Driving back home, neither of them said anything until they were clear of the hacienda village and Caleb quietly asked, "What do you think he will do?"

Domingo laughed out loud. "Did you see the look on his wife's face when she heard what would happen to her lovely hacienda? You are a married man, Señor Bender—you tell *me* what he will do."

Caleb couldn't suppress a grin, though the ethics of it bothered him a little. "It was wrong to lie to him, Domingo. El Pantera doesn't have a hundred men."

Domingo met this with a shrug. "It was not exactly a lie. I only asked what he will do *if* El Pantera comes with a hundred men. I did not say he would."

In the evening, just before sundown when the Benders were gathered at the supper table, Caleb heard hoofbeats rounding the house and went to the back door to see who it was.

Diego Fuentes, Hidalgo's right-hand man and overseer of his estate, cantered up to the corral on his big black Friesian. As he climbed down from his silver-studded saddle Caleb strolled out to see what he wanted.

"I have something for you," Fuentes said, handing him an envelope bearing only the name Montoya on the front. "I am told it contains a letter and a *cheque*. Don Hidalgo instructed me to give it to you, and that you would know what to do with it. He said he would have attended to the matter himself but he is far too busy with the affairs of his estate just now."

Caleb smiled, running a rough thumb over the fancy wax

seal. "The haciendado is a proud man. Tell Don Hidalgo it will be done, and tell him *muchas* gracias."

Caleb hitched the surrey and left two hours before daylight the next morning, picking up Domingo in San Rafael and making it to Arteaga in time to catch the afternoon train to Monterrey. They arrived in the bureaucrat's office bright and early the next morning. Once Caleb presented Hidalgo's cheque he found Montoya much more amenable than he had been on Caleb's last visit. There were no federales available at the moment, Montoya said, but he promised an entire company within a fortnight.

"I only hope they will not come too late," Caleb said.

They caught the train back to Arteaga before nightfall, shaving a whole day off the trip—a good thing, since there was planting to be done. Camping by a little stream outside Arteaga for the night, Domingo seemed preoccupied. The young native had never been talkative, but for the last two days he'd said virtually nothing. Sitting across the campfire from him that evening, Caleb found out why.

"Señor Bender, I need to talk to you about something very important," Domingo said. The night air was chilly, and he held his palms to the fire.

Caleb chuckled. "More important than bringing the federales to the valley to keep bandits from killing us all?"

Domingo considered this for a moment, but he did not smile at Caleb's little joke. "A different kind of important," he said. "I am in love with your daughter."

Caleb was sitting on a log, elbows on knees. Now he straightened very slowly and his head tilted, staring at his young friend.

"Miriam?" It could only be Miriam. Rachel was promised, Ada was simpleminded, and the other two were too young.

"Sí. Miriam. We are in love, and we are planning to be married."

Caleb blinked and his head recoiled as if he'd been slapped. "You want to marry her? How did this come about?"

Domingo looked up and there was a note of sadness in his eyes. "How do such things *ever* happen? It was fate, Señor Bender—too strong. Neither of us could resist it."

Caleb was stunned speechless for a moment as scraps of memory flashed through his mind. He had seen the signs— the glances, the quiet words exchanged when they thought no one was looking—but blinded by his love for his daughter, and for Domingo, he'd told himself it was nothing, told himself they were only friends.

He saw the future, too. Amish girls had married outsiders before. The outcome was always the same, inescapable. Miriam would be *banned*.

"I'm sorry, Domingo, but I cannot give my blessing to this union. I must refuse."

The young native shook his head and spoke gently. "You misunderstand me, Señor Bender. This is not a *petición de mano*— I am not asking you for her hand—but out of great respect for you I am simply telling you what is about to happen. Miriam has told me what to expect, and I assure you I am grieved by it as deeply as you. But our course is set, the decision made. I already know you cannot give us your blessing."

Caleb nodded absently, staring into the fire. "I admire your honesty, at least."

Then a thought occurred to him, a slim but fervent hope.

"Domingo, have you considered becoming Amish? You would be welcomed with open arms."

But Domingo shook his head. "It would only be a lie. I was raised to be a warrior, Señor Bender. I cannot change, and I will not pretend to be something I am not."

"But I have seen you make the sign of the cross. Have you become a Christian?"

"Sí, your God came to me at *El Paso de los Pericos*, and He has changed my life, but I am too much like my Nahua father to ever be a pacifist. The Catholic Church does not require it of me, and besides," he added with a chuckle, "Father Noceda says I am not even a very good Catholic."

Caleb's rough hand rubbed the tired muscles of his neck as his eyes wandered, lost. "I don't think you understand how difficult this will be for Miriam. And for her mother."

"Perhaps not. But it can only be as difficult as you make it. Miriam's feelings for her family will not change."

There was nothing more to be said. His mind reeling, Caleb got up and went for his bedroll, though he already knew he would not be sleeping much this night. Most of all, he dreaded breaking the news to his wife.

Chapter 4

It was the end of a school day. The children had all gone home and Miriam was straightening up the buggy shed when her dat came home from Monterrey. The whole family turned out to welcome him, but after he corralled the horse he came to put the buggy away. Alone with Miriam in the buggy shed, he sat down on one of the school benches and patted a spot beside him.

"Domingo told me," he said, and then took off his hat and rubbed his bald head the way he did when he was very tired or very worried. There was a great sadness in his eyes.

"I'm sorry," she whispered. "I know it's terrible news to you, but, Dat, I love Domingo more than anything."

"More than your family?"

Coming from her father, the question pierced her heart. She took a deep, shuddering breath and fought back tears.

"Dat, I didn't choose this. Things just . . . happened. The time I spent alone with Domingo and Kyra in the mountains was like heaven on earth, and I was overwhelmed. Domingo is *the one*. I believe Gott himself put us together, and I want to spend the rest of my life with him. Everything else will just have to work itself out. It makes me very sad to think of the grief it will cause my family. I only hope you can all forgive me."

On the verge of tears, he whispered, "You're still my daughter—at least until the church says otherwise—but this is a hard thing, Miriam. A very hard thing. How many of my children will this country *take* from me . . . ?"

Miriam couldn't hold it back. She wept for a lost brother, and for a softhearted father whose pain she felt as keenly as her own.

"I will not try to stop you," he said wearily, "but you already know what is coming, and you know I will not defy the church. As for Domingo, I only wish I could have talked him into joining us, but—"

"I know. He's a warrior. Dat, he was raised in a different world, but in his heart he's as good as any man I know."

He nodded grimly. Neither of them spoke for a minute as a sad resignation settled over them both. Finally he asked, very quietly, "When will it happen?"

It, he said, the way he would ask a doctor how long before someone died. Staring at the dirt floor she thought for a moment.

"In a few weeks, at Iglesia El Prado. We'll have to go talk to the priest first."

There was another long silence before he said, "Perhaps it won't be so bad, since there is no bishop here."

She knew what he meant, and she appreciated it. He was saying perhaps the family could bend the rules a bit after she was banned. There would be restrictions, yet beyond those the law was somewhat flexible, especially in the absence of an official overseer.

"Thank you for that, Dat." Then another thought occurred to her. "Will you let Domingo keep working for you?"

He seemed surprised, caught off guard by the question, but then he shrugged. "As long as the others don't complain.

Domingo is a good hand. Besides, he has done nothing wrong, except to fall in love with my daughter. I can't hardly hold that against him."

The word was out, and it divided Miriam's heart right down the middle. Mamm was deeply hurt, as expected. She managed to function, cooking dinner as always, but she spoke only when necessary and sniffled off and on through dinner. She ate very little, refusing to even look at Miriam.

But Ada misbehaved at dinner. Confused by the somber mood she kept making little attempts to stir things up and create the lively banter she was accustomed to seeing around the dinner table. When she spilled her water—on purpose—she laughed too long and too loud until Mamm finally shushed her with a stern word. Then she sulked, pooching her bottom lip and refusing to eat another bite. Even Miriam's younger sisters were all deathly quiet.

Breakfast the next morning was no different. A black gloom hung over them all, and Mamm still wouldn't eat. Miriam couldn't take it. As soon as she finished her chores she told her mother she needed some time alone.

Mamm nodded without looking at her. Miriam crept silently out the back door, past the barn and up along the face of the ridge.

Even now she was wracked with doubts, and as she wandered aimlessly along the tree line her soul cried out. Where was Gott in all this? Was it not Gott who led her to Domingo in the first place, and he to her? Was this not Gott's will? Was it only selfish desire? She knew in her heart that desire played a part in her choice. She was young and unmarried—how could it not? And if Gott led her to this place, where was He now? Why did she feel so utterly alone, so deeply wounded by the

43

silence of her family? These questions, and others, poured from the deepest recesses of her soul as she fought with herself, even now, resisting what lay ahead of her.

It was not too late to turn back. She had said no vows; she was still Miriam *Bender*. But if she turned back now what would it do to Domingo? To hurt him like that would crush her even more than the disdain of her kin. And what of her future, knowing as she did that this was her one chance for happiness? Even if she abandoned Domingo at this point she knew his shadow would remain forever, and she would never love another. No man would ever measure up to Domingo, and she would remain alone for the rest of her days, an old maid schoolteacher.

No matter what promises she'd made on the day of her baptism, did her family or her church really have the right to demand such a price? How could she have known then—on the day of her baptism, as a seventeen-year-old who had lived all her life in Salt Creek Township—that she would one day be forced to move to Mexico, or that such a man as Domingo Zapara even existed in the whole earth? Only Gott knew such things.

And where was Gott now?

She wandered along the face of the ridge, oblivious to her surroundings, and she was more than halfway to Emma's house before it dawned on her that this was where she'd been heading the whole time. Emma would know. She was the second wisest person Miriam knew, and in this case Emma had a distinct advantage, even over her father.

She was a woman.

Levi was on his planter way down by the main road. Focused on his work, he didn't see Miriam. She heard the sound of a baby screaming in pain and hurried down to the kitchen garden where she found Emma squatting on the ground with Clara, picking at the toddler's fingers. Clara wailed louder when she saw Miriam.

She knelt down to help, scooping up the child and holding her still for Emma.

"What happened?"

Emma glanced up. "I edged the garden with prickly pear cactus to keep the pests out, but it got poor Clara instead. She didn't know not to grab it."

Three-year-old Mose stood back, glowering from under his hat while infant Will lay nearby in a wooden wheelbarrow, sleeping soundly through the whole ordeal.

"Best way to learn, I guess," Emma said as she plucked the last of the spines from her baby's fingers, then hugged her close until the wailing turned to snuffles. Five minutes later the child was playing in the dirt with her brother and Emma was heading toward the house for a fresh diaper.

Miriam stayed with the children, watching them torment an ant lion. Staring at nothing she tumbled back into her tangled, bleak thoughts. She didn't hear Emma return.

"Where *are* you?" Emma asked over her shoulder.

Startled, Miriam glanced at her, then looked away again, shaking her head.

"What's wrong, Mir? You can't hide it, you know. I saw it on you when you first came up. It's in your shoulders, your eyes—"

"I'm going to be married," Miriam moaned, fighting back tears.

Emma took her by the shoulders and spun her around, but Miriam refused to meet her eyes. Emma's head tilted, confused at first. An announcement of marriage wasn't usually cause for grief. Then her eyes widened and the diaper flew up to cover her open mouth.

"Oh, Mir, I'm so sorry," she said, drawing Miriam into a tight hug. "It's Domingo, isn't it?"

Miriam nodded against her sister's shoulder.

"Poor child," Emma said. "Oh, what you must be going through."

Emma held her for a minute, saying nothing, just holding her tight. Finally she backed away and dabbed at Miriam's face with the diaper.

"It's just too cruel," Emma said. "You never had a chance, did you? You're suffering, and will suffer more, over something you cannot help."

Miriam blinked. "You knew?"

"That you were in love with Domingo? Of course."

"Was it that obvious?"

Emma shrugged. "To me, jah. To others—I don't know. But marriage?" She shook her head. "I can never read Domingo. I wasn't sure how he felt about you, and I never dreamed he would ask you to marry him."

"He loves as fiercely as he fights," Miriam said.

Emma lifted her chin with a finger and looked into her eyes. "Are you sure this is what you want?"

Miriam's head tilted forward a bit and she glared, hard, from under her eyelids.

"Right," Emma said, smiling. "Dumb question. Why would you face the ban if you weren't sure."

"Such a terrible, heavy price. How can I bear it?"

"Do you have a choice?"

"No."

"Then you will bear it. Maybe it won't be so bad."

"How can you say that? To be put out from among my family, my people?"

"Oh, Mir, you'll still see your family. They'll still talk to you. Just because you can't sit at the same table—"

"Even that. The very thought of it chills me. The dinner table is the center of our lives together."

"But it's not like you can't see them or talk to them. I don't know about Dat, but I will wink at the ban."

"Then they'll ban you, too."

"Psh, no they won't. I know how much I can get away with." Emma was smiling now. She always knew what to say.

"You would do that for me?"

"Jah," Emma said, "and so will the rest of the family, sooner or later. You'll see."

"But why?"

"Love. Your family loves you, Miriam. Listen, the *ordnung* is a good thing, but it's not greater than Gott. Gott is love, and love forgives. I have already forgiven you, and I know my father's heart. He will forgive you too, in time."

⁂

The next morning Miriam saddled a horse and rode over to the house on the back side of San Rafael. The house belonged to Kyra and her two young sons, but Domingo and his mother lived there as well. Domingo's mother greeted Miriam at the door, her face still aglow from Domingo's announcement. She kissed Miriam's cheeks, hugged her and called her *mi hija preciosa*—my lovely daughter. Uncle Paco and Aunt Maria were there too, waiting to meet her. Paco was tall like Domingo and bore a striking resemblance to him but for the short hair and full mustache. Maria was a plump little woman like Mamm, but full of mirth, her hair tied back in a tight bun, just beginning to gray at the temples. She laughed at everything and was giddy with the news of her nephew's betrothal.

Gripping Miriam's face in her chubby hands, Maria beamed. "Domingo, I see why you chose this one. She is *beautiful*! Like Kyra," she said, casting a glance at Domingo's sister and bursting into laughter, "only younger, and not so feisty!"

"Uncle Paco and Aunt Maria will be our sponsors for the wedding," Domingo explained. "Our *padrino* and *madrina*."

"Sponsors?" Miriam had never heard of such a thing.

"Sí, it is custom. They will help us in many ways. The madrina will help you with your dress and the planning of the wedding. The padrino drives everyone to the church and gives away the bride."

This was something of a relief. Knowing absolutely nothing of an Englisher wedding, let alone a Mexican one, she was delighted to learn she would have an official guide.

"Today we will go with you to the magistrate's office for a license, and then we will all go visit the priest," Paco said.

Maria took Miriam's arm and spoke in a low, conspiratorial tone. "The priest will ask you a few silly questions, a mere formality. But I am the one who will teach you the things you will need to know if you are to be married to a Zapara." With a mischievous glance at her husband she added, "It is a vexatious path you have chosen, my child."

Riding arm in arm with Domingo in the back of Paco's cart, Miriam began to relax and sink into her new world. Basking in the warmth and acceptance she felt from his family, for a time she was almost able to forget her impending departure from all she had ever known and loved.

Domingo leaned close and whispered, "Are you sure you want to do this?"

She studied his eyes—steady and confident. There was no fear in him, no regret, only compassion. He knew what she was going through.

"Sí," she said. "I am certain."

Over the next few weeks she spent every spare moment in San Rafael with Kyra and Maria, fretting over a thousand wedding details and giggling over a thousand family secrets. Already they had made her a member of the family, and it was a joyous time. But at the end of the day she returned to her father's house in Paradise Valley, where a gray mood lay heavily on the Bender home. Mealtimes remained silent and grim, as if her family were already mourning, as if she were already banned. For the time being she could still eat at the table with the rest of them, but the future loomed over them like a dark cloud.

One night, when she and Rachel lay awake after the others had dozed off, Miriam rose up on an elbow and spoke softly to her sister.

"Rachel, I wish we could talk. I know this is hard on you, but—"

"It's hard for us all, Miriam." Rachel turned to her in the dark. "Not just me, but Mamm, Ada, Barbara, Leah—even Harvey can't stand the thought of losing you. We're your *family*, Mir. Think of all you will lose!"

"Maybe it won't be as bad as you think," Miriam whispered. "And think of all I will *gain*. I wish you could have been there, at Los Pericos. For two weeks I walked and talked with Domingo in a place as lovely as the Garden of Eden, and it was wonderful. No matter what tomorrow brings, I will always remember those days as the best and brightest of my life. Rachel, I love this land. I love these people. I love teaching the Mexican children—another thing Micah wouldn't have me do, by the way. I love Domingo, and I love his family. I could live here forever."

"You could live *here* forever," Rachel countered, denting the mattress with a forefinger. "Without breaking all our hearts! Mir, when I wanted to go back to Ohio for Jake, you were the one who made me stay. You remember what you said? *Family!*

You said family is everything, and now you're going to run off with Domingo and abandon your family?"

"There's more to it than that, Rachel. Gott has led me here. He led me to teach the children and gave me the gift. He led me to Domingo through a dream, and Domingo to me the same way. I have found the life I was born to lead—a pearl of great price—and if Gott led me to it shall I not follow, even if it costs me everything?"

Rachel was silent for a moment, and when she spoke her voice was choked with tears. "Miriam, I am part of the everything you will lose," she said.

Miriam slid an arm around her sister, laid her head gently on Rachel's shoulder and whispered, "I want you to promise me something."

"What."

"When I am gone—after I'm married and gone from here—I want you to promise me that you will always be my sister." She rose up to kiss Rachel lightly on the cheek. "No matter what. Always."

Rachel didn't answer. Full of hurt, she turned away and burrowed into her pillow.

❧

They were the longest days of Caleb's life, full of dread and waiting. He kept himself busy with work, and thanked Gott there was plenty of planting to do. Every morning he watched in silence as one of the young men climbed the ridge behind the house and another left on horseback for the western heights to keep a lookout for bandits. The men had worked out a schedule for the sentries, and so far the women didn't even know about the looming threat. If they did, none of them had said anything.

The company of federales Montoya promised them had still

not arrived, and with every passing day Caleb's anxiety grew. What if the bandits attacked before the troops came?

Then there was Miriam. On the days she wasn't holding school in the buggy shed she would ride off to spend the day in San Rafael. She was already halfway gone, her chores divided among siblings as she slipped away to another world.

In the evenings he would often find time to go up and sit on his rock alone, partway up the ridge where he could look over his valley and all the lives, the farms, the busyness and work, ten families toiling and carving out homesteads here, because of him. And now, more than ever, he wondered if he had done right by bringing them here.

Gott's will could be a burdensome thing.

Sunday morning, a church day, and the others were all out doing chores an hour before daylight. Miriam had the upstairs bedroom to herself for a while, a rare and piercingly lonely circumstance for a girl with a large family on the day of her wedding. She dressed herself in her best dress and kapp, the only Amish clothes she would take with her, and perhaps the last time she would wear them. She was ready to go when she heard the padrino's horse and carriage arrive to pick her up. After one last long look at the spare dresses and kapps in the drawer she slid it shut and left them behind. She would not be needing them now, and one of her sisters could make use of them. A small drawstring bag containing her scant possessions hung loosely from one hand as she went down the stairs. Only Mamm and Ada were in the kitchen, cooking breakfast.

Mamm glanced at Miriam, at the bag in her hand, then her attention turned quickly to her frying pan. Ada looked up from cracking eggs and gave Miriam a big smile, oblivious.

Miriam laid a hand on her mother's shoulder. "My ride is here," she said softly.

Mamm nodded, once, without looking, her hands busy turning salt pork. "Go on, then."

Miriam waited a beat. Mamm swallowed hard, fighting back tears, but she was biting her lip and it was clear she would say nothing more. Miriam gave Ada a hug as she passed, and said goodbye, though it was never clear whether or not Ada really comprehended what was happening.

Uncle Paco was waiting for her out back by the corral fence. He'd borrowed a fancy open-top carriage from somewhere, low-slung with a little entry gate in the middle, and plush upholstered seats. Pausing beside the carriage in the predawn stillness Miriam could hear her father's hayfork scraping the boards up in the barn. He'd gone there on purpose to avoid this moment. He would have heard the carriage come. They all would. They knew why Paco was here, and yet they all stayed out of sight. Not one of them came to see her off. Not even Rachel.

Miriam's heart was breaking. Rachel had not said a word to her, not even so much as a goodbye. If this was a taste of what lay in store, she didn't know if she could take it. In exchange for everything that awaited her she could bear to be shunned by all the world, but not Rachel.

Please, Gott, not Rachel.

Her padrino was decked out in his wedding clothes, tight knee-breeches and a trim waist-length gold-trimmed jacket over a ruffled white shirt. He grinned widely and made a grand gesture of offering his hand to help her up, and then he took his seat, pulled the reins and turned the carriage around.

As the carriage rolled slowly past the house Miriam sat ramrod straight with her hands folded on her lap, eyes forward, refusing to look back. The future was all that remained now.

But just as the horse broke into a trot at the top of the lane she heard footsteps, someone running hard, gaining on them. Paco must have heard too, because he looked over his shoulder and pulled up short.

Rachel caught up with them and stood holding the side of the carriage for a second, panting, and then jerked open the little door and climbed up onto the padded seat opposite Miriam. Gripping her shoulders, Rachel leaned close and kissed her lightly on the cheek. Foreheads touching, she locked eyes with her sister and whispered, "No matter what. Always."

Then, without another word, she jumped down out of the carriage and disappeared into the darkness.

Chapter 5

K yra's little house became the center of a whirlwind once
Miriam arrived. The men, already dressed, waited outside while the women took over the entire house to get
themselves ready. Kyra and Maria swept Miriam into the back
bedroom and fitted her into the same white cotton dress Kyra
had worn on her wedding day, the same one her mother had
worn. The loose-fitting dress was decorated around the yoke
in intricate red Aztec patterns, embroidered near the bottom
with a ring of red roses the size of her hand. They let her hair
hang loose and full down her back. Leaving her face exposed,
they draped her head and shoulders in a sheer lace mantilla
veil, secured by a wreath Kyra had woven for the occasion out
of delicate little vines salted with tiny white blooms. They put
white satin shoes on her feet and filled her hands with a thick
bouquet of white flowers.

When they went outside to load into the carriages, Miriam
came last. Watching Domingo's face, the other women parted
to let him see his bride, and the first glimpse took his breath
away. Broad-shouldered and erect in his fancy jacket, with his

hair tied back, his regal bearing didn't change when he saw her, but he swallowed hard, and for an instant Miriam thought she saw tears in his eyes.

It was a fine spring morning, yellow and purple wildflowers dappling the fields, cactus beginning to bloom, and birds swarming through air scented with flowers and ringing with songs and laughter as the wedding procession wound its way into the hacienda village and up the narrow streets to the church.

Two little girls sprinkled flower petals in front of them as Miriam's padrino escorted her up the church steps alongside Domingo. Father Noceda met them there on the portico, and the crowd in the churchyard fell silent as the ceremony began.

Miriam's departure left a hole in Rachel's heart, and she sat through services in the Bender barn that morning stiffly, listening without hearing. Perched on the backless bench behind her mother, Rachel knew she wasn't the only one thinking of Miriam. Mamm sighed deeply every minute or two and kept a handkerchief at the ready the whole time, occasionally dabbing at the corners of her eyes. Again, she had eaten hardly a bite of breakfast. Mamm's dresses hung loosely on her these days, and Dat worried about her. She endured church with a sullen, vacant look in her eyes, staring at nothing, as if she were watching Miriam's wedding from a distance.

Miriam's wedding. Even the words sounded disjointed and ironic to Rachel. When they first came to Mexico, of all the Bender girls except Ada, Miriam was the one with the slimmest hopes of ever finding a husband. Rachel, on the other hand, already knew whom she would marry, and yet in the absence of a minister three years had passed without the opportunity. Now here she sat, nineteen and still single.

And Jake wasn't in church this morning, another disquiet-ing sign. There had been rumors whispered between the women for the last month. They knew something was going on because every day a couple of the younger men would disappear on horseback before dawn and return at dusk without saying where they'd been—a different pair every day. They did this even on Sunday, a breaking of the Sabbath that Rachel had never witnessed in her entire life. Esther Shrock had finally gleaned from her son that the fathers had assigned sentries to the heights on the north and west, but he would say no more than that. If the men were frightened enough to post lookouts on Sunday it could only mean that whatever was out there threatened the lives of everyone in the valley.

Halfway through the service, while John Hershberger was reading aloud from the Bible, all their questions were answered. Hershberger paused to take a breath, and into the little silence fell the distant but unmistakable echo of a gunshot.

Heads turned, and the men started to rise. Every one of the men, the heads of household, scrambled outside as quickly as they could. Hershberger stopped reading, closed the Bible and started after them. He hadn't even reached the door when another shot rang out, this time closer.

Now even women and children got up and surged toward the door to see what was happening. Rachel elbowed her way to the front of the crowd. The fathers stood in a cluster at the edge of Caleb's field, watching the road to the west.

It was Jake, on horseback, charging hard across the fields with a rifle in his hands, the barrel pointed straight up in the air. The gunshots were warnings. Jake was sounding an alarm. He shouted something, over and over, and the wind finally carried his words to her.

"They're coming!"

Caleb stood in the edge of his field, his heart pounding.

"We should go," Ira Shrock said, his voice high-pitched and full of angst. "Most of us came on foot, Caleb. It will take time to get back to our houses and hitch up. Oh, this couldn't have come at a worse time!"

"Wait," Caleb said. "Let's see what Jake has to say."

Jake made a beeline across the field, sliding the rifle into its scabbard. He pulled up right in front of them, his horse prancing sideways.

"They're coming! Bandits. I counted maybe thirty-five of them."

"How long before they get here?" Caleb asked.

"Not long. Maybe ten minutes. I'm sorry, they came from a different trail than what I expected and I didn't see them until they were only a few miles away."

Caleb gave orders, scattering the men. Most of them bolted away on foot while one or two borrowed horses from Caleb's corral and took off bareback.

Caleb went up to the crowd of women and children gathered by the barn.

"An army of bandits is coming," he told them, perhaps a little too bluntly. The women gasped and clutched at each other. He raised his hands, trying to calm them.

"The men will bring the buggies. Go down to the road as quickly as you can and wait for them. We will all flee to the hacienda, where we'll be safe."

Turning away, he called to his son. "Harvey, the surrey won't hold our whole family. Get a team of Belgians and we'll hitch the wagon." He could ill afford to lose his draft horses anyway.

Ten minutes later a line of buggies and hacks and wagons

converged in the road in front of Caleb's farm, and a caravan began slowly trundling out of the valley to the east.

Caleb brought up the rear in his farm wagon. He'd gone no more than a mile when Harvey, standing behind him, tapped his shoulder and said, "I see them."

Caleb looked back. At the far end of the valley a line of men on horseback charged down the hill and headed for the nearest farmhouse—Levi and Emma's place. He could hear the faint pop of pistols as they stormed the house and barn, slaughtering cattle and horses.

Caleb snapped the reins, urging his draft horses into a trot as he shouted to the buggy ahead of him. The warning was passed up the line and everyone picked up the pace.

When Caleb looked back again he could see a plume of smoke trailing from the roof of Levi's barn, but that wasn't the worst of it. El Pantera had apparently spotted the escaping Amish. His army had regrouped and turned toward the wagon train. Now they were galloping flat out in pursuit.

By then the caravan had made it past the crossroads, but they were still a mile from the gates of the hacienda—and the bandits were gaining on them. It was going to be close.

☙

Standing on the portico of the old Catholic church in her antique Mexican wedding dress, Miriam's emotions warred against one another. She was giddy with joy over finally being united with the only man she had ever loved, yet haunted by twinges of unspeakable grief over the absence of her family. The entire morning went by in a disoriented blur, right up until the moment when Father Noceda asked quietly, "Who gives this woman?"

Her padrino answered, "I do," then placed her hand in

Domingo's and stepped back. As Domingo's fingers closed around hers she looked up at his face and felt herself falling straight through those dark confident eyes, into his soul. His unshakable devotion calmed her, instantly and completely—a love that would weather any storm without complaint, for her. Domingo was the embodiment of grace and patience wrapped in a towering strength, and all of it laid freely at her feet. She could trust him. He would always be there for her. Miriam was at peace, her mind no longer divided, and it was in that precise moment that she and Domingo Zapara became one.

She kept her eyes on Domingo while they repeated the vows spoken by the priest. Words. She barely heard them. In her heart she was already married.

The ring bearer, one of Kyra's young sons, handed a long pink ribbon to the priest, who tied the ends together and draped the loop over their shoulders, a symbol of binding.

Domingo took a small leather pouch from his pocket. Maria had told her about the *arras* in advance, so she knew what to do. When he opened the pouch she held out her hands, fingers splayed, and he poured thirteen little gold coins into her palms, a symbol of abundance. But it was only a ritual; the coins were, and would remain, the property of the church. The priest's helper held out a basket to catch the coins as she let them slip through her fingers, a symbolic offering to the poor.

As the young robed assistant whisked the basket of coins away the ring bearer opened a small hand-carved box and held it up to the priest. Father Noceda took a gold band from the box and slid it onto Domingo's finger, then handed him a smaller duplicate, which Domingo slipped onto Miriam's hand. This too Maria had told her about. Gold rings were expensive, so for a peasant wedding such as this the church provided the rings, but only for show. They would be returned in three days, replaced by leather bands like all the peasants wore. It didn't matter. A ring was, after all, only a symbol.

After the priest blessed them and pronounced them man and wife, Miriam and Domingo kissed and turned about, arm in arm, to be saluted as a couple by the throng of family and friends in the courtyard.

The ceremony was only half done. There were still certain religious rites to be performed inside the church, but as the priest threw open the huge front doors a commotion rolled through the streets.

A barefoot peasant charged out from the main street across the churchyard, one hand holding his sombrero in place as he ran, shouting something to the guards on the parapet wall around the hacienda grounds. Miriam couldn't make out the words, but Father Noceda brushed past her and flew down the steps, through the crowd and across the yard to see what was happening.

Domingo froze, listening.

Then she heard it— the unmistakable sound of gunfire in the distance. She gripped Domingo's arm.

"*My family!*"

"Come with me," Domingo said, pulling her with him through the big doors into the narthex, then pressing her shoulders against the stone wall.

"Don't move!" he commanded, and then dashed through a side door and up a spiral staircase to the belfry.

The commotion outside grew, and in a moment Domingo flew back down the stairs, burst into the narthex and whisked her out into the churchyard.

"Bandits," he said. "We must get everyone behind the walls of the hacienda. Come."

Fifty yards from the church, the massive iron gate in the

hacienda wall swung wide. Bedlam ensued as everyone from the wedding and most of the people in the hacienda village crowded through. Miriam dropped her flowers and struggled to keep up in her wedding dress and satin shoes. She stopped. When Domingo's hand tore away he skidded to a stop and came back to her. Hastily stripping the dainty shoes from her feet, she gripped them in a fist as she hiked her skirts.

"Now I can keep up," she said. And she did.

Once inside the gates most of them kept running, on up the hill away from the walls. Domingo stopped and pointed.

"Go up there with the others. I will stay here and do what I can to help. Go!"

Terrified, she did as her husband said and ran up the long hill to join the wedding party by the stables. When she finally looked back her heart leaped. A flood of Amish poured through the gates in wagons and hacks and buggies and on horseback—all the Amish in Paradise Valley. Something truly horrific must have descended upon them.

When the last of them were behind the walls one of the haciendado's men closed and barred the gate. Diego Fuentes, the superintendent, stood in the back of a wagon down near the wall, handing out rifles and ammunition. Domingo's tall figure was easy to spot in his wedding finery, already manning a parapet on the crenelated wall with a rifle at the ready.

She spotted her dat, driving up the hill in a farm wagon—the last one through the gate before it closed. Mamm sat beside him, and the rest of her family was safe in the back of the wagon—Ada, Harvey, Rachel, Barbara and Leah. Caleb turned the wagon aside near the stables and stopped less than twenty yards away from her. Standing among a crowd of locals and dressed as she was, no one in her family even noticed her.

Except Ada. Ada stared straight at Miriam with a wide

childish grin on her ample face. Ada's grin finally caught Rachel's attention and she too spotted Miriam.

Rachel did a double take, but then she glanced at Mamm and Dat on the bench up front. They were looking the other way, watching the walls. Rachel beckoned with her fingers.

Miriam shook her head. *I can't face Mamm and Dat. Not now. Not dressed like this.*

Rachel took another quick peek at her parents, then jumped down from the back of the wagon and trotted over to the stable. Miriam ducked behind a wall.

Rachel rounded the wall and ran right into her. Miriam grabbed her shoulders.

"What's happening?"

"Bandits," Rachel said, breathless. "El Pantera attacked us, and it looks like he brought his whole army."

Horror-stricken, Miriam half wailed, "Is everyone all right?"

"Jah. Jake was watching from the ridge and warned us in time. They chased us all the way to the village—and *shot* at us too, but no one was hit."

Miriam's knees almost buckled. "What will happen now?"

"I don't know. Dat said we are safe here because there are not enough of them to storm the hacienda." Rachel took a deep breath and added, "But they will probably go back and burn our houses and barns."

Miriam started to answer, but her words were drowned out by a booming barrage of rifle fire, thick and close—the men on the hacienda walls.

The bandits were attacking the hacienda.

Chapter 6

When the rifles roared Caleb instinctively herded his family down off the wagon and into the stables, where the smoothly stuccoed walls were plenty thick enough to stop stray bullets. Townspeople and Amish alike ran for cover, screaming, crouching as they ran. Some gathered behind the superintendent's house and a great many ran clear up the hill to take cover behind the main mansion. Caleb and his family mingled with the panic-stricken throng pouring through the big double doors of the stables.

He rushed his brood to the other end of the long building, mother and daughters huddling together in sheer terror. The guns thundered steadily. Men were fighting and dying *right there* on the other side of the hacienda walls—an unimaginable horror.

Counting heads, Caleb suddenly missed Rachel. Scanning the crowd in the stables he saw several white kapps, but only one with flame red hair. She was at the far end, by the doors, talking to a couple of Mexican women. In the shadows of the stables it didn't immediately dawn on him that the Mexican woman in the fancy white dress with the roses embroidered on it was Miriam. Before he thought about it he pointed her out to Mamm—a big mistake. Mamm turned her face to the wall, fetching a handkerchief from her pocket as her shoulders began to shake, weeping.

Caleb leaned close and whispered in her ear, "She is still our daughter, Mamm. I must speak to her. You stay here with the girls."

Mamm nodded without turning.

When Caleb walked up, the plump Mexican woman between Miriam and Rachel was complaining bitterly about her husband.

"My Paco is up on the walls with Domingo. In his *wedding clothes*! Just try to keep a Zapara out of a fight, Miriam. You'll see. Silly old goat."

Miriam was listening intently when Caleb walked up. It was a tense moment. He wasn't sure whether Miriam was ignoring him or just didn't see him. He studied her embroidered dress for a minute—the white satin shoes in her hand, the lacy mantilla veil over her undone hair.

"Miriam Bender," he said softly.

Miriam's mouth flew open in shock, but she collected her wits quickly. "*Me llamo* Miriam Zapara," she said, and there was a hint of respectful sadness in her eyes. "I am Domingo's wife. This is Maria, his aunt. She is my madrina."

So it was done. "Are you all right?" he managed to ask.

"Sí, Dat. I am unharmed, but I am afraid for Domingo. He is on the wall with a rifle."

Caleb gazed in the direction of the gate. "Sí, he would be. I hope he doesn't get himself killed."

There was a commotion by the door as a Mexican in fancy clothes stumbled into the stable clutching his shoulder. He dropped to his knees in the dirt, his face ghostly pale.

Maria wailed. "Paco!" She ran to her husband and peeled

off his jacket to reveal a shirtsleeve soaked in blood. Kyra went to her aid, kneeling beside Maria and ripping away her uncle's shirt before they laid him down on top of his ruined jacket.

Paco smiled weakly up at his wife. "A flesh wound, Maria. The bullet passed through. I have been hurt worse shaving."

Feigning anger, Maria's eyes widened and she hissed at him, "Sí, you will live, but you will *still* be an old fool!" Her hands never stopped working, wiping blood, applying pressure. Kyra ripped Paco's wedding shirt into long strips to make bandages.

Caleb went over and knelt in the dirt beside the wounded man's head.

"I am Caleb Bender, Miriam's father," he said. "Perhaps you can tell me, Señor . . ."

"Zapara. But Miriam's father may call me Paco."

"Paco, if you are able, can you tell me what happened out there? I didn't think the bandits would attack the hacienda."

"They didn't, at first." Paco winced as Maria jerked a bandage tight. "The *bandidos* stopped short of the town when they saw all the rifles on the walls. They turned around to go back to your valley, but three wagonloads of federales came down Saltillo Road and blocked their retreat. The bandidos had no choice but to take cover in the village where they were caught between the hacienda walls and the federales, taking fire from both sides."

As he spoke, the rifle fire from the walls grew sporadic, then stopped entirely.

"The troops have come, then," Caleb said. "This is good."

Paco gave him a doubtful look and half shrugged with his good shoulder. "Maybe. We will see."

A shadow fell across them both, and when Caleb looked up, Domingo was standing in the door, rifle in hand. Miriam ran to him and opened his jacket, searching for wounds.

The echo of a pistol shot came from beyond the walls, and a few seconds later, another. Caleb watched the men on the walls. None of them seemed alarmed by the shots. They didn't even raise their rifles.

Domingo put an arm around his bride and smiled.

"I have no wounds, Cualnezqui, but you are welcome to keep looking for one if you wish." Then he spotted Caleb. His arm dropped away from Miriam and he suddenly became serious again.

"Your federales arrived just in time, Señor Bender. Half of the bandits fell in the streets and the rest have taken refuge in the church. The battle is all but over."

Another solitary pistol shot echoed from the distance. "Then why are they still shooting?" Caleb asked.

Domingo shrugged. "The troops are cleaning up."

"Cleaning up?"

"Sí. Some of the bandits were only wounded. The federales finish them."

"No! They can't do that!" Horrified, Caleb went to the door to see for himself. From the height of the stables he could see over the walls to the far edge of the town below. The street was full of smoke, but in the distance he could make out what he thought were a couple of men, lying prone in the hazy street. The silhouette of a soldier appeared through the smoke and dust to stand over one of the downed bandits. The man on the ground moved, raised a hand. The soldier aimed his pistol, his arm recoiled, and a second later Caleb heard the sharp report. The bandit's hand dropped lifeless into the dust.

Caleb stormed out the door and down the hill toward the gate. The haciendado's men parted for him as he stalked up to the gate, hoisted the bar aside and heaved open the heavy iron gate.

He could see rifles lining the rooftops and protruding from

windows, all pointed at the church. Four bandits lay scattered in the open ground between him and the church, none of them moving. Across the way he saw a clutch of federales gathered in the lee of the nearest building on the main street. One of them was peeking around the corner, watching the church.

He headed straight for the federales, striding purposefully and erect across the thirty yards of open ground. Halfway there, a shot rang out from the belfry of the church, and dirt flew up in front of him. He didn't flinch, didn't break stride. A second shot tore open the front of his coat but didn't touch his flesh. He kept walking, and this time a barrage of rifle fire answered from both sides, peppering the stone tower. Five yards short of his goal Caleb was tackled from behind and driven to the ground. Domingo grabbed his arm and yanked him roughly past the corner of the building, then helped him to his feet.

"You are *loco!*" Domingo said, pointing. "The men in that church came here to kill us. Did you think they would not shoot at you?"

Caleb ignored him, turning to the half-dozen soldiers who stood gaping at him in confusion. They wore brown uniforms with a thick belt on top of their shirts, and flat-top military caps. Apart from that, and the leather shoes on their feet in place of sandals, they looked nearly as ragged and desperate as the bandits.

"Who is in charge here?"

One of the federales stepped forward, bowed slightly and tipped his cap. A short hawk-faced man with a pencil-thin mustache, his dull brown tunic bore markings and medals the others didn't have, though Caleb didn't know what any of them meant.

"*Capitán* Soto, at your service." The captain waved casually at the open ground Caleb had just crossed and added, "I must say I agree with your young friend. You are indeed loco, Señor . . ."

"Bender. Caleb Bender. Captain Soto, you must stop your men from shooting the wounded. It is *murder*, plain and simple. I am the one who sent for you, but I would never have done it if I knew your men were going to slaughter people like pigs. I will not tolerate—"

"Tolerate? You will not *tolerate?*" Soto took a step closer and his eyes narrowed. "You have an American accent. You are not even *Mexican*, Señor Bender. I was told the haciendado sent for us, but it does not matter. I answer to my commander, and he to his, all the way up to *el presidente* himself. We do not take orders from the haciendado, and certainly not from some gringo. My job is to kill bandits. I think you should go hide someplace and let me do my job."

One of the soldiers peeked around the corner the whole time, keeping watch on the front of the church. Now he turned to Captain Soto and said, "Capitán, they are waving a white flag."

Soto turned his back on Caleb, straightened his tunic and stepped out from the corner to see for himself. He looked back at Domingo and snapped his fingers.

"*You*—come here."

Domingo and Caleb both stepped out to where they could see the church. A handkerchief fluttered in the crack of the door, and a head protruded. There was a skullcap on the back of his head.

"Who is this man?" Soto asked.

"Father Noceda," Domingo answered. "The parish priest, and a good man. He must have been trapped in the church when the bandits took it."

Soto cupped his hands around his mouth and shouted, "What do you want, priest?"

The door opened a little wider and Father Noceda stepped out, dressed in the full cassock he'd worn for the wedding.

"These men have requested sanctuary," he shouted back, "and I must grant it to them. You must not attack this building. It is *God's* house."

Captain Soto shot a sarcastic glance at his clutch of officers and they broke into quiet laughter, shaking their heads.

He shouted back, "You are mistaken, priest. Things have changed. Perhaps you have not heard that we have a new presidente. His name is Plutarco Calles, and he does not cower before your God. I am afraid even *you* will not find sanctuary behind your stone walls. I am hereby decommissioning your church and appropriating the building in the name of the federal government."

Soto glanced aside at his men, chuckling. "It will make a good barracks, don't you think? Easily defended, plenty of room, and there is even a rectory in the back for me and my lieutenants." He turned his attention back to Father Noceda. "I will give you one minute to make up your mind whose side you are on, priest. After that, we will treat you the same as the murdering thieves who are hiding behind your skirts."

The priest surveyed the line of rifles pointed at him from both sides. Without another word he turned slowly and went back inside, but a few seconds later the door opened wide and he was hurled out. Noceda bounced across the portico, cassock flying, and tumbled down the front steps all the way to the bottom.

He picked himself up very slowly, retrieving his skullcap from the bottom step and dusting it off. The door creaked nearly shut before a shot came from the church door, kicking up a little cloud of dust by the priest's feet. He jumped back and scurried away as quickly as he could to the nearest building.

The shot was enough to drive Soto back behind the wall of the store, along with Domingo and Caleb.

Captain Soto glanced at Domingo. "Who is their leader?"

"El Pantera."

"El Pantera! I have heard of this man. He led a company under Pancho Villa during the Revolution. He is a fierce warrior."

Soto stuck his head around the corner and shouted, "El Pantera! Or should I call you Captain Aguilar? It seems the panther has lost his teeth. You are surrounded. There is no escape. Will you surrender?"

A hard voice growled from the crack in the door. "Come and take me."

"Captain Aguilar, I think maybe you have not given enough thought to your predicament. You have chosen a fine place to make your last stand, but now you are trapped between the guns of the hacienda and seventy-five federales. You cannot escape, and it would be foolish to waste the lives of my men attacking such a fortress, so it seems we are at an impasse. I am sure we could devise a way to burn the building down around you, but it's such a *pretty* building and I really hate to destroy my new barracks."

He chuckled at himself for a few seconds, and his men laughed with him.

"I think I will wait," he shouted. "I am a very patient man, Aguilar. Without food or water you will be dead in a few days anyway, and then I will have only to burn the bodies."

Silence. The church door closed, and remained so for a good five minutes.

One of Soto's lieutenants grew impatient, cocked his rifle and said, "We can storm the church if you wish, my capitán. Anytime."

Soto calmly rolled a cigarette between his fingers, licked it and stuck it in his mouth. "No," he said as he struck a match. "No more of my men will die today. Aguilar is no fool, and he has no choice. Be patient. He will try to bargain with us."

The raspy voice called out from the church door, "*Oiga,* Federale!"

Captain Soto stuck his head out and shouted, "Sí, I am still here. Have you reconsidered?"

"If we lay down our guns, will you let my men live?"

Soto smiled. "Of course! I am not a monster, Aguilar."

But Caleb was beginning to wonder. From where he was standing he could see precious little difference between those who attacked him and those who came to defend him. Before today he could not have imagined feeling a twinge of sympathy for the bandits who killed his son.

Chapter 7

Rachel didn't realize her father was gone until she looked out the door and saw him halfway to the gate with the stride of a man on a mission. She had no idea what angered her dat but she knew that walk, that posture. Nothing could stop him when he got like that. By the time she realized what he was doing he'd reached the gate and thrown the bar.

"Domingo!" she shouted, and pointed out her father. Domingo sprinted after him. They were both outside the gate when she heard shots fired, and the rifles on the walls thundered again. And then silence.

She and Miriam clung to each other in terror. Dat and Domingo were out there somewhere in the middle of all that shooting. The sisters held each other and began to pray.

Afraid to leave the protection of the stable, Rachel and Miriam waited by the door for what seemed like hours, watching, listening. Finally, their father walked calmly through the gate and up the hill as if nothing had happened. Rachel burst from cover and ran halfway down the hill to meet him.

"Dat, what's happening? Where did you go?"

"I had to speak to the commander of the troops, that's all. The battle is over. The bandits have surrendered."

Miriam's voice came from behind her, high-pitched, quavering. "Where is Domingo?"

"Your husband is unharmed, Miriam. The captain detained him to identify some of the bandits. Captain Soto has never seen El Pantera's face before."

"I have, and I don't care to see him again," Rachel said. "So it's done, then?"

"Jah, we can go home now. It's safe."

Miriam started toward the gate, but Caleb grabbed her arm. "Domingo will be back shortly," he said. "You don't want to see what's out there right now."

The whole family loaded onto the wagon and was starting toward the gate when Jake appeared on horseback, trotting along beside them. He reached out to touch hands with Rachel, relief written plainly in his eyes.

"Is everyone all right?" he asked.

"Jah, we are fine," she said. She wanted to tell him about Miriam but her mother was right there, still distraught.

After they emerged from the gates into the open courtyard Rachel saw why her father had stopped Miriam from going out alone. The scene in the churchyard was horrific, bodies lying about in the dirt, soldiers lining the rooftops with rifles held at the ready. A handful of federales led a line of bandits away in chains, most of them wounded, limping. Mamm buried her face in her hands while Rachel's sisters averted their eyes.

Halfway across the open ground between the gate and the village someone called out from the church. "You there! Come here!" One of the federales—a small sharp-featured man—beckoned to them from the portico of the church, and now she saw

Domingo standing next to him. She also saw the fear and loathing in her father's eyes as he slowly turned the wagon. Jake's horse trotted alongside.

The wagon pulled up in front of the portico, and her dat stared hard at the soldier. "You need something from me, Captain Soto?"

The officer grinned, but there was a hollowness in it that sent a shiver up Rachel's spine. His grin reminded her of El Pantera. The captain motioned to one of his men, who stepped inside and shoved a lanky bandit out in front of him. The prisoner's hands were tied behind him and his head was bowed as he stumbled onto the portico, hat missing, hair hanging loose. It wasn't until he stopped and looked up at her that she saw the long jagged scar angling down across that odd, milky eye.

El Pantera.

Terrified, even now, she shrank down behind her father. Jake reached over from his horse to brace a hand on her shoulder.

Captain Soto said, "*Lo siento*, but it wasn't you I wanted, Señor Bender. I was calling to your young friend. Our horses were scattered in the fight and my men are still rounding them up, so I will borrow this one. For El Pantera. He will not need it long—only a few minutes, señor, and then you can have it back."

Rachel flinched and her face turned deep red as she spotted a clutch of soldiers near the hacienda wall tossing a rope over the stout horizontal limb of a big oak tree. There was a noose on the end of the rope.

"You gave your word," Dat rasped, his eyes sharp and fierce. "You promised you would let them live."

Captain Soto shook his head, still grinning. "No, my *yanqui* amigo, I promised I would let his *men* live. Perhaps next time Captain Aguilar will choose his words more carefully."

The captain was *laughing*.

"You can't have my horse," Jake said. "Not for that."

But two of the federales were on him before he knew what was happening. One of them grabbed the reins while the other pulled Jake from the saddle and flung him roughly to the ground. Two others dragged El Pantera down the steps and hoisted him up into Jake's saddle.

Jake rolled onto his back and sat up, shaking his head as if to clear it.

El Pantera glared down at him, and as soon as he steadied himself on the horse he leaned out and spit on Jake.

"Coward!" he hissed. "All these months I thought it was Domingo Zapara who murdered my guard in the barn that night, but when I confronted him a few minutes ago I saw the truth in his eyes. He was not the one. That leaves only you, you spineless worm. You won't fight, but you will sneak up behind an unarmed man in the dark and choke him to death with a chain!"

Jake crabbed backward on the ground, eyes wide in stark terror, glancing desperately from Domingo to Rachel and back to El Pantera.

"But the guard lived!" Jake cried. "He was *alive*—they *said* so!"

As a soldier tugged on El Pantera's reins and led him away, the bandit twisted around in his saddle and spat at Jake one more time. His gaunt face was purple with rage, cursing Jake to the last.

Jake pulled himself to his feet and grabbed the side of the wagon with both hands, his anguished eyes pleading with Rachel, imploring her to refute the bandit's accusation.

"Rachel, tell them!"

But she couldn't do it. She knew the truth, and she couldn't bear the hurt in Jake's eyes, the pain of betrayal. Rachel covered her face and wept.

Her father clucked at the horses, and she felt the wagon lurch to the left, turning away from the scene. No matter what else plagued his thoughts in that moment, her dat would never have his children bear witness to a hanging.

But Rachel raised her head and looked back. The noose was around El Pantera's neck now, that white eye still glaring, that gravelly voice still railing at Jake.

"Stand and watch, coward! I will show you how a *man* dies!" El Pantera roared through gritted teeth as he spurred the horse out from under himself and swung, kicking.

Horrified, Jake sank to his knees in the dusty churchyard while Caleb drove away without looking back.

Rachel couldn't bear it. She hid her face, but even above the rattle of harness and the rumble of wheels she could hear the faint groan and creak of that rope, the sounds of a man dying.

Domingo and his nephews finally managed to round up the carriages and horses, and the wedding party regrouped behind the church. The troops took over the church building exactly as Captain Soto had promised.

Father Noceda limped up to the party as they were helping Uncle Paco into the carriage.

"Is everyone all right?" he asked.

Miriam stared at the trickle of blood working its way down the priest's forehead.

"Sí," she said. "Uncle Paco is wounded, but he will survive. What will *you* do, now that you have no church?"

Two soldiers pulled up next to the rectory in a mule-drawn wagon full of boxes and started carrying supplies inside.

"He has no *home*, either," Domingo said, laying a hand on

Father Noceda's shoulder. "Come with us, Father. We will find you a place to stay."

"But it's your wedding day," Noceda protested.

"Not anymore," Miriam said, glancing around at the carnage.

Domingo put an arm around her and smiled. "Miriam, this is *our* day, and I will not let El Pantera steal it from us. He has taken enough."

She looked at herself, tugged at the sides of her wedding dress. "But there is blood on my dress—"

He lifted her chin with a finger. "You would have changed it anyway as soon as the party started. I hate to spoil Kyra's surprise, but there are two more dresses you must wear on this day. *Beautiful* new dresses."

"But look around, Domingo. Men have *died* here today."

"Then we will light a candle for the souls of the dead. But life must go on, and what better way to put all this behind us? The house is already decorated, the feast prepared. I have waited all my life for this day, Cualnezqui, and so have you. In our new home we will find peace, and the joy of sharing our new life with our family."

She stared at him for a moment until she felt herself melting under his astonishing strength.

"Sí," she said softly, and then remembered the priest. "Will you come with us, *por favor?*"

The priest gazed longingly over his shoulder for a second. There were soldiers wandering in and out of his rectory, laughing, smoking, cursing.

"Sí, I might as well. I have nothing left here," he said, and climbed into the carriage.

Domingo drove the lead carriage himself, since Paco was wounded. Miriam sat up front beside her husband on the driver's seat.

As soon as they got under way Domingo leaned close and muttered, "Lo siento, Cualnezqui. I would have done anything to keep this darkness from your wedding day."

She smiled, tightening her grip on his arm. "We are together. I am content."

They rode along for a little ways before she asked, "Domingo, what will we do with Father Noceda? Your house is too crowded already. I wasn't even sure where *we* would sleep, and now there is another."

He grinned. "I was going to save the surprise for later, but now I think it is best to go ahead and tell you. Over the winter my nephews made bricks, and in the evenings I built you a house. It is only two rooms, but big enough . . . for now."

Warmth flushed through her and she blushed, knowing what he meant.

"I know how to make bricks, too," she said. "When the time comes that we need to add on, we will do it together. Together, we can do anything."

Shocked speechless by all she had witnessed, Rachel didn't say a word all the way home. Her father pulled up to the corral, stopped, and just sat there for a minute, watching smoke rise from the ruins of Levi's barn a quarter mile to the west.

"Harvey, leave the wagon hitched and wait here. You and me will be going to Levi's shortly." He set the brake and climbed down from the wagon. "Rachel, come with me."

She followed her dat without a word, head down, past the corral and up the ridge, almost to the tree line. This was about Jake, and she knew it. She'd seen her dat's wheels turning as he pieced it all together during the ride home. He knew she had lied to him. Trailing along in her father's footsteps as he trudged up the steep face of the ridge she couldn't help thinking of Isaac, following Abraham.

Please let there be a ram, she prayed.

He sat down on an outcropping of rock overlooking his farm, took off his hat and patted the rock beside him.

"Sit," he said.

She sat.

He was silent for a minute or two as he gathered his thoughts, and then he said, quietly but sternly, "I want you to tell me the truth."

She tugged at her kapp strings, thinking. There would be no more lies, but her whole future might very well depend on how she shaped the truth.

"Do you remember when I told you about the night I was chained in El Pantera's barn at Diablo Canyon?"

Caleb nodded curtly. "Jah, I remember well. You said Jake knocked out the guard and that was how you escaped."

"There was more to it than that."

"Tell me the whole truth, Rachel. I want to know everything."

"The guard came to me alone in the middle of the night. To harm me." She hesitated then, embarrassed.

"You don't have to say any more about that," her dat said. "I understand."

"He came into the stall where I was chained, put his hand over my mouth and told me what he was going to do. He would have done it, but Jake came and stopped him. Jake caught him from behind with his handcuff chains and choked him."

"Jah, so that much was true, but it wasn't the *whole* truth, was it?"

She took a deep breath and her gaze dropped away from her father. "No, Dat. The guard was dead. Jake never *meant* to kill him, but it was dark as pitch and he couldn't see. He only wanted to stop the man, to make him pass out, but Jake was half crazy with fear and I guess he held the chain too long, too tight. I lit a match and . . . it was awful."

"Are you sure the man was dead?"

Recalling the sight, she was overcome with emotion for a moment. Finally she managed, "Jah. There was no doubt. I only saw his face for a second, but it was a horrible sight. When Jake came to his senses he ran away to the other side of the barn. He didn't see what I saw."

"So Jake believed the guard was still alive?"

"No, not at first. He was so sure he killed a man that he nearly lost his mind. The flames of hell flashed before his eyes and he couldn't think of anything else. He didn't hardly know where he was after that." Now she clutched at her father's arm, pleading her case. "Dat, we only had one chance to escape and we needed Jake to be alert. Domingo saw how shook up he was, so he lied to him. Domingo told Jake he saw the guard breathing, that he was only unconscious."

"But Domingo knew the man was dead?"

"Jah, he took the guard's weapons. He knew. When Jake asked me if Domingo was telling the truth, I lied, too. I said yes, the guard was alive, and Jake believed me because he trusted me. He was all right after that. Dat, I don't believe we would ever have made it out alive if we hadn't lied to Jake about the guard."

Her father's jaw tightened and he stared straight ahead.

"So why didn't you tell him after you got home? It's been seven months, Rachel. The boy you love has been walking around in danger of hell's fire for seven months, and he didn't even know it. All because of you. Why didn't you tell him the truth?"

She hung her head and began to cry softly. "I was afraid he would be sent away and his father wouldn't let him come back. I didn't want to lose him."

Her dat stared into space a bit longer, and then as he jammed his hat back on his head and started to rise he said something that cut her like a knife.

"The truth is more important than what you *want*, child. I'm disappointed in you."

The dam broke then. Rachel Bender could bear almost anything, but not her father's disappointment. She lay on the rock with her face on her arms and wept.

"Jake will confess," her father snapped. "He will have the chance to repent before Gott and his brethren, and cleanse his soul. A man's soul is no one's plaything, Rachel."

Then he stalked off down the hill and left her alone.

Chapter 8

Emma clutched baby Will tight with one hand and hung on to the buggy rail with the other. Levi was pushing the horse harder than he should, his eyes fixed on the thick column of smoke in the distance. Little Mose and Clara clung to each other in the back seat as the buggy jostled hard over rocks and through ruts, flying past the other buggies and wagons.

She tried to calm him, once. "There's no need for such haste, Levi. What's done is done."

But Levi only leaned forward and whipped the reins harder. "You never know. We might still save something."

He let out a long wail of anguish as soon as they were close enough to see. The barn had already collapsed in on itself, a tangled mass of charred rubble still belching smoke and flame from between the adobe foundation walls. A lone mule and a draft horse looked up at them from the kitchen garden as their buggy bounced into the yard. A few chickens pecked at the dirt by the smokehouse, but there were no other signs of life. Dead horses and cows lay scattered in the barn lot.

The open front door of the house hung by one hinge, smoke crawling out the top of the doorframe. The roof was still intact.

Levi jerked the buggy to a stop and leaped out, running. He grabbed a bucket from the back porch, filled it from the horse trough and rushed into the house. Two other buggies rolled up as Levi stumbled out the door and doubled over, coughing and gagging.

They found more buckets, and the women carried water while the men doused the flames and dragged smoldering cabinets out of the house.

"It's only the cabinets," Levi wheezed. "The rafters never did catch, and adobe walls don't burn."

By the time Dat and Harvey arrived the fire was out. Levi had destroyed his coat beating out the flames, and one of the cabinets left a nasty burn on his forearm, but the house was still standing.

In the barn lot, the men loaded two dead cows onto wagons to be strung up and butchered. Even though it was a Sunday, they couldn't afford to waste the meat.

In the evening, after everyone left, Emma walked out to the barn lot where Levi stood alone, leaning on a shovel outside the smoldering ruins of his barn. He was completely exhausted, his beard singed, his shirt filthy and torn, but beneath the weariness she could see rage in his eyes.

"It could have been worse," she said softly, holding little Will on her hip. "We still have our house, and the fields were too green yet to burn."

Levi sighed heavily, glaring at the carnage. "Besides our stores of hay and grain we lost a good mule, a milk cow, a yearling Guernsey bull, a fine kid-broke draft horse, a wagon, a harrow and a planter. All gone," he said, his voice a raspy whisper from fatigue and smoke. "Was this Gott's doing, Emma? Punishment for our unconfessed sin?"

She rubbed his shoulder. "Aw, Levi, everything bad that happens is not Gott's punishment. Sometimes it's just bandits. There are bad people in the world."

He still refused to look at her. "Then why did they only burn *our* barn? Why not someone else's?"

"Ours was the first one they came to, that's all."

"A lot of hard work, wasted."

Emma shook her head, put an arm around him. "But it's only work, Levi. Our children are safe. The things we lost are only things, and we have family and good neighbors to help us rebuild. We're going to work every day of our lives anyway, no matter what comes, and even now, with the help of Gott and neighbors we will want for nothing. We will still have food to eat and a roof over our heads. We are blessed."

Watching his eyes, she saw that he remained unconvinced. From birth, his heavy-handed father had pounded it into him that no sin would go unpunished, ever. She could see it still, in Levi's angry eyes, and she knew his thoughts. The two of them had sinned before Gott and had never confessed publicly. In Levi's world, every ill wind was divine retribution.

"We are cursed," he said.

Shifting Will to her other hip she smiled patiently and kissed his cheek.

"No, Levi. We are blessed. In time, you will see."

He looked down at the baby she was holding and gently ran his blackened fingers through Will's curly brown hair. When his eyes met hers she saw it—the glimmer of hope, the beginning of faith. Levi trusted her. In time, he would come to know the Gott of love and forgiveness that she knew.

In time.

The butchering of Levi's cows kept some of the men busy all afternoon, but they managed to gather in Caleb's barn that evening. Because of everything that had happened there would be no youth singing, although the church benches remained in place.

They were all there except Levi, sitting shoulder to shoulder on a couple of benches in the back—Caleb's son-in-law Ezra, John Hershberger, Ira Shrock and the five new men. Caleb stood before them, and with grim determination told them everything Rachel had confessed about what happened that night in El Pantera's barn at Diablo Canyon. There were gasps of astonishment, along with a few grunts and groans as he talked, but no one interrupted.

"The question that is in my mind," Caleb said, "is what do we do now?"

Ira Shrock was the first to speak. "If the boy killed somebody he will have to be put in the ban, it's as simple as that. We cannot abide a murderer in our midst. But we don't have a bishop, and it don't look to me like we're going to have one anytime soon."

"That might change," Mahlon Yutzy said hopefully, "now that we got rid of those bandits."

"They're not the only bandits in the land," Ira huffed.

Atlee Hostetler chimed in. "Jah, but now that we have troops in the valley we won't be having so much trouble. We should write and tell the folks back home. Maybe a bishop will come at last."

Caleb nodded, but he didn't share their enthusiasm for the troops. They had not seen the things he'd seen.

"I will write them," he said. "But just now we have to decide what to do with Jake."

Hershberger, the man who was working Jake as a hired hand and knew him best, raised a finger and said, "I think we should take things in order here. We haven't heard from Jake, nor have we heard from two witnesses."

"Did you bring him?"

"Jah, just like you asked me to. He is waiting outside. What about the witnesses? Two witnesses are needed for a proper hearing."

"I don't think there *were* two witnesses," Caleb answered. "Only Rachel. Domingo knows the truth, but he's not one of us."

"We can't have a proper hearing anyway, since we don't have a bishop," Hershberger said. "So let's bring Jake in here and see what he has to say for himself. We can listen to Rachel, too. We should hear this from the lips of those who were there, don't you think?"

Several of the men mumbled words of assent.

Caleb motioned to Ezra, who stepped outside and returned in a moment with Jake trailing behind.

They questioned Jake at length. He freely admitted his guilt, and it was clear from his demeanor that he felt deep and terrible remorse, though he respectfully maintained that he never meant to kill the man.

As soon as Jake was allowed to leave, Ezra fetched Rachel from the house and they interviewed her. She confirmed everything Jake had told them, holding nothing back, even when they asked her why Jake attacked the man in the first place.

"The bandit was on top of me," she said. "He came to me in the middle of the night to—" she hesitated, blushing, but then straightened herself—"to do terrible things to me. He tried once before, when we camped in the mountains, but El Pantera stopped him then."

The men stirred and muttered among themselves.

Ira Shrock raised an eyebrow. "Why was this bandit so interested in you? Did you do something to provoke him?"

Caleb gave him a hard look, but said nothing.

Rachel met Ira's stare. "I was forced to ride with him, sitting in front of him on his horse for hours, traveling through the mountains. He said many awful things to me about what he planned to do. I said nothing, did nothing. My hands were tied."

Ira nodded. "You did *nothing*? Sin begins with tempta—"

"Enough," Caleb said. "She was *bound*, Ira—a prisoner. She had just seen her brother killed by these same bandits, and I'll thank you to remember that she's my daughter." He didn't raise his voice, yet his tone was clear and firm.

Ever the peacemaker, Hershberger broke in before Ira could say anything else and started a different line of questioning. "Jake says he didn't mean to kill the man, that he only meant to put him to sleep. Do you believe this is the truth?"

Rachel nodded. "I'm sure of it."

"How can you be certain? Can you read Jake's thoughts?"

"No, but I saw El Pantera trick him when they were wrestling by the campfire. That's why—"

Ira broke in again. "Jake *wrestled* with the bandits?"

Rachel's mouth flew open and she looked to her father for help, but Caleb only said, "Answer him."

"Jah," she said reluctantly, "but they forced him to do it. El Pantera held a knife to my throat and said he would kill me if Jake didn't fight him. So Jake agreed, but only to wrestle. He would have won, too, but El Pantera tricked him. Jake got him from behind, with an arm around his throat, choking him, and El Pantera pretended to pass out. When Jake let go he jumped up and started hitting Jake with his fists."

Ira smirked. "So the man in the barn was not the *first* bandit Jake strangled."

Rachel's eyes narrowed and her lips tightened into a thin line. "He never had a choice, Ira, and he never meant to kill that bandit."

Ira's expression didn't change. "But, woman, he fought with a bandit, and the bandit died. Gott's Word does not say, Thou shalt not *mean* to kill; it only says thou shalt not *kill*."

Caleb sighed heavily. "Jake's transgressions are between him and Gott, who knows his heart. We are only trying to decide what *we* should do. I think there have been enough questions. Rachel, you must leave now, so we can talk."

She found Jake just outside, leaning back against the wall of the barn with his hands in his pockets. It was the first time she'd seen him since that morning in the churchyard, and the forlorn look was still in his eyes. He barely glanced at her.

"You lied to me," he said.

She made sure no one was looking before she took his arm. "Jake, I'm sorry we lied to you, but there was nothing else we could do. You were acting like a dead man, the way you're acting right now. None of us would have escaped if we hadn't lied to you. Would you rather I was sold as a slave?"

He thought for a moment, then shook his head slowly. "No. I suppose a lie is better than that. But you could have told me after we got home."

"Jah, and then what?"

He looked at her, shrugged. He didn't see it.

"Then they send you to Ohio to face the bishop," she said. "And you never come back. I didn't want to lose you."

His eyes widened as understanding took hold. Gripping her shoulders, he looked deeply into her eyes. "Rachel, you *can't* lose me. Did you learn nothing in Diablo Canyon? We can be separated for a time, but I will come to you. No matter how far, no matter who stands in the way, if I can draw breath I will find my way back to you."

Overcome with emotion, she couldn't answer.

"Anyway," he said, "you're forgetting something. In less than a year I'll be twenty and then I can make my own decisions."

This was true. In their district a boy became his own man at the age of twenty. He could keep the money he earned and go wherever he wanted.

A kiss brushed her forehead. It was the lightest of kisses and yet it rolled through her like a warm wave. Forgiveness.

"Jake, what did they say to you?"

He sighed deeply. "They just asked a lot of questions about what happened. I will be banned, I could see it in their eyes. But not for long. I'll repent and be forgiven. What about you? Are you in any trouble?"

Rachel hung her head. "Only with my dat. He was upset about the lies, but the church won't do anything since I haven't been baptized."

He nodded. "Jah, I forgot. Maybe I would be better off if I hadn't got baptized when I did."

She heard the shuffling of feet, the murmuring of voices, and let go of his arm. "They're done. Here comes my dat."

Caleb walked up to them slowly with his head down, his wide hat hiding his face. When he finally looked up, Rachel saw the worry lines deepened around his eyes. Miriam's wedding, the battle with the bandits, and now this. It had been a very trying day.

"It was as I feared," Caleb said. "No one here is able to deal with such a thing—or wants to. They were all in agreement that I should write to the bishop back in Ohio and see what he would have us do. But there is another thing on which they all agreed. I must also write to your father, Jake, and tell him everything."

"What will happen now?" Rachel asked.

"Most likely Jake will have to appear before the church and the bishop, where punishment will be decided. He will probably be banned, at least for a time."

"Will the bishop come here?" Jake asked.

"We won't know that until we get a letter back from him," Caleb said. "I'll write him tonight and maybe we'll have an answer in two or three weeks."

Chapter 9

Miriam braced herself for the inevitable culture shock of going from American Amish to Mexican peasant, but nothing could have prepared her for the wedding party. Domingo said only relatives and close friends would be there, so she was shocked when half the population of San Rafael turned up at Kyra's house. Red was the color she had chosen for her wedding, to match the roses on her dress; the whole house and yard were trimmed in red banners and clay pots of red cactus flowers. Half of the women wore red dresses. When she and Domingo climbed down from the carriage the guests lined the walk for the ritual entry of the new couple into his mother's home—or in this case his sister's home where his mother lived.

"The whole clan is here," Kyra said when Miriam finally made it to the house. "Oh, there will be dancing and singing far into the night."

"But, Kyra, I've ruined my lovely dress."

Kyra's eyes sparkled. "No matter. Come, let's get you cleaned up and then I will show you the *new* dresses Maria and I have made for you."

"New dresses?" Miriam had no trouble feigning surprise, for Kyra's sake.

"Sí. A bride always shows off her finery at the wedding feast—it's the custom. Come!"

There was something different about the bedroom, but in the excitement Miriam didn't realize what it was until after she'd already changed and was about to make her grand entrance.

The dresser was gone. The night she and Kyra left to search for Domingo they had put on Kyra's father's clothes, and she remembered taking them from a lovely little dresser with brass pulls on the drawers and fancy inlaid designs. It seemed out of place in a peasant house—far too elegant and expensive. Kyra said her father had salvaged it from a raid on a hacienda. Until now, in the mad rush of her wedding day, Miriam hadn't even noticed it was missing.

"Kyra, what happened to the little dresser that was here before?"

With a curiously sad smile Kyra took her hand, ran a thumb over the gold ring on Miriam's finger and said, "You are wearing it."

Miriam shook her head. "No, Maria told me about the rings. They belong to the church and will have to—"

"No, *mi hermana*. My mother and I did not want that for you, so we sold the dresser. The ring is bought and paid for. It is yours to keep."

"But that fancy dresser was all that was left of your father! You said it was the only thing the Revolution gave you in return for his life—how could you bear to part with it?"

Kyra smiled. "Miriam, the thing itself was not important, only what it represented. It was a symbol. *This*," she said, touching a fingertip to Miriam's ring, "is a much better symbol. My father is smiling because this is what he himself would have done. He would have loved you so much."

Miriam turned the little gold band on her finger, staring at it in wonder, too moved for words.

"I have never owned a ring before," she finally said. "My people don't wear jewelry. Thank you, sister. Your father lives on in his children, and already I feel like one of them."

Miriam made a grand entrance in her new dress, then sat on a woven mat beside Domingo's chair as the guests filed by to offer best wishes and present their gifts, usually a few pesos.

A trio of guitar players circulated among the crowd outside, the wine flowed, and the singing and dancing began. Miriam did her best to follow Domingo's lead, but her Amish feet betrayed her. Her new family laughed at her, and then *with* her, and when they took it upon themselves to educate her in proper dance steps they did it with such grace and charm that her Amish feet actually learned some of it.

She hadn't laughed so hard in years. Even Paco joined the festivities with his arm in a sling, and she marveled at his great good humor, despite the wound, until he confessed that he'd allowed himself a touch of tequila.

"Only for the pain," he said with a wink.

Domingo cut a striking figure in his wedding clothes, and his pride in his new bride showed in every glance. Dancing close to him at one point, she asked, "Are all Mexican weddings like this?"

"No, usually there is more, but we had to leave out the parts involving the family of the bride." Then, when he saw the sadness in her eyes, he drew her close, kissed her neck and whispered, "It's all right, Cualnezqui. Your new family loves you just as much."

The Zapara women had laid out a huge feast on tables in the backyard, and as the sun went down the wedding party dined by torch and candlelight on fire-roasted beef and all kinds of Mexican delicacies.

It was a raucous, joyful celebration unlike anything she had ever known, and it all flew past her in a colorful blur, like one great long dance. More than once the Amish part of her felt a twinge of guilt at the worldliness of it all, but then at least a dozen times she caught herself thinking, *If only Rachel could see this, she would love it.*

Long after dark it was Kyra who sang the *entrega* to the newlyweds, and it was over.

The guests all said their goodbyes and departed.

Miriam took her husband's arm, and he walked her to their new home.

Her new life.

$$\mathcal{C}_\circ$$

After evening prayers everyone wandered off to bed except Dat. Rachel paused at the foot of the stairs when she saw him set the lantern on the kitchen table. He took paper and envelopes down from a cabinet, along with the little hinged box containing fountain pen and inkhorn, then sat himself down and put his face in his hands.

When he looked up and saw her watching him, she thought surely he would order her up to her room, but he didn't. There was deep regret in his eyes as he motioned to her and said softly, "Come. Sit."

She sat across from him at the table, eyes downcast, unable to face him.

"I want you to know I have forgiven you," he said. "All day I have been thinking about what I must say to the bishop, and

I have learned how hard the truth can be. I don't blame you anymore."

He stared at the blank paper in front of him. "I only wish I didn't have to do this thing. Jake Weaver saved your life, and Domingo's. It grieves me to know that a man died by his hand, but I know Jake. I know he would never kill anyone on purpose. It could only be an accident. Anyway, if Jake didn't do what he did none of you would be here, and now he is to be punished for it."

Dat gave no hint that he wouldn't write the letter, only that he regretted it. The first and most important thing was that Jake's soul was in peril, and the only path to safety was through repentance.

Clinging to a fragile hope, she looked up at him. "Tell me what you really think, Dat. Will the bishop come here?"

Her father knew her too well. She saw his face soften as he read the hope in her eyes like an open book.

But he shook his head sadly. "No, child. I know Bishop Schwartz. He's too old and frail, and anyway he'll want to confer with his ministers and the other bishops on such an unusual matter. He'll never come to Mexico. Jake will have to go to him."

She lowered her gaze. "That's a pity. If the bishop would just come for a visit, there are those of us who would like to be baptized and join the church."

Her father leaned back from the table, his eyes widening. "You have decided, then?"

A nod. "Jah, I am ready. My course will not change."

He studied her for a minute, then reached across the table, lifted her chin with a forefinger and looked into her eyes. "I must know one thing, Rachel, and I want you to tell me the truth. This is not the time for secrets."

"I will."

"Are you only wanting to be baptized so that you can be married?"

The question itself was out of bounds, but these were extreme circumstances. Her father was taking her to a whole new level of trust. Her gaze was steady, her voice firm.

"I'm nineteen years old, Dat. I was barely sixteen when we moved to Mexico, and I have never complained, though it was not my choice to come. If there was a bishop here I would have joined the church already. Do I want to marry Jake? Jah, I do. It is time. It is right. But do I want to be baptized *only* so I can marry? No, that's not the truth. I want this life, and all that comes with it. I want to marry in the faith."

The words hit him like a thunderbolt. Rachel would never dream of trying to intentionally manipulate her father, but it occurred to her now that this was Miriam's wedding day, and she could not have chosen a better time to say the words *marry in the faith.*

He rested his chin in his palm and sat thinking for several minutes. She waited in silence.

"There are problems," he finally said. "You will have to go through instruction classes."

This was routine and she already knew it. Joining the church was a serious matter. All applicants were required to take classes outlining the beliefs and practices of the Amish, the Confession of Faith. There would be nine classes, held during the Sunday service every other week.

"That's more than four months before you could be baptized," her father said. "Even if the bishop did come to Mexico, he would never stay that long."

She still said nothing, and they stared at each other across the table for a moment—long enough for her father to catch up with her thoughts.

A sad smile crept onto his face and he shook a forefinger at her. "You want to go to Ohio with Jake, don't you? But even if you go back and stay long enough to finish the classes, you still won't be able to get married—"

"Because my family won't be there," she said. "That's true, and I've already thought about it. I wouldn't want to be married without my family. What would be the point of having a ceremony at all if not for them? But I *could* be baptized, and then I will be ready if the day ever comes that me and Jake and my family and a bishop are all in the same country at the same time."

The rare hint of sarcasm brought a smile to his face. "All right then. But we will wait for the bishop's letter. *If* he says Jake must go to Ohio, then I will think about it."

Rachel was stunned speechless. Never in a million years could she have seen this coming. Clutching at the neckline of her dress she rose from the chair, turned her back to her father and started across the room on uncertain feet.

"You're welcome," her father's voice said from behind her.

She stopped and looked back, making no effort to hide the tears of joy. "Thank you, Dat," she whispered. "Thank you."

Nothing was the same for Rachel now that Miriam was gone. Leah moved into the vacant spot in the bed, balancing things out a bit. Now Ada, the oldest, and Barbara, the youngest, slept in one bed while the middle two girls slept in the other. Rachel loved her younger sister, but Leah was a flighty seventeen-year-old who liked to talk, and as Dat often said, people who talked all the time very seldom said anything.

Rachel crawled into bed and lay awake for a long time, thinking, her mind running through endless possibilities. She was bursting to talk about it, but Miriam was gone and this was not something she could discuss with Leah.

On Monday morning, though she had barely slept, she got up an hour before daylight to do chores and again felt Miriam's absence. Leah helped with the milking, but she was not Miriam. Sometimes chattering took the place of working.

When the chores were done Rachel went to the kitchen to help Mamm put breakfast on the table. Mamm was nearly as absent as Miriam and kept forgetting where she put things. If Leah talked too much, Mamm made up for it by not talking at all, staring out the back window for minutes at a time while the biscuits burned. When the family sat down to eat, Mamm took one look around the table and her sagging face melted even further.

Since the carnage in the hacienda village, she had spoken very little, eaten almost nothing and never smiled. The color was gone from her cheeks, and she always looked as if she was about to cry.

Not so many years ago, when all her children were still living and at home, there had been thirteen faces around Mamm's table—a thriving, happy, noisy clan—and she was the center of her children's lives. She had always laughed so easily, Rachel recalled, constantly entertained by her hearty brood. Now there were only five children left at home. During breakfast Mamm tilted her head and stared at the empty chairs as if they spoke to her.

When the breakfast dishes were all washed and dried and put away Rachel helped her mother haul out the laundry and set up the washing machine on the back porch. A bone of contention with some of the Amish, the wringer machine was driven by a pulley, powered by a separate little gasoline engine that some said was "worldly." Dat disagreed, and until a bishop told him otherwise he would let her use it.

Mamm fed Caleb's and Harvey's work pants through the wringer in dark silence. The only time she said anything at all was when Rachel was helping hang dresses on the line and she rambled morosely about how there wasn't nearly so much to wash as there once had been.

Even Levi noticed it. Since Emma's kitchen was still a wreck, he and Emma came over for supper that evening, and after dinner Levi and Caleb walked outside in the gathering dusk and leaned on the corral fence to talk. Rachel was taking clothes off the line right next to them and overheard part of the conversation.

"Mamm's not right," Levi said. "She didn't hardly eat a bite of supper."

Caleb put a foot up on the rail. "She'll be fine. She'll eat when she's hungry."

"I can't blame her for being upset, I guess, after all that's happened lately. Dead bandits in the streets, a man hung, my barn burned."

Caleb picked at his teeth with a bit of straw as he watched a colt prance in the corral. "Jah, those things were bad, but not so bad as seeing Miriam in her Mexican wedding dress. That hit her mighty hard."

"It's a terrible shame," Levi said quietly, staring at the ground as if he couldn't bear to intrude on his father-in-law by looking at him just now. "That Miriam was a fine girl."

Rachel dropped the last dress into the basket, picked it up and headed silently for the house, but she'd been wounded by that one word, uncontested by her father.

Was. As if Miriam were dead.

Chapter 10

On Wednesday afternoon Caleb brought the harrow up to the barn and was putting away the draft horses when he heard hoofbeats. Four soldiers on horseback escorted a wagon into the backyard and hailed him as he came out of the barn.

Captain Soto dismounted, shook hands and greeted him like an old friend.

"*Buenos días*, Señor Bender. I trust everyone is well?"

Caleb nodded, a little suspiciously. The knot in the pit of his stomach was the same one he always got when bandits came around. "Sí," he said, rather tersely. "What can we do for you?"

Might as well get to the point. He was not inclined to engage in small talk with this man.

Smiling, the captain waved vaguely toward the wagon. "We are trying to get settled into our new headquarters, my amigo, and things are going very well except that we have found some necessary items in short supply, so we have come to purchase what we need from the local campesinos. What better way to establish a bond between my men and the people we have come to serve, no?"

Caleb nodded slowly, one eyebrow creeping up. "What do you need?"

"Only a few sacks of grain to feed our horses, señor, and perhaps a few ears of corn. Oh, and we will need to purchase six saddle horses—broken, of course."

"I don't have six saddle horses to sell."

Soto laughed. "No, Señor Bender, I can see that, but there are other settlers here."

Caleb eyed the other three soldiers, all mounted on pinto ponies.

"But you got the bandits' horses, didn't you?" He'd seen soldiers corralling the ragged ponies on the outskirts of town as the remainder of the bandits were led away on foot.

"Sí, this is true. We have rounded up all of their ponies, but there are seventy men left in my command. There were seventy-five, but some of my brave men died protecting you from the bandidos. If we are to defend your valley properly my men will need mounts, and we are short six horses. I will buy that one." He pointed to Caleb's best buggy horse, a standard-bred gelding that stood staring at him over the pasture fence.

"He's not for sale."

Captain Soto glanced over his shoulder, then leaned a bit closer and spoke in a low conspiratorial tone, as if sharing a secret he didn't want his men to hear.

"Señor Bender, you must understand my position. I am a company commander in the Mexican National Army, and I have the authority to take whatever I need. Now, I offer to pay you out of kindness, because I don't wish to be a burden to the yanqui campesinos." Then his head tilted and he shrugged. "But if you dishonor me in front of my men . . ."

Caleb was no fool. He could see where this was going.

"All right," he said. "I'll sell you the horse."

Soto grinned and clapped him on the shoulder. "*Muy bueno!* I will pay you a hundred pesos. Corporal, fetch this fine animal from the pasture and put my saddle on him."

"A hundred pesos?" Caleb said, perhaps too indignantly for his own good. "He's worth at least twice that."

Now Soto's smile turned condescending, as though he were talking to a child. "Perhaps in America, but this is Mexico, and things are different here. A hundred pesos is a whole month's pay for a peon or a soldier. But if this paltry sum offends your dignity I can always keep the money."

Caleb glared at the little captain, but he knew from experience it was useless to argue with a thief. He held out a hand, palm up.

Beaming, the captain pressed the coins into Caleb's hand and closed his fingers over them. But Soto wasn't done. While he bargained with Caleb his men climbed up into the barn, and now they began tossing down sack after sack of grain. In the end Soto paid for this too, perhaps a fourth of what it was worth.

"It has been a pleasure doing business with you, Señor Bender," the captain said, "but now I'm afraid we must go. We have other farms to visit, other purchases to make." Soto tested the girth strap to make sure the saddle was properly secured on his new mount, and as he hooked a foot in the stirrup he glanced over his shoulder at Caleb. "By the way, we took care of the rest of the bandidos for you. El Pantera's rabble will trouble you no more."

The wagon driver made some kind of remark that caused a ripple of subdued, sinister laughter among the others.

The knot tightened in the pit of Caleb's stomach. "What did you do?"

Soto's head tilted, puzzled, as if the question made no sense.

"We sent them to the garrison in San Luis Potosi, where they will be hanged."

"You promised you would let them live," Caleb seethed, his nostrils flaring.

Soto spread his hands wide and looked to his *compadres*. "Sí, and I kept my promise! I *did* let them live. I even made the commander of the garrison at San Luis Potosi promise that he would give the bandidos a fair trial before he hangs them."

Caleb's fists clenched white, remembering the words of a Jewish grocer he'd once known in Ohio. The old Jew told him a strange story handed down by his ancestors about when the Red Sea swallowed the Egyptian army. The refugees were jubilant until Gott himself asked them, *"Why do you sing when my children lie drowned in the sea?"* Caleb hadn't quite understood it until now. Try as he might, he could not remain silent.

"I'm starting to think the only thing in this country worth less than a man's life is your word, Captain Soto."

The smile disappeared, and Soto's face reddened as he leaned toward Caleb. "They were bandidos, gringo. Outlaws, murderers, thieves. Five of my men lie dead because of them, and three of the peasants in the village. What would you have me do, release them so they can kill again? Or perhaps I should build a nice jailhouse for them and make myself their servant. Would you have me bring them eggs and toast for breakfast every morning for the rest of their lives? Life is hard here, gringo. Mercy is a luxury we cannot afford, especially for men who only make life harder. I have no sympathy for these men."

"You will answer to Gott one day," Caleb spat.

They laughed at this, the captain and his men, as if it were an old joke.

"Señor Bender," Soto said, still chuckling, "I think perhaps this has been the problem in my country for far too long—too much God and not enough common sense. But the new presidente is taking steps to correct the problem. He will bring order. You will see."

Captain Soto spurred the horse he had just stolen from Caleb, and his men followed him down the lane toward Hershberger's place.

The soldiers had just left when Domingo rode up to the barn on a mule-drawn planter. Climbing down from the seat the young native wiped his forehead with a bandanna.

He pointed with a thumb. "Wasn't that one of your horses?"

Caleb nodded, holding out a hand to show him the coins.

Domingo raised an eyebrow. "A hundred pesos?"

"Not nearly enough for my best buggy horse."

"Better than nothing," Domingo said, instantly grasping the alternative.

Caleb pocketed the money. "I'm starting to wonder if maybe the federales are worse than the bandits. Twice now I have heard Captain Soto say the new president does not fear Gott. What does he mean?"

"Presidente Plutarco Elias Calles, who won the election and took office just before the New Year. He is an atheist, and he has sworn to break the church's grip on Mexico."

"Why?"

"Because he, and many others, see the church as the tool of European imperialists."

Caleb stared at him. "Do you?"

Domingo thought for a moment before saying, "I did, once. Father Noceda disagrees with me, but I have come to believe there are *two* churches. One of them is the buildings and the land, the money and power that attracts evil men and corrupts good ones. The other church is the real one, the one in the hearts of common people who only want to raise their crops and children in peace. They seek only absolution, and hope. Such a hope binds people to each other in ways that men like Captain Soto will never understand. I have only recently come to understand it myself. I am afraid for the *true* church, Señor Bender. Our new president will attack the power, but in the end it will be the common people who suffer. It is always so."

Caleb nodded slowly. Amish or not, his son-in-law was a man of keen perceptions.

℃

On Thursday morning Miriam laid two outfits on the bed, one Amish and one Mexican.

"What should I wear?"

It was an hour before daylight, and Domingo was already dressed in his cotton work clothes and sandals. Miriam had not seen her family since the wedding, apart from the madness at the hacienda, but today was a school day.

School would be held, as always, in her father's buggy shed. Miriam couldn't help being nervous about how she would be received. *Very* nervous.

Domingo wrapped his arms around her waist, kissed her ear. "If you are asking what I would like to see you wear, it does not matter—you make *everything* beautiful. And if you are asking what will upset your family the least, you would know that far better than I."

Now, with Domingo's arms about her, the choice became clear. There was no going back, and no sense in pretending. The plain black dress and kapp would never be seen as accommodation, but hypocrisy. With great trepidation she put on the printed skirt and white blouse, draped a shawl over her shoulders, twisted her hair into a single thick braid, uncovered, and slipped sandals onto her feet.

Domingo went to his mother's barn and hitched his horse to the cart while Miriam dressed. Kyra's two boys sat in the back as the rickety oxcart jostled out of San Rafael and around the end of the ridge, arriving at the Bender farm as the sun peeked over the low hills in the east.

When Domingo pulled up to the buggy shed and stopped, Miriam hesitated, staring at the house.

"Domingo, are you sure about this?"

He took her hand in his. "No. I don't know what will happen, but I do know that whatever it is, it must happen sooner or later. It was a little awkward being around your father the last two days, but he doesn't seem angry. Sad, maybe."

A glimmer of lamplight shone through the cracks of the buggy shed—Rachel, already there. Miriam took a deep breath, steeled herself and climbed down from the cart.

As soon as she stepped through the door, Rachel met her with a hug, then held her at arms' length. "You look lovely," she said. "Marriage must agree with you because you're glowing."

Miriam smiled demurely, but shook her head. "The blush in my cheeks is only nerves. This is a tense moment for me."

But Rachel only smiled. "You're not banned yet, sister. People may talk, but there's nothing they can do. Not yet. Relax."

"How is Mamm?"

Rachel darkened and gave a little shrug. "Not so good. Give her time—she'll get used to the idea."

They were almost done arranging the benches and tables when the children started coming in, and Miriam began to sense that Rachel might be wrong. There *was* something they could do. The Amish were usually the first to arrive, but when it came time to start, the only children in her classroom were Mexican.

Not a single Amish child showed up.

Clutching her shawl about her Miriam went outside to look.

111

From the slight rise where the buggy shed sat she could see the entire lane, and the lanes from the other houses down to the main road. There were no children in sight, anywhere.

Her father came out of the house and headed for the barn, but when he spotted her he changed course. She could hear her own heart pounding as he walked up.

"Buenos días, Señora Zapara," he said. She would have taken it as a kindly greeting if he'd been smiling, but her father's eyes were hard.

"Good morning," she croaked.

"You needn't be looking for the children, Miriam. The Amish grapevine has done its work. I've already heard from most of the fathers that their kinner won't be coming to your school anymore."

Fighting back tears, she clutched her shawl tighter and merely nodded.

He leaned closer and his voice lowered ominously. "What did you expect, Miriam? You want to know what they said? They said they came to Paradise Valley so their children wouldn't be influenced by outsiders all day in school. Every family here— *every one of them*—sold out and picked up and moved a thousand miles, just for that. And now their children are going to be taught by an outcast? A baptized woman who chose to walk away from the church? What did you *think* would happen?"

When she saw her father in the hacienda stable right after the wedding he hadn't seemed angry, only a little sad. But the Amish grapevine had indeed done its work, and now she saw in his eyes the disapproval, perhaps even the scorn, of his brethren. She had shamed him. She couldn't hold back the tears, but she clung to one last hope.

"I am not yet banned," she whispered.

"You will be. You've broken from your church, and *they* know it even if you don't. These people don't need a ban to tell them who they should allow to teach their kinner."

Her eyes drifted down, away from his hard glare, as tears tracked her cheeks. "Shall I continue to use your buggy shed, then?"

"Do as you wish until the ban comes, but you'll only be teaching Mexican children."

He walked away, but after a few steps he stopped. Half turning, he looked her up and down. "And don't go into the house dressed like that," he said. "It would only upset your mother."

It took her a few minutes to collect herself. Then, wiping the tears from her face, she went back into the buggy shed. She had a class to teach.

At lunchtime Rachel went to the house to eat while Miriam stayed behind. A few minutes later Domingo came into the buggy shed carrying two plates.

Shocked, Miriam asked, "Did they put you out?"

He shook his head, smiled. "No, but I am a free man. I choose to eat with my wife."

Somehow she made it through the day, and somehow her brother and sisters managed to avoid her the entire time. But she had time to think. None of this was the children's fault, and it was unfair to deprive the Amish children of an education. Devastating as it was, there remained only one solution.

"One last thing," she said as the Mexican children cleared their tables, preparing to leave. "After today I will not be coming here anymore. From now on *Señorita* Rachel will be your teacher. I want you to treat her with respect and listen to her, okay?"

The children took it in stride, granting Miriam only a brief parting hug before they bolted into the sunshine, oblivious to her anguish.

But Rachel knew. She didn't have to be told what the

boycott of the Amish children meant, and that Miriam had no alternative but to withdraw.

"Miriam, I'm so sorry. What will you do now?"

She sighed. "I don't know. Maybe I can start a school for the Mexican children in San Rafael. There is a great need."

Miriam remained in the buggy shed after the children left, waiting for Domingo, puttering around, straightening up, saying goodbye to the place where she had discovered her greatest gift. Apart from Rachel none of her family came near, but when Domingo finally brought the cart around and she went to get on it, Ada spotted her. Ada's face lit up as she lumbered across the yard and threw her arms around Miriam, nearly knocking her down.

After a day of such heartbreak and disappointment, Ada's unfettered joy caught Miriam off guard and it pierced her heart. When her big sister backed away beaming, innocent as a child of all but the simplest of rules, she saw the tears in Miriam's eyes and hugged her again.

"Shhhh, little one," Ada whispered. "Gott knows."

Chapter 11

omingo and Miriam went to Kyra's for dinner on Friday, and Father Noceda was there without his cassock. He wore ordinary dark clothes, the only marks of his priesthood the stiff collar around his neck, and his skullcap. Kyra and her mother served up some kind of spicy Mexican mixture with tortillas and beans, and only after Miriam tasted it did she realize it contained fish instead of the usual chicken.

"It's Friday," Kyra explained, glancing at the priest across the table.

Miriam was confused, and when Kyra saw the question in her eyes she added, "We don't eat meat on Friday."

"Fish is not meat?"

Father Noceda smiled. "It's an old Catholic tradition—our little way of fasting. We mustn't neglect our traditions just because we no longer have a chapel."

This, Miriam understood. "The Amish are full of traditions, but they have *never* had a chapel. They meet in each others' homes and barns."

Father Noceda nodded. "Admirable. This is how it was done in the first century."

With his mouth full, one of Kyra's boys asked, "*Padre*, why did the soldiers take your church?"

Noceda smiled, tousled the boy's hair. "Because they could. You must understand, child, the rulers of our country are a little confused. They think everything bad that happens in Mexico is because of the church, so they take the property of the church in the name of the state. Sometimes they take the priest, too."

"This is true," Kyra said. "I've heard there are many towns where they have lost not only their church but their priest as well."

Miriam gaped in astonishment. "And this is the law of the land?"

Domingo nodded. "It has been so for a long time. Eight years ago the government adopted a new constitution making it against the law to teach religion in schools or to worship in a public place. The church has no legal right to property, and priests have practically no rights at all." He waved casually toward Father Noceda. "He is not even allowed to wear his cassock in public."

"But we have been here for three years and there has been no trouble in El Prado," Miriam said. "If the laws have been in place for eight years, why are things suddenly so much worse?"

It was Father Noceda who answered. "Because troops are here now, and they serve the new presidente. The old one, Obregón, was a cautious politician who didn't like to stir up the people in places where the church was strong. But this Calles, he doesn't care. He is out to destroy the church. So now I have no building."

"What will you do?" Miriam asked.

The priest chuckled. "I will do as the Amish do—my flock

will meet in a barn. There is a man who owns an old warehouse in San Rafael, where he once stored beans and grain but he doesn't use it anymore. When he heard what happened he offered his building to the church. It needs a bit of work a new roof, some paint, and we'll have to borrow a few things for the Communion table—but under the circumstances it is a great blessing."

"I know the place," Domingo said. "We can't thatch a roof that size, and tin is expensive. You walked away from Iglesia El Prado with nothing but the clothes on your back."

"Not quite," the priest said with a wry smile. "You're forgetting that it was your wedding day. I came away with thirteen gold coins in my pocket."

"So you will have a building where people can come for church?" Miriam asked.

"For mass, sí. It won't be like the beautiful stone chapel in El Prado, but God will bless even a warehouse if His children gather there."

Miriam had barely touched her dinner. Since her own people forced her out of her beloved school, she had thought of almost nothing else. Now she began to see a new path, and the idea intrigued her. She pushed back her plate and laid down her fork.

"Father Noceda, the children of San Rafael have no school. Do you think it might be possible to start one in your warehouse?"

Father Noceda gave a shrug and stared blankly for a moment. "It's against the law . . ."

She sighed and nodded, her gaze falling away from him, a fledgling hope shattered.

Domingo saw her disappointment and squeezed her hand. With his eyes on the priest, he said, "Miriam, Father Noceda was born and raised in Mexico, so perhaps I hear more than you do of what he does *not* say. He only said it was against the law; he did not say he wouldn't do it."

Noceda laughed out loud. "My young amigo knows me too well, Miriam. Sometimes we must obey God rather than men. I think it would be wonderful if you could teach the children of San Rafael to read and write, and I will do everything I can to help you. But it *is* against the law to have a school in the church. The only reason I did not defy the law at Iglesia El Prado was because there a school would have been impossible to hide. Perhaps we can get away with it here in San Rafael, but we will have to do it quietly."

Emma watched Levi closely because she knew him well. When the bandits burned his barn it was a watershed moment for him, a time of rare and deep reflection that Emma felt certain, in the end, would sway his mind one way or the other. He didn't say much, but he spent every spare moment cleaning out the shell of the barn, hauling off charred remains, sifting through drifts of ash and brushing black soot from the adobe foundation walls. Levi was a relentless worker who never shirked and never wasted time, though occasionally amid the remains of his barn she would see him stop and stare, hands on hips, for minutes at a time.

Thinking.

Once or twice he said something, only a word or two, but enough for her to know. He was still wrestling with his own understanding of Gott.

Emma knew what she believed, but Levi had been raised by a father who judged his every move, his every thought, and with mathematical precision meted out punishment for the slightest infraction. In time, it had become Levi's picture of Gott.

She understood this, too. Right or wrong, what boy's image of Gott was not carved in the shadow of his father? Here, in the ruins of his barn, she saw a chance to show him the truth. It was a delicate moment, and she knew better than to preach to her husband about the limitless mercy of the Father, the all-encompassing sacrifice of the Son. Levi didn't trust words. Better to let him see the reflection of the truth in the deeds of those who understood it.

Emma went to see her father. It only took a moment, a word or two, as the lightest step in the right place can trigger a landslide. Late in the afternoon her father drove up in his hack while Levi was out by the barn. He only stayed a moment, then returned to his hack and went home. Standing in the back door of the house with Will on her hip, Emma saw them talking. Though they were too far away for her to hear what was said, she knew. She saw the change in her husband's face—first confusion, then disbelief, then wonder, and finally a profound gratitude. When Caleb left, she saw her husband start for the house and then stop and turn about. Even this, she understood. Levi was a man; he would let no one see him with tears in his eyes.

Later, after he washed up on the back porch and came in for dinner, he hung his hat on a peg by the door and said bluntly, "Your dat said they're going to rebuild my barn."

"Oh, that's wonderful, Levi! But surely it's not a surprise. Our friends always do this for each other."

"But they're bringing the lumber, too," Levi said. "Your dat said they all got plenty left over and they'll pool their money and buy what's needed from Hidalgo. They want to start tomorrow—everybody. All the men and boys."

"Well then, I better start cooking." She took a pot of new potatoes from the stove, set it on the table, and picked up Clara. When she looked around, Levi was still standing there, staring at her.

"Emma, your dat—I think maybe he's a very wise man."

"Oh? Why?"

"He told me these bandits were like a storm. He said a storm don't care whose barn it tears down, so it's up to the lucky ones to help him rebuild. He said that's why we're here, to see each other through the storms." Levi shook his head, staring at the pot of potatoes on the table without seeing them. "Your father and mine—they're not much alike, that's for sure."

Smiling, she reached up to kiss Levi's cheek. "You'll understand him in time," she said. "In due time."

They came in wagons at first light, one after another, bearing heavy loads of lumber and tools. Boys unloaded lumber and stacked it in the yard while men hauled down chests of tools and broke out hammers and saws and planes and mallets and razor-sharp wood chisels. They worked with purpose and precision, every man knowing his place and every boy helping, learning, watching, anticipating needs so that no one had to wait for anything.

It wasn't exactly a barn raising. Back home it was not uncommon for more than a hundred men to show up from surrounding districts for a barn raising, but the total population of Paradise Valley was only about a hundred, including women and children. In Mexico there simply were no other districts, and this was the busiest time of year for farmers, so the work would be spread out over weeks instead of days. Back home a barn raising would have been planned far in advance, all the joints carefully measured, cut and shaved to a precise fit before the actual construction began. Here, it would all have to be done on-site.

They were setting the main posts in the middle of the barn when a quiet fell, and Emma stepped outside the back door of the house to see what was happening. An oxcart drawn by a standard-bred horse trundled up the lane with Domingo driving and Miriam by his side. She was dressed Mexican, her hair braided down her back with no covering. Levi stood near the barn, watching.

Everyone stopped what they were doing and stared at the oxcart. Emma hurried out to her husband, knowing instinctively that this would be one of those moments.

"What are *they* doing here?" Levi asked, his eyes fixed on Miriam.

"They have come to help," Emma said. "To do good."

"But she's not one of us anymore." His eyes were hard.

"Miriam is my sister, Levi, and I love her. She's still welcome in my home."

"When she was baptized she promised to marry in the faith. She broke her promise. How can we forget that?"

This was Emma's moment and she knew it. She took his arm. "We don't have to forget; we only have to forgive. The Book says who has been forgiven much, loves much. Look around you, Levi. We have been forgiven, you and I. These people, these *friends*, are Gott's surest way of showing us that. Gott is love, and love forgives. Who are we if we don't do the same?"

He had no answer. She watched his eyes and saw a seismic change as her words washed over him and through him, the inkling of mercy. It was frail and tenuous, but it held.

Levi nodded slowly as he watched Domingo help Miriam down from the cart. His head turned and he took in all the men and boys looking down on the scene, staring at him, staring at Miriam. There was tension in the silence. No one knew what to do, how to react, and they waited to see what Levi would do. It was his house.

When Levi turned back to Miriam his mind was made up. Emma followed as he strode purposefully over to the cart and offered his hand to help Miriam down.

"I'm glad to see you," he said, with a clumsy smile. He shook hands with Domingo, then walked him up to the work site with a hand on his shoulder, talking to him like a brother, pointing, bringing him up to speed on what was being done.

The tension broke then, as the noise of hammer and saw resumed and everyone went about their business, the show over.

Emma put an arm around her sister and walked her toward the clutch of women waiting by the back door of the house. "Thank you for coming," she said. "We'll need your help with lunch."

It was a delicate moment, and Emma wondered at first if she should say more, but then she saw the thin line of silver at the bottoms of Miriam's eyes and knew that it was forgiveness enough.

For now. Emma ushered Miriam into the house and didn't realize until they were inside that the other women had not followed. Her first thought was that they refused to go into the house with Miriam, but then she looked up and saw Mamm in the kitchen. The other women weren't being standoffish after all; they were just giving Miriam a moment to face her mother alone.

When Mamm turned around and saw Miriam her eyes went wide and her mouth opened as if to cry out, but she made no sound. She took a half step backward, and Emma, afraid her mother might collapse, rushed to her side.

Mamm and Miriam stared at each other, neither of them moving.

Emma whispered in her mother's ear, "She's still your daughter."

"I'm sorry," Miriam said softly, with tears in her eyes. "I never wanted to hurt you, Mamm. You must believe that."

Emma could feel her mother straightening, stiffening herself. Her arm rose, shaking, and her fingers beckoned to Miriam.

Miriam glanced from her mother to Emma, then slowly closed the distance between them. Mamm reached up and touched her fingers to Miriam's dark braid, then slid her arms around her and drew her close.

With her head on her mother's shoulder, Miriam couldn't hold it back any longer, and she wept.

"Shhhh, little one," Mamm whispered, stroking her daughter's back. "Shhhh."

Chapter 12

The letter from the bishop came on a Saturday afternoon, and the next morning Caleb stood up in church and read it to the whole community.

"'I regret that I cannot come there to visit with you, and I know what a terrible burden it must be for the brethren in Paradise Valley to miss Communion another spring yet, but I have grown old and frail. My health will not permit it, and I think I might not survive the trip.

"'I have discussed the matter of Jake Weaver with the ministers, and we are in agreement that he should come here to face discipline. When he comes we will gather together the local bishops to decide what should be done. It is too great a matter for one man alone.'"

Caleb folded the letter without reading the rest of it, and so deep was the silence that everyone in the barn could hear the little sound as he slid it into the pocket of his Sunday coat. "So Jake must go back," he said. "I will take him to Arteaga tomorrow and put him on the train myself."

Jake sat on the back row with his head bowed, painfully aware of the men turning to stare at him. Caleb glanced at him and cleared his throat.

"The young man is still here among us, and I can see for myself that he is sorry for what happened. I'm sure when the bishops hear the whole story and talk to Jake they will want to see him through this time of separation, so he can be restored in fellowship with Gott and man. My Rachel will be going, too. She wants to be baptized, and since the bishop cannot come here I have decided to let her go to Ohio for instruction classes. It breaks my heart that we won't be there for her baptism, but it can't be helped. My daughter's hope of heaven is more important than my feelings."

"What about the other matter?" It was Ira Shrock who spoke, his eyes fixed hard on Caleb. "Your *other* daughter."

Caleb felt a twinge of shame then, and he hung his head, unable to meet Ira's glare. "I didn't tell the bishop about that yet," he said. "I wanted to wait and see if he would come here, and it seemed to me that we put enough of a burden on him already with the Jake Weaver matter. I will send a letter with Rachel."

Caleb knew it was a flimsy excuse, and Ira looked at him a little suspiciously, but he said nothing else. Ira knew—they *all* knew—that Miriam would be banned and, unlike Jake, there would be no opportunity for repentance and reentry into fellowship. The ban was inevitable, and permanent. Since divorce was a banning offense, the only possibility for restoration would be if her non-Amish husband died and she came back to the church on her own, seeking forgiveness, though certainly none of them would entertain that wish. But until such time as the bishop sent the written command to his flock in Paradise Valley, Miriam was not officially banned. Caleb knew in his heart that most of them didn't blame him for putting it off as long as possible. They would have done the same.

"We should pray for safe travel for Jake and Rachel," Caleb said, and without another word everyone went to their knees.

Before sunrise the next morning Rachel and Jake loaded their meager belongings into the surrey while Caleb hitched the horse, and after parting hugs with the family they headed out. A mile from the house they met up with Domingo on his way to work.

Caleb stopped the buggy and explained what was happening. Domingo didn't know the letter had come or that Rachel was leaving.

"If all goes well I'll be back late tonight," Caleb said. "I need you and Harvey to cut hay in the south field. Leah and Barb can help."

Domingo nodded. No one had to tell Domingo he was in charge. Since Aaron's death, Caleb had treated him like a foreman.

Domingo's dark eyes focused on Jake and Rachel. "We will miss you two," he said. His horse pranced nervously, but Domingo held him in check. "Jake, you take care of my little sister. Whatever your people decide, in *my* world you did no wrong in defending her. You're a good man, Jake. Hold your head up."

"Thank you," Jake said quietly, and Rachel heard the things that were not said. Jake had saved Domingo's life in Diablo Canyon, a debt Domingo repaid at El Ojo. An unbreakable bond existed between them.

"I will be back by harvest," Rachel said, "and no matter what happens Jake will be back by spring planting. Give our love to Miriam, won't you?"

"I will." Domingo spurred his horse, Caleb tugged on the reins, and they parted.

Rachel was afraid to mention it for a while because she really didn't know how her dat would react, but when they rounded the end of the ridge and the village of San Rafael came in sight she turned to him and said, "I haven't seen Miriam in a week."

Dat didn't answer. He kept his eyes on the road ahead.

"She doesn't know I'm leaving."

He still didn't answer, his face a blank. But when they came to the little dirt road that passed through the heart of the town he turned the horse. Dogs barked and chickens scurried out of the way as the buggy rumbled between peasant hovels, heading toward Miriam's house.

"Maybe it's best," her dat said, without looking at her. "By the time you get back . . ."

He didn't finish the thought, or need to. Rachel knew. By the time she got back from Ohio Miriam would be banned, and her involvement with family would be strictly limited.

Miriam was hoeing weeds in her kitchen garden when they drove up. Caleb and Jake stayed where they were, waiting, while Rachel jumped down. Miriam dropped her hoe and ran to meet her.

Rachel hugged her sister and, before they pulled apart, reassured her once again. There were tears in Miriam's eyes as their foreheads touched and Rachel whispered, "No matter what. Always."

&

Rachel's sister Lizzie Shetler met them at the train station in Ohio, with her husband, Andy, and their five children. Jake's folks were there too, and when the two families parted Jake and Rachel went separate ways. She held his hand and looked into his eyes for a moment before he climbed into his father's buggy.

"It will be all right," she said. They had talked it through for a thousand miles and she had said these same words a hundred times.

He took a deep breath and blew it out. "I know. I'll see you at church I guess, but I may not get to speak to you for a while yet. That will make it even harder for me."

"I'll take my portion," she said, "and be waiting at the end."

He knew what she meant; she could see it in his eyes. They shared each other's thoughts and clung to each other's hopes. The sad smile as he turned away and climbed into his father's surrey almost made her break down, but she stiffened her spine and kept the tears in check—for Jake.

Rachel hadn't forgotten an inch of the road to the house she grew up in, but having grown accustomed to Paradise Valley over the last three years she *had* forgotten how spectacular Salt Creek Township could be in the springtime, how deep the green of endless forests and how brilliant the fields, as if they drank sunlight and glowed in gratitude. There were flowers in bloom everywhere, bright colors bordering kitchen gardens and hugging front porches. The sky was deep blue and the air full of the chatter of birds, calling to each other as they guarded their nests and fed their young.

When the old house first came into sight at the top of the hill she almost wept with joy. Almost, but not quite. While she would always see the house where she grew up as the repository of a million warm memories, it surprised her to find that she no longer thought of it as home. Home, she suddenly realized, was not made of houses and barns and trees but of faces and voices and laughter around a dinner table, of whispered secrets in the night, and tears behind the smokehouse. As homesick as she had been, and as precious the sight of the old house, home, for her, was Paradise Valley. Home, for her, was Mamm and Dat, Ada and Harvey and Leah and Barbara and Mary and Emma.

And Miriam. She missed Miriam most of all.

The following Saturday a group of ministers and bishops came to talk with Jake and Rachel. Jake was taken into a separate room to be questioned. They kept him in there a long time, then called in Rachel for a few questions because she had witnessed everything with her own eyes. She spoke the truth exactly as she had seen it, but she also made a point of telling them it was dark and Jake was excited.

He never meant for the bandit to die.

Jake's feet felt like lead that Sunday morning, his heart like ashes. Willing himself into the barn for the service he took a seat alone on the back row, thankful, at least, that the council meeting had been held weeks earlier. At council meeting the preacher always talked about how to deal with an errant brother, the sermon always ending with the same chilling admonition: "Therefore put away from among yourselves that wicked person." Even now, the words rang in Jake's head. He felt Rachel's compassionate eyes watching him from across the barn, but he could not make himself return her gaze.

It was a normal service, except that at the end Bishop Schwartz asked all the members to remain seated while the rest were dismissed. He caught Jake's eye and motioned for him to leave, too. The bishop had an announcement to make, for members only. Filing out the door behind the children and youth Jake's ears burned from the stares of those who knew what was coming. Word had spread.

Rachel was waiting for him in the sunlight just outside the

door. She took his hands in hers and made him look at her as she whispered, "It'll be all right. I'm with you."

He nodded grimly, but her words warmed him. She was his anchor. Even now, even in the coming storm, he knew his anchor would hold. As long as Rachel drew breath, he would never really be alone.

Nothing else needed saying. They both knew what was happening inside. The bishop would announce to the members that Jake Weaver had been banned, but that he had acknowledged his sin and his willingness to accept punishment. After a few agonizing minutes, the deacon emerged and came straight up to Jake.

"You are banned," he said with a formality that was not natural to him. "We will come and speak with you before next meeting." He punctuated this with a sharp nod, then turned away and went back inside.

It went exactly as Jake had anticipated, and yet an awful weight still settled on him. To be shunned by all his family and friends was a daunting prospect. He would be forced to take his meals in another room, apart from his own family, eating from separate bowls. But that was not the worst of it. The real horror was that during the ban he would be separated from Gott himself.

Rachel visited as often as she could during the ban, to try and cheer him up, but Jake was inconsolable. He could find no way to escape his own thoughts. Since no one was allowed to do business of any kind with him, he couldn't even work his father's fields or do chores to keep his hands busy and his mind occupied. He had no appetite; food had no taste. On long walks through woods and fields even the brightness of high spring faded to brown, as if Gott had turned His back. Throughout the whole ordeal he clung to his memories, recalling moments spent with Rachel in these same surroundings three years ago.

In some ways it seemed like yesterday, as though no time had passed at all, and in some ways it felt like a lifetime, as though he and Rachel were not even the same people anymore.

℈

Two weeks felt like a hundred years for Jake, but the time did finally pass and the second Sunday arrived. At the end of the service the nonmembers—this time including Jake—were once again dismissed while the members remained seated.

He found Rachel tending a group of children outside and stood with her, waiting nervously while the members voted on whether or not to allow him back into the fold. With a reassuring smile she took his arm, leaned close and whispered the words he'd heard a hundred times.

"It'll be all right. You'll see."

A deacon came out shortly, summoning everyone back inside. As Rachel and Jake filed in behind a long line of children and teenagers, the deacon caught Jake by the shoulder. His heart stopped until he saw the little smile in the man's eyes.

"The vote was unanimous," the deacon said. "Not one person here thinks of you as a murderer."

He very nearly wept with relief.

℈

As Rachel was taking her seat on the backless bench, Bishop Schwartz began reading the story of the prodigal son from the Bible. When he was done, he called Jake to the front and asked him to kneel.

The bishop asked a few pointed questions, which Jake answered from the heart. His contrition was clear. When Jake rose to face them, the bishop said, "I encourage you all to forget that this ever happened. This man is forgiven, and you should hold nothing against him."

There was one point during Jake's confession when Rachel almost got herself in trouble. When she heard Jake promise out loud before the church that he would "seek to do better," in essence he was promising that in the future he would do his best to avoid killing anyone. She very nearly laughed at the absurdity—as if Jake were a murderer, as if there were the remotest chance he'd ever find himself in that situation again. But she managed to catch herself and lower her face to hide the smile.

And then it was over and Jake was restored to fellowship, a member in good standing.

After the service one of the bishops pulled her aside. It was Abe Detweiler, one of the younger ones newly ordained in another district and a second cousin of Lizzie's husband, Andy. His face was ruddy, his beard as red as Rachel's hair. She was afraid for a minute that he'd seen her smiling during Jake's confession and was going to give her a scolding, but it wasn't that at all.

"I read your father's letter. It's a shame about Miriam," he said gravely. "We will have little choice, but we'll give it time before we do anything. A grace period is customary because you never know—something could happen to Miriam's husband and she could return to the fold. Of course it's up to Bishop Schwartz, but I'm sure he'll want to wait a while. Perhaps when you finish your instruction classes and are ready to return to Mexico, then we'll decide."

"Thank you," she said. "Miriam and I are very close. I have to tell you, after all we've been through I cannot find it in me to fault her for marrying Domingo. I know she made a promise when she was baptized, but how could she have known she would be hauled off to the mountains of Mexico where there were no Amish? No one knows what it was like for her. She never really had a choice. Mexico is a different world."

He nodded and, despite his position as a bishop and a defender of the faith, there was deep sympathy in his eyes. "I have heard," he said. "Your family has been through terrible trials . . . especially the death of your brother Aaron. We here can't know what it must be like having to deal with bandits all the time. Do they still plague your valley?"

"Oh no. A detachment of soldiers came to El Prado not long ago. There was a battle, and the bandits lost. Word has already spread about the troops, so I don't think we'll have any more trouble with bandits."

He stroked his rusty beard, staring at the floor. His eyes narrowed in thought and it hit Rachel suddenly that he was thinking about Mexico.

And he was a *bishop*!

Abe Detweiler was young for a bishop—only about forty—but he had several school-age children who were being forced to attend public school five days a week. She resolved to be careful with her words. It was just possible that Abe Detweiler was the answer to a thousand prayers.

"I have to go and help with lunch," she said, "but I would love to tell you more about our home in Mexico. Perhaps you and Sarah could come visit sometime."

He nodded, smiled. "I would love to hear more about it. And I will pray for Miriam."

Miriam's loss would be deeply felt by all, and none so deeply as Rachel, but on this day Jake was restored to fellowship, his sins washed away and forgotten. It was a day for joy. She and Jake went to the youth singing that night, together, and afterward they slipped away into the darkness for a little reunion of their own.

Chapter 13

Emma saw a change in Levi that summer, and she nurtured it with great care and patience—the way she watered her trees, and for the same reason. When the men came and helped Levi rebuild his barn he began to step a bit lighter and smile more often. Taciturn by nature, he said little to Emma about the lifting of his spirits, but she knew. The grace of Gott was at work in her husband, and he was finally beginning to see it.

Domingo came by sometimes in the late afternoon when his work was done, toiling until dark, nailing boards on the outside of the barn and helping Levi cover the roof with new sheets of tin, paid for and delivered by his neighbors. Miriam came on those afternoons too, for she knew—had always known—that Emma held the key to her father's heart.

"They work well together," Miriam said one evening, watching from the back door of the house.

The sharp reports of hammers on tin told Emma what they were doing. She dried her hands on a dish towel as she went and watched over Miriam's shoulder.

"They're so different," she said, "and yet in some ways they're two of a kind. Strong, quiet, hardworking and honest."

"You left off stubborn," Miriam said.

Emma chuckled. "Jah, that too."

"I'm glad to see them finally getting to be friends."

"Levi's come a long way in his thinking lately. When he saw that Gott has forgiven him he finally forgave himself, and it felt so good to him that he started forgiving other people. It's all new to Levi. I only hope he doesn't change his mind when the ban comes."

"He won't have any choice," Miriam said. "Nobody expects him to disobey the church—least of all me. I won't have anybody getting in trouble because of me."

Emma took her sister's shoulder and turned her until their eyes met. "Listen, Miriam. You know as well as I do that people bend the rules all the time, and your family will bend them as far as they can. The ban won't be so hard. The only one you ever really had to worry about was Levi, and look at him now."

They both glanced up at the barn roof just in time to see Domingo slip. He was high up near the peak, with Levi a little lower and off to one side. Domingo went to step sideways when the board he was bracing his foot against broke away. Domingo went belly-down on the steep tin roof, scrambling for a handhold as he started sliding.

Emma and Miriam both gasped, but then they saw Levi's arm fly out quick as a snake, grabbing Domingo's wrist and stopping the slide.

Two hammers clattered down across the tin roof and plummeted thirty feet to the ground as Levi strained to pull Domingo back up to a safe foothold.

It happened so fast neither of the women even had time to move. They just stood there with their mouths open, shaking their heads in disbelief. There was nothing they could have done anyway, and by the time the panic subsided the danger was past and their husbands were laughing at themselves.

"Laughing," Emma said, "Look at them. They're *laughing*! Have they lost their minds?"

"No," Miriam said, her hand still pressed against her beating heart. "They're men. They don't think the same way we do, and after all we've been through I'm glad for it."

$\approx$

Rachel didn't see Abe Detweiler again until she was halfway through her instruction classes, but on a Sunday afternoon in midsummer his surrey pulled up the drive. The children all went out to play with Lizzie's brood while Abe and his wife, Sarah, came in to visit.

Jake was there too, which was fortunate, because Abe wanted to hear more about what had happened in Diablo Canyon. Despite Jake's interrogation, there were a great many details Abe didn't know.

They exchanged pleasantries while Lizzie served coffee and apple pie at the kitchen table. She was well prepared; Sunday afternoon was when people would drop in for a visit unannounced, and Amish women prided themselves on spending their Saturday baking for just such a contingency. Lizzie was a little flustered nonetheless. It was a rare honor to have a bishop drop by.

"I don't mean to dredge up unpleasant memories," Abe said, a fork poised over a half-eaten slice of deep-dish pie, "but I'd really like to hear the whole story about how you came to be in a bandit's barn so far from home."

So Rachel told him. She started at the beginning, about how she, Aaron, Ada, and Little Amos were on their way back from Agua Nueva when El Pantera and his men overtook them on the road.

"It was horrible," she said. "Ada and Little Amos run off to who knows where, and Aaron is stabbed. I was so worried about them I just didn't think much about myself."

"When Ada came home the next morning we went looking and found Aaron," Jake said. "Caleb and Harvey brought him home, and me and Domingo went after Rachel on horseback. We trailed the bandits all the way to their hideout in Diablo Canyon, but then they caught us."

Sarah's eyes went wide in terror. "So you were captured?" She had heard only the barest outline of what happened.

"Jah," Jake said. "That night they chained us all in the barn, but I got loose. That's when I . . ." His face darkened, his voice trailed off and he leaned over his apple pie, picking at it with his fork. "I don't remember much after that," he mumbled.

"It's all right," Abe Detweiler said, and there was compassion in his eyes. "It's all behind us now. All is confessed and forgiven."

Still grieved by the memory, Jake didn't offer anything more, so Rachel told them the rest of the story about her escape, including Domingo's stand at El Ojo. Abe and Sarah sat back wide-eyed, captivated, forgetting their pie and coffee.

"I've never heard anything like that in my life," Sarah said. "It's a wonder you weren't all killed."

"Gott protects His children," Abe said softly. "But you were right in what you told me, Rachel. Everything that has befallen you and your family there—it's all so different from how we live here. Almost unimaginable. Hearing what it's really like down there makes it a lot harder to judge people's actions. We just can't know."

But Rachel hadn't forgotten her main objective. She was watching their eyes, gauging the bishop's reactions and those of his wife. In the end, Rachel knew Sarah was the one she would have to persuade.

"But the bandits don't bother us anymore, now that the troops are there," she said. "And there are a lot of good things about Mexico, too. Dat says the soil in Paradise Valley is as rich as any he's ever seen. Wheat grows like hair on a dog's back. The winters are milder, and since we're in the mountains the summers aren't so hot."

"I thought Mexico was a desert country," Sarah said.

"Not all of it. It's nice in the mountains. There aren't as many trees as here in Ohio, but Emma has planted trees everywhere. Someday our valley really will be a paradise." A little smile came to Sarah's eyes then, and Rachel decided it was now or never. Time to run out her best argument. "We even have our own school," she said.

Sarah's eyes widened. "No! You have your own *school?*"

Rachel nodded casually, wiping her mouth on a napkin. "We teach Amish kinner reading, writing and arithmetic, without all the other stuff they fill their heads with in public school. And we teach them Spanish, just like the schools here teach Amish children to speak English."

"But who is the teacher?" Abe asked.

"Well, Miriam started the school, and she was amazing with those children—truly gifted. But after she married Domingo the others didn't want her teaching their kinner anymore, so now I'm the teacher. Sometimes Leah and Barb help."

"I didn't know this," Abe said, sitting back in his kitchen chair as if the thought itself knocked him slightly off-kilter. "I never would have thought of it. Everyone knows the school issue is why you went there in the first place, but I never dreamed you would start your own. This is a very good thing."

Rachel could see it in their eyes. The seed was planted; Abe and Sarah would discuss it between themselves later. Now, she judged, it was best to change the subject, not to belabor the point.

"Our houses are adobe," she said. "They cost practically nothing because we make the bricks out of mud and straw."

Sarah's nose wrinkled. "Your houses are made of mud?"

The look on her face made Rachel giggle. "Jah, but you should see them. We plaster over the inside walls when we're done, and then whitewash the whole thing. It's really kind of nice once you get used to the idea. The men cut trees in the mountains for the roof, and we even found stone to build a basement."

Abe's brow furrowed. "Is there a market where you can sell your cash crops?"

Jake perked up, now that the conversation had gotten away from bandits, and it was he who answered the question.

"Well, we trade little things like milk and butter in the hacienda village, but we have to take our cash crops to Saltillo. It's fifty miles, but they're supposed to be building a railroad down our way. It'll be much easier then."

Abe and his wife asked questions all afternoon, clearly fascinated by life in Mexico. Jake and Rachel answered them all, and when the children came bursting into the house later in the afternoon Sarah took her youngest under her arm—a little sandy-haired boy named Eli—and whispered to him, "What would you think about going to a school where there were only Amish children?"

The bashful boy said nothing, but he looked up at his mother with a wide-eyed grin and nodded vigorously.

The look that flashed between Rachel and Jake was brief and wordless, yet there was an unmistakable gleam of hope in it.

Emma's babies were asleep, the lights out, and she and Levi lay awake in bed.

"I saw Miriam today, in town," she said. "She told me Domingo and the priest went to Saltillo for tin, and they're ready to roof the building they're going to use for a church."

"That's good," Levi mumbled, and she could tell by the drowsy tone that he was already near sleep.

"It's a lot of work. They'll be needing help."

He didn't answer for a moment, and she was afraid he'd drifted off until he stirred. "And you want me to go help them?"

"Domingo helped you roof your barn."

"A lot of men helped with my barn."

"Jah, but Domingo more than the others. You owe him."

Levi raised himself up on an elbow. "Emma, I like Domingo. He's a good hand, and he don't talk too much. But he's an outsider who married your sister, and the ban is coming. To help Domingo is to help Miriam, and you know we can't do that. What will people say?"

She smiled patiently. This kind of thinking was still new to him. "They'll raise their eyebrows and wag their beards, but they can't do anything more. Even if Miriam was banned there's no money changing hands, so it's not like you're doing *business* with them."

"But it's a *Catholic* church."

"It will also be a school for the poor children of San Rafael."

"Mexican children."

"Children are children, Levi. The little ones can't help that their parents aren't Amish. Gott loves them all, and so should we."

He didn't answer right away. She held her breath, waiting, because she knew her husband well. Though he loved Emma more than all the world and would always listen to her, he would never do something he thought was wrong merely because she asked him to. It was his right as a man, and his duty as the head of his house. But if he thought it over and decided it was the right thing to do, nothing would stop him. Not even the raised eyebrows of the Amish.

He sighed deeply and said, "I knew you were a troublemaker when I married you. When will we go?"

⁓

There were lots of local people helping fix up the warehouse in San Rafael, but only one Amishman. Every morning, as soon as chores were done, Levi and Emma and their three babies showed up early and spent the day.

The women—Miriam, Kyra, and Emma—made sure everyone got their share of tortillas and beans at lunchtime, and carried water all day long.

They were filling buckets from the well one afternoon when they paused for a breather and fell to watching the men work on the roof.

"You know," Kyra said, "Father Noceda swings a hammer pretty well, for a priest. But he's no match for Domingo and Levi."

Miriam smiled, and there was a note of pride in it. "When those two work side by side, no one is a match for them."

"*Esto es verdad*," Kyra said. *This is true.* "But I'll say this for Father Noceda—he's every bit as good-looking as they are. Too bad he's a priest."

With an embarrassed grin Miriam slapped her shoulder. "Kyra, you shouldn't even *think* such a thing."

Emma's head tilted. "Why?"

"A priest cannot have a wife," Kyra answered. "He is married to the church."

142

"Ahhh, I see. An Amish minister would never put up with that."

"Nooo," Miriam said. "If an Amishman didn't have a wife he'd starve to death."

They all laughed. Looking at the two of them side by side, Emma said, "You know, Miriam, I never realized how much you and Kyra resemble each other. In those clothes you look more like her sister than mine."

"*Ella es mi hermana,*" Kyra said with a smile. *She is my sister.* "Which I guess means you are my sister, too, Emma. I can't thank you enough for bringing Levi to help with the work. From what little I know of Levi, I never thought he would help work on a Catholic church."

Emma smiled. "He and Domingo are getting to be very good friends these days, and he's only repaying a favor. Anyway, Levi doesn't think of it as working on a Catholic church." She glanced at Miriam with a trace of pride. "He's helping to build a school for the *niños.* What he doesn't know is that he's the first student. Levi is learning a lot."

Chapter 14

A squad of soldiers passed through Paradise Valley every morning heading west on patrol, and every afternoon they returned. Caleb watched with growing irritation, in the beginning because one or two of them were always riding standard-bred horses they had practically stolen from the Amish, but later because of their increasingly arrogant disregard for the farmers. On their way back to the hacienda village the soldiers would always stop and water their horses at one of the Amish horse troughs. Caleb didn't mind this—he wouldn't begrudge a thirsty horse no matter *who* was in the saddle—but they also walked their horses through cultivated fields. As the summer deepened and the crops grew, the patrols began walking their horses right through the oats and letting them graze, trampling a different stretch of field every day.

When no one protested, they grew bolder, raiding kitchen gardens and taking eggs from chicken coops. In the beginning they had at least made a pretense of paying for what they took, but as time wore on they stopped offering even a pittance in exchange. They just took it, as if they had a right.

Most of the newcomers didn't speak enough Spanish to complain, but they wouldn't have said anything anyway. They were not in the habit of arguing with armed men.

❧

Mamm was still not herself, morose and silent most of the time since Miriam and Rachel had left. Miriam came by to visit almost every Sunday afternoon, and Mamm gradually got used to seeing her in Mexican clothes. Miriam's visits helped, but now Mamm worried about Rachel. So much violence and uncertainty had entered her world that she seemed incapable of the kind of serene faith she had known before Aaron's death. If a child of hers was out of her sight Mamm was never quite convinced that she would ever see them again. Once in a while she muttered something to Caleb about Rachel and he reassured her that her daughter was fine, that she would be back by harvest and all would once again be right with the world.

But privately he was worried about Mamm. She still had no appetite and she was losing weight.

She perked up a bit in August, when her kitchen garden was at its peak and she got busy with the girls canning vegetables for the winter. Her workload was a bit heavy then, with only Ada and the two youngest daughters to help, but Caleb knew it was better to be too busy than to think too much.

He went into town one afternoon to get a horse shod at the blacksmith shop, and got a surprise when he came home. He found Mamm fuming in the kitchen.

"Those soldiers!" she cried. "They came to my garden and took half of my vegetables!"

He hadn't seen her so animated in months. "What soldiers?" he asked, rubbing her arm, trying to calm her. Her face was very red.

"The ones who patrol every day. They just came and took my vegetables. They cut a bunch of cucumbers and squash and all the ripe tomatoes, and they even took the basket of peas I had already picked! I won't have those scoundrels cleaning out my kitchen garden," she said with tears in her eyes. "How will I feed my family?"

Something had to be done, and Caleb knew it. Things were getting out of hand. "I'll talk to the others in the morning," he said calmly, "and we'll go see Fuentes." He thought about going directly to Captain Soto, but given his past experience with the crooked little officer he figured it was better to let Fuentes deal with him. A native Mexican might have better luck with the captain, and Fuentes, as the haciendado's right-hand man, had the weight of authority behind him.

"They ride horses, carry guns, and steal from us," John Hershberger said. "Sometimes I think the only difference between a bandit and a soldier is the uniform."

Caleb had gotten the men together at Hershberger's farm, and now they stood in a cluster near the barn, chewing on straws and complaining to each other.

"He's right," Ira Shrock said. "These men take more from us than bandits ever did."

Caleb stroked his chin. Ira had not lost a son to bandits. "The soldiers never killed any of us yet, Ira. And I wouldn't forget that if they didn't come here when they did, the bandits would have killed us all."

Ira nodded thoughtfully. "Jah, I guess you're right, but they're getting to be a real nuisance, that's all. Something has got to be done. When they're not busy soldiering, those guys stand around in the hacienda village and drink, right out in the open."

Atlee Hostetler seemed to shrink back a little when Ira said this, and his attention wandered. There had been rumors back home that Atlee was a little too fond of hard cider. Now his self-conscious tics made Caleb wonder.

Hershberger backed up Ira's complaint. "Jah, and when my girls go into town to get the mail or go to the store, the soldiers say rude things to them. It's getting so I'm afraid to let them go alone."

Caleb nodded. "My girls have told me the same thing, and they say it's getting worse. I'll go and talk to Fuentes about it. Maybe he can do something with them."

They all nodded in agreement, and Hershberger volunteered to go with him. Atlee Hostetler never said a word.

Driving through town they saw the usual clutch of idle soldiers tossing dice against a wall outside the dry-goods store, and there was a ceramic jug sitting prominently on the sidewalk between them—at ten in the morning—though Caleb never actually saw anybody take a swig. The soldiers grinned and whispered to each other, watching as Caleb's buggy passed by.

The old stone church in the clearing just short of the hacienda walls didn't look much like a church anymore. The troops had built sandbag barricades around it and split-rail fences to contain their horses. A Mexican flag flew from a new flagpole atop the belfry.

They found Diego Fuentes in the hacienda stables, rubbing down his big Friesian after a hard morning's ride.

"Buenos días, Señor Bender!" he said with a big smile and a handshake. Fuentes had always treated Caleb with respect.

They exchanged a bit of small talk about crops and weather, and Fuentes informed them the haciendado was currently in Paris with his family, though Caleb already knew this.

When they finally got down to business Caleb said, "What we came to see you about is those troops."

Fuentes's brush stopped halfway down the big horse's flank and he looked over his shoulder at Caleb. "What about them?"

"They're getting to be a problem."

Fuentes straightened to his full height, picking horsehair from the brush. "Really?"

Caleb listed his complaints— how they had extorted the best buggy horses from the Amish and then grazed them in the fields, trampling crops, and how they'd begun raiding kitchen gardens and chicken coops.

"One of our men says they even took half his laying hens last week," Caleb said. "I guess maybe they're starting their own coop."

Hershberger told him about the girls, and how every time his daughters came to town little groups of soldiers leered at them and said rude things.

"I won't have my girls threatened," John said.

Fuentes's eyes narrowed. "You will not *have* it?" His voice rose in anger, and he pointed at John with his currying brush. "Let me tell you something. You *asked* for this. Would you rather have bandits? Have you forgotten that these troops saved all your lives and that my haciendado *paid* for them to come here? And he did it at your request! He paid a hefty sum for their protection, but as you have already seen, we did not need their protection for the hacienda. We can protect ourselves."

"But surely they can be made to behave in a more civilized manner and treat us with respect," Caleb offered gently.

Now the angry eyes turned on Caleb. "You are in *Mexico*, Señor Bender, not America. Perhaps our country is not so *civilized* as yours, but we have just suffered through ten years of war, and because of the Revolution our government is a mess. Supplies don't always come when they should, and soldiers are poorly paid. They don't have time to farm for themselves because they are out on patrol keeping your people safe from bandits, so somebody has to support them. Would you have the haciendado give them everything they need to live? It only makes sense for you to do your share, even if Mexican soldiers seem a little *rude* to you."

Fuentes turned his back on them and resumed brushing his horse, but then he stopped for a second and glared at Caleb over his shoulder. "Think of it as taxes," he snapped.

They were driving back through the hacienda village on their way home when John finally spoke his mind.

"I suppose Fuentes is right. We are the ones who asked for the troops, and if they need help, why then I guess it's up to us to help them."

Caleb chewed on this for a while, gripping the reins in his fists, his jaw working. "Taxes. We already pay our fair share of taxes. They tax our land, they tax our produce, they tax our doors and windows. Pretty soon they'll tax the air we breathe. And the money Hidalgo paid to get the troops here wasn't a proper tax; it was a bribe paid to a corrupt government official. John, we weren't the ones who brought corruption to this place."

"No," John said pensively. "I'm thinking that would be Satan."

Rachel and two boys followed the ministers into the *abrode* on the morning of her baptism, and the three of them faced old Bishop Schwartz. He talked to them gently for a bit about humility and trust, the honor and sanctity of Gott's church, and the meaning of commitment.

"You are about to make a promise before Gott to your family and your brethren, and it is a holy vow that will bind you for the rest of your life. To break this vow is a very serious thing."

He looked right at Rachel as he said this, but she knew he wasn't really looking at her. He was looking at Miriam.

"Are you ready for such a commitment?" he asked with a gentle smile. He already knew the answer, for they had all been through instruction classes. Once or twice Rachel had known of a boy deciding the commitment was too great and changing his mind at the last minute, but in such a case the boy simply didn't show up for church. If they got as far as the abrode, they never turned back.

Rachel looked the bishop in the eye and said simply, "Jah. I am ready."

The boys did the same.

It all went by in a blur, and when it came time Rachel knelt alongside the two boys. One at a time, they answered publicly the questions the bishop had already put to them in private.

When it was Rachel's turn she bowed her head and someone took off her kapp. The deacon dipped water from an oak bucket, poured it into the bishop's cupped hands, and the bishop poured it on her head. This was repeated three times—once for the Father, once for the Son, and once for the Holy Ghost. Then they lifted her up, and the deacon's wife gave her the holy kiss. Rachel was now a member of the church.

Later that evening Jake gave her a kiss of his own and said, "In a couple weeks we'll have Communion, and you'll be able to partake with us. I'm proud of you, Rachel."

"Jah, it's wonderful." She said this with a sigh, a hint of sadness in her eyes. "I know I shouldn't be having selfish thoughts on such a day . . . but two weeks is all the time we have left."

"I'm having the same selfish thoughts," he said. "After Communion your business in Ohio is finished."

She nodded. "I'll be going back home the next morning like I promised my dat."

Jake held her close, his arms about her waist, and looked into her eyes. "It's only for six months, Rachel. In March I come of age, and I promise you, from that day forward we will never be separated again."

Chapter 15

Rachel's last two weeks with Jake flew by. They saw each other almost every evening, but it only made the time pass faster.

The day of her first Communion was a crisp, beautiful fall day, slanting sunlight painting a landscape of brilliant reds and golds. Abe and Sarah Detweiler visited that Sunday, and after lunch they pulled Rachel aside to talk to her.

"It was an honor to have you with us at Communion this morning," Rachel said.

Abe smiled warmly. "It was an off Sunday at my church, so I thought it would be good to join you. We have many friends here. But it was you I really came to see. I wanted to tell you that Sarah and I have talked it over—"

"And over and over," Sarah added with a smile.

"And we have decided to give Mexico a try. We want our children to grow up without so much interference, without being influenced by outsiders every day. It's important to us."

Rachel fought hard to keep from jumping up and down with joy. *A bishop in Paradise Valley!*

"My father will be so happy to hear that," she said. "We have been without leadership for a long time."

"Well, you'll have to wait a bit longer," he said, scratching his rusty beard. "We'll need time to find another bishop to tend my flock, and I'd like to get another crop in the barn before I go. I don't want to leave my family in too hard a way, though I'm sure the church will take care of them in my absence."

Rachel glanced at Sarah. "You're not going?"

"Not at first," Sarah said. "Abe wants to go down and get settled, find a place for us and get started."

"And to be honest," Abe added, "I want to make sure it's safe—you know, what with bandits and all. Make sure it's a place where we can live in peace."

"I understand," Rachel said, though she felt a twinge of doubt now that she knew it was to be a trial visit. She'd known of Amishmen in the past who went to a new place, took one look and got right back on the train to go home.

"Also," he said, "Freeman Coblentz came to see me yesterday. They're having a hard time of it since they came back because he wasn't able to sell his place. He tried to sell it to the newcomers last year, but he set the price high because he'd already put so much work into it."

"Jah, I remember. The walls of his house are half built, the well already dug, and some of the fences up. I don't blame him for wanting more money."

Abe nodded. "But it was a risk, and nobody wanted to pay his price, so it sits there. Anyway, when he heard I was going down he offered to let me use his place if I finish the house, and then if I decide to stay I can buy it."

"I'm sure you'll love it there," she said, "and we'll make you very welcome. So when will you be coming down?"

"In the spring," he said, and her heart soared.

❦

Later, Bishop Schwartz came to see Rachel, pulling her aside as she was helping clean up after lunch. "I hate to do this on the day of your first Communion," he said grimly, "but it cannot be helped. I want you to take this to your father."

He pulled a sealed envelope from his coat pocket and handed it to her. She ran her thumbs over it, knowing what it was without having to read it. The bishops had met. The matter was decided now, and final. Miriam was banned. All that remained was the delivering of the letter to her father.

She met his gaze and nodded solemnly. "I will give it to him."

"I'm very sorry," the bishop said. "We had no choice."

❦

She got a chance to talk to Jake that evening after the singing and told him about the letter.

He nodded. "Even knowing this would come, it still hurts."

"But there is good news, too," she said, and then told him about Abe Detweiler.

"*Spring*, Jake! Bishop Detweiler will be in Paradise Valley in the spring when you come down, and we can finally be married!"

"Gott has smiled on us," he said. "I been thinking about something else, too. I'm thinking when I get back I'll go to work for your dat. He's been shorthanded since Aaron died, and he's got extra room, too. After we're married we can live in his basement while we save up for a place of our own."

She hugged him fiercely. "That's a wonderful idea, and you're right," she said, kissing his cheek. "Gott has smiled on us."

❦

The next morning Lizzie agreed to let Jake take Rachel to the train station. She said her goodbyes to the family at home, then had the luxury of saying goodbye to Jake alone at the station.

Rachel boarded a passenger car, found her seat, and looked out the window. Jake was watching her from the platform, his broad hat tilted back, his eyes steady and dependable as ever. Their future together was assured.

Touching her fingertips to the glass she mouthed the words, *Till spring.*

He smiled and raised a hand. *I love you*, his lips said.

⁓

Caleb hitched the buggy and left well before daylight for Arteaga, to pick up Rachel at the train station. He traveled alone and without fear. There was little need to fear bandits any longer. The greatest danger in any trip north to Arteaga or Saltillo had always been El Pantera and his men. As he drove north in the cold dawn Caleb thought with a chill that if El Pantera and his men still haunted those hills, it would only be as ghosts. Even now, he caught himself watching the ridgetops for that bicolored Appaloosa.

Everything in his world seemed divided these days. He was glad the bandits were gone, but deeply grieved by the thought that he had caused their deaths. He could not find it in himself to celebrate the death of any man—even the one who had taken Aaron from him—and the troops who displaced the bandits filled him with a growing sense of trepidation.

Even his excitement over Rachel's return was overshadowed with foreboding. Though he missed Rachel sorely and couldn't wait to see her again, he knew about the letter she carried, and knew what it would say. The return of one daughter meant the loss of another.

He handed Rachel the reins as they left the station, and then slowly, willing his hands and eyes to do a work nearly as grim and unspeakable as burying a child, he took out the envelope, opened it and read the letter. Even knowing what it would say, seeing the words there on the paper in the familiar jerky handwriting of old Bishop Schwartz nearly broke his heart. Unable to speak, he folded the letter carefully and slid it back into the envelope. He said very little the rest of the way home.

Darkness had fallen by the time they reached San Rafael, but there was still lamplight in the windows of the houses. Caleb turned down the street toward Miriam and Domingo's house.

"No sense putting it off," he said, and Rachel turned her face away from him. He pulled up in front of the house and handed Rachel the reins.

"You wait here," he said. "I won't be long."

They were sitting at the kitchen table when the knock came, Domingo reading a book by lamplight and Miriam sewing, patching a pair of work pants. It was a small two-room house, and the sound of her father's knock was still hanging in the air when Domingo opened the door. They just stood and looked at each other for a second, and Miriam knew. Even before he came in she could tell by the expression on her father's face why he had come. It was the same look she'd seen in his eyes the day he buried Aaron. Domingo stepped back, waving him in.

Miriam laid aside her sewing and rose to her feet. Her father had not set foot in her house since she married Domingo. He walked stiffly, perhaps tired from the long day's drive, but more likely making a conscious effort at formality. He took off his hat, and without a word of preamble opened the letter and read it to her, word for word.

157

Domingo came to her as her father read, slipping an arm around her waist and gripping her with purpose. A deep and terrible grief welled up in her as her father read. Her knees betrayed her, but Domingo held her erect. Her husband knew her well.

When her father finished reading he folded the letter and slipped the envelope back into his coat pocket.

"You are banned," he said flatly. "You may no longer share Communion with our church or have fellowship with your family. You will now be treated as a heathen, an outsider."

She steeled herself and managed not to break down or weep, though she could not hide the grief in her eyes or the heaviness of her breathing. There was no use in pleading, no answer, no words that could begin to heal the rift that had opened between them. All she could do was weather the storm and wait.

She fully expected her father to turn his back on her and leave without another word, but there was more.

"Domingo," he said, and now his voice almost broke, "you may no longer work for me. The men came to me and said after Miriam is banned it won't do for her husband to earn his bread by my hand because it's too much like I'm supporting her. I'm not to do business with her, and not with you either."

Domingo nodded. "What about the others? Ezra, Levi."

Caleb shook his head. "I don't expect any of them will hire you. The rules are the same for all of us."

"That's not fair," Miriam said softly, and it surprised her to hear her own voice. "Domingo has done nothing wrong, and he is not a member—"

"He is the *husband* of a banned woman," her father said, "and shares her fate."

"But he has done only good things for all of us," she moaned, though a quick hard glance from her father made her amend her words. "I mean you—all of *you*. Over and over Domingo has proven faithful. He has saved all our lives more than once, kept you from harm many times, worked to help you build a homestead, and been a friend to all the Amish. He has worked as hard as any—"

"You think I don't know that?" her father shot back. He actually raised his voice, and there was a new fire in his eyes. "Do you think I *wanted* this? I have no choice in this matter, Miriam, I'm only the messenger. These are the consequences of your actions, the natural result of your *choice*. You brought this on yourself, and you *knew* this day would come!"

Domingo held out a calming hand. "We will be all right, Señor Bender," he said quietly, and the compassion in his voice forced Miriam to look up at his face. Though her husband was proud and quick to anger there was not a trace of it in his eyes, and it suddenly dawned on her that he had sensed something in her father that in her grief she had missed.

Pain. Dat said it himself—none of this was his choice. And it was killing him. Caleb Bender was hurting, and Domingo felt it.

"You know you can trust me," Domingo said gently. "I give you my word, as long as I draw breath your daughter will be well cared for. No harm will come to her, and she will never know hunger. She will never want for anything so long as I live."

Caleb held his gaze for a long moment, and in that moment something profound passed between them that even Miriam felt. Her father said nothing else. He nodded once, curtly, then turned his back on her and snugged his hat on his head as he went out the door.

It seemed to Miriam that most of the air in the room swirled out the door in his wake, and a fair portion of her world with it.

Chapter 16

Rachel sat with her face in her hands most of the way home from Miriam's, devastated. Miriam's ban cast a shadow over everything. Even coming home from Ohio a baptized member of the church and bearing news of a bishop coming in the spring, all she could think about was Miriam.

But that changed when they came in sight of the house.

"They're waiting for you," Dat said as he turned the buggy up the lane. They were the first words he'd spoken since leaving Miriam's. A little smile came to him as the front door opened and lanterns began bobbing outside.

Before the buggy stopped rolling Rachel leaped out. Ada reached her first, and nearly knocked her down with an exuberant bear hug. They were all there. Mary and Ezra had come up with their five children, and Emma and Levi with their three. Even Lovina Hershberger came to welcome her home, but then Rachel knew for a fact Lovina would use any excuse to spend time with Harvey.

Mamm stepped out of the crowd and clutched Rachel's face in her two hands. Rachel stifled a gasp. Mamm had lost so much weight she didn't even look like the same person. Her face—a face that had always been round and red and cheerful—had become thin and drawn. There were dark circles under her eyes, and her skin was pale.

The difference was alarming to one who had been gone for nearly five months, and Rachel couldn't hide her fears. "Mamm, are you all right? Have you been sick?"

"No," Mamm said, but even her voice sounded strangely high and frail. "I just missed my little girl, that's all."

The whole crowd migrated inside, and since Rachel and Caleb had not eaten supper the women set about heating up leftovers. They all crowded into the kitchen and gathered around the table while Rachel and Caleb ate, which they hardly had time to do because they were forced to answer a barrage of questions from all angles.

"How are Lizzie and Andy?"

"Who does her new baby look like?"

"How's the farm doing?"

"Did anybody else get baptized?"

"Did you miss us?"

"I missed you all so much," Rachel said. "I thought I was going home until I got there and realized home is where my family is."

But in the middle of answering, Rachel noticed an unnatural hush had fallen, and only then did she see that Mamm had filled a plate and sat down beside Dat at the table.

And she was eating. Mamm was packing away the vegetables, eating the way none of them had seen her do in months. Mamm finally noticed the stares, the silence. She looked up wide-eyed, with her mouth full, and muttered, "What?"

They laughed, a bit nervously until Caleb took a chicken leg from his own plate and laid it on hers.

"Pay no attention to them," he said. "Eat up."

It was a joyous reunion, and Rachel was full of news about how the crops had done, who was courting whom, who had gotten married and how all the children had grown. They sat around the stove in the living room on hard-back chairs and talked and laughed and cried for two hours, hungry for news.

The whole time Rachel noticed her father watching Mamm. Her mother didn't talk much, but she seemed suddenly alive again, as if some spark of her old self had ignited, some small ember of hope. As she watched her father watching her mother, Rachel realized it was hope she saw in *his* eyes, too.

The house emptied out when Mary and Ezra and Emma and Levi left with all their children, and Rachel's siblings wandered off to bed. After the others retired Rachel caught her mother alone in the kitchen putting away the last of the dishes.

"Mamm," she said, touching her mother's shoulder, "I need to tell you something—a secret, just between us."

Folding a dish towel, Mamm turned to face her. There was a trace of the old fear in her eyes then, as if she had forgotten that news could sometimes be good.

"Jah?"

"I need your help," Rachel said, a smile creeping onto her face. "Jake will be coming back in the spring when he comes of age. I didn't tell the others yet, but a bishop is coming, too. Abe Detweiler is coming down in the spring to see if he wants to live here."

"Oh, that's good," Mamm said. "We have waited a long time for a church leader." She said it almost absently, her brow furrowed in confusion. "That's your secret?"

She hadn't taken the hint.

"Mamm, Jake has asked me to be his wife. We're going to be married when the bishop comes in the spring. I'll need your help to get ready."

Mamm just stared for a few seconds as if she still didn't comprehend, but then something happened. She blinked. Her eyes widened a little, and Rachel watched as that small ember of hope in her mother's heart burst into flame, as if she suddenly remembered who she was. Mamm came alive in that moment.

"Oh my stars!" she said, clutching her cheeks. "Rachel, we have so much to do! You know it's harder having a spring wedding because we can't plant everything we need in the winter."

"I know," Rachel said. "We'll have to do without a few things, but that's how it's got to be. We'll publish the first Sunday after the bishop gets here, and not one minute later. Jake and I have waited long enough."

It was harvesttime and, without Domingo, Caleb had to work twice as hard. Barbara, his youngest daughter, was driving while he and Harvey walked along behind a mountain of hay on their way back to the barn when Caleb looked up and saw the platoon of federales cutting across his fresh-mowed field.

Captain Soto rode at the head of the column.

"Buenos días, Señor Bender," the captain shouted as his men rode up alongside the draft horses, grabbed the reins and brought them to a stop.

Caleb nodded, but declined to return the captain's cheerful greeting.

Undeterred, Captain Soto grinned broadly, leaning on his pommel and looking down at Caleb. "It is a fine crop you have here," he said. "I was wondering if perhaps you can share some of your bounty with us. We have no place to pasture our horses, and they will need a lot of hay for the long winter ahead."

Caleb eyed the captain cautiously. He already knew how this would go. "How much are you going to take?" he asked bluntly.

Soto shrugged. "I was thinking it would save us a lot of time if you could just let us borrow your wagon and team, since the hay is already loaded. We will take this load to our barn and have your wagon back in an hour."

"Pity you couldn't show up a little earlier and help with the harvest," Caleb said.

Soto shrugged again, and his men chuckled among themselves. "We are not farmers, Señor Bender; we are soldiers. We are here to *protect* farmers."

Caleb's jaw worked and he chewed on his bottom lip to keep himself from saying what he was thinking. Soto and his men were here to protect farmers from those who would steal, but the soldiers stole more than the bandits ever did.

"Take it, then," he said, and motioned Barbara down from the seat.

"Muchas gracias, Señor Bender. Of course this one load will not be enough to last the winter, but I see others in the valley bringing in their hay. We will only need this one little wagonload from you."

The captain actually tipped his cap and grinned at Caleb as he turned away, and one of his men climbed up into the seat to bring the wagon about.

They brought the wagon back empty in two hours, and Caleb watched as they headed straight for Hershberger's farm. John was on his way to the barn with a big load of hay.

Think of it as taxes, he thought.

They came back a few days later and took a wagonload of corn.

~

Rachel was glad to be home, but it seemed to her now that her world was fractured, divided into three distinct pieces. Part of her was with Jake in Ohio, and part of her with Miriam in

San Rafael. Miriam hadn't come around since the ban letter arrived, so Rachel hadn't seen her at all. Her name was rarely even mentioned at home. Her name brought the darkness back to Mamm's face, a thing which they all learned quickly to avoid. Better not to speak of Miriam at all.

But ban or no ban, she was still Rachel's sister, and Rachel missed her sorely. Already, after only a week at home, she'd caught herself turning over in bed a hundred times to say something to Miriam, only to remember that she was gone. She loved Leah, but Leah was not Miriam.

She finally got a chance late one afternoon to take the buggy into town to do the trading at the *mercado* and pick up the mail. Leah went with her, talking the whole way, but it occurred to Rachel as she was tying the horse to the rail at the mercado that she couldn't recall a single thing her seventeen-year-old sister had said.

Rachel traded her eggs and butter for a bag of salt and the cloves that Mamm had requested, then hurried back to the buggy, but Leah wasn't back from the post office yet. She untied the horse and drove slowly down the main street, watching for her sister. As she passed a narrow alley she happened to glance down it and saw Leah coming toward her, escorted by an Amishman. The man didn't look up, but that pointed black beard and small stature were unmistakable. Atlee Hostetler. He was holding Leah's arm, and the look on Leah's face was one of abject horror. Rachel could also see a little group of uniformed men farther down the alley, staring at Leah's back, laughing and gesturing.

Before they emerged into the main street, Atlee looked up and saw Rachel waiting there with the buggy. He gave Leah a little shove and then turned about, ducking his head as if he thought he could keep from being recognized.

"What happened?" Rachel asked as her sister climbed up into the seat.

Leah only shook her head, pale as a ghost. "Go," she said, waving at the horses. "Go!"

By the time they were clear of the town Rachel finally got her sister calmed down enough to talk.

"I was on my way back from the post office," she said, drawing a packet of mail from the deep pocket of her dress, staring at it. "Three of those soldiers stopped me, took my arm and dragged me into that alley."

She broke down and cried for a minute, then sobbed, "I thought they were going to kill me! I don't know what would have happened if Atlee hadn't come along. He told them to leave me alone, and they let me go."

"What was Atlee doing there?" Rachel asked.

Leah shook her head, dabbing at her eyes with a handkerchief. "I don't know, but I did smell liquor on his breath. I think they were all drinking."

"Atlee was drinking with the federales?"

"I guess so. I don't know what else to think."

Rachel thought about this for a minute, and nodded. "It makes sense, I guess. There are rumors about Atlee's drinking. They say that's why he came down here, to get away from his reputation and maybe straighten up. I guess if you're looking for a drink, a bunch of soldiers would know where to find it. Are you okay?"

Leah nodded. "Those men are pigs. You should hear the things they said."

Rachel shook her head. "I don't want to, but I can imagine. It's okay. You're safe now. I think from now on we'll have to have a man come with us when we go to town. Dat will hear about this, and I'm thinking he'll want to have a word with Atlee."

Despite the problem with the soldiers they'd made good time in town, and when Rachel came to the crossroads, instead of going on straight toward home she turned right, toward the little town of San Rafael.

"Where are we going?" Leah asked, still upset.

"To see Miriam."

"Really?" Leah said, a little shocked.

"Jah, she's still our sister." She gave Leah a hard stare. "You're not to tell Dat about this, you understand?"

Leah shook her head, still sniffling. "I won't."

They found Miriam in her kitchen with Kyra, canning the last of the produce from the garden. Kyra opened the door, and when Miriam heard Rachel's voice she almost knocked over the big boiling pot in her excitement.

Miriam gave Rachel a big welcome-home hug, but when she went to hug Leah she held her at arms' length for a second.

"Have you been crying? What's wrong?"

So Leah told her the whole story about the soldiers while Rachel pitched in with the canning.

Kyra listened in. Wiping her hands on a rag, she said, "You mustn't go to town unescorted. Any of you. Those soldiers are no better than bandits, especially when they've been drinking."

"Sometimes I think they're worse," Rachel said over her shoulder. "But at least they haven't killed anybody yet."

"They killed a whole bunch of bandits," Leah said. "Dat was pretty upset about that." But now she was craning her neck, already distracted. "Your little house is very nice, Miriam. I like it a lot."

As she helped fill jars with peppers Rachel remembered one of her main reasons for coming.

"I have some really good news, Miriam. Abe Detweiler is

coming down in the spring." And then, as if Miriam needed a hint, she added, "He's a bishop, you know."

"I know," Miriam said quietly. There was a trace of sadness in her eyes. "I know exactly what that means for you . . . and for Jake. I only regret that I can't be there for you."

Miriam's kitchen was very small. There was only room for two at the stove, so Leah stood back and watched. But now Rachel stepped aside and wiped her hands, beckoning Leah to take her place. She went to Miriam and took her hands.

"Miriam, you know there's nothing in the world I'd like better than to have you at my wedding," Rachel said. "It won't be the same without you, and I know you would be there for me if you could."

Miriam's eyes fell away for a moment, thinking. "Maybe I *can* be there— in a way," she said pensively. "Come to the bedroom with me. I want to ask you something."

Rachel followed her back to the bedroom. A crude, hand-made chifforobe stood in the corner. Miriam opened the door and brought out a dress.

An Amish dress.

"I wore this the morning of my wedding day," she said. "But only to leave home. It's new. Mamm made it for me when I was courting Micah. It was supposed to be my wedding dress, but . . . well, you know."

"You want to *give* this to me?" Rachel asked.

Miriam shook her head. "No, you can't accept a gift from me now that I'm banned. But if I leave it out back on the burn pile and someone takes it, well . . . it's no great loss."

Rachel giggled, holding the dress against her body, gauging the fit.

"Are you sure it's okay?" Miriam asked. "Would you *want* to wear it?"

Rachel's grin disappeared. When she looked up, tears sprang to her eyes. "Miriam, I would be *honored* to wear your dress. It'll almost be like you're there with me."

Miriam hugged her, the dress pressed between them, and Rachel whispered four words into her ear.

"No matter what. Always."

Chapter 17

The rains were kind that year, and the bean fields yielded a bumper crop. But that fall, for the first time since coming to Mexico, Caleb Bender did not bring his Belgians and his spring-toothed harrow to help Domingo. The men of the church would have frowned on it.

Domingo and his cousins labored in the sun for two days, prying the vines from the ground by hand and piling them in neat rows to dry in the sun. Miriam and Kyra helped, and Kyra's boys, who were growing into strong young men. Everyone worked long hours, for the beans were vital to survival. When game was scarce in the winter, when the canned vegetables ran out or worms fouled the cornmeal, the beans were always there. For every peasant household in San Rafael, dried beans became a hedge against starvation.

It was midafternoon and Miriam was bone weary, but the work was almost done. Nearly all the vines had been pulled and stacked when Miriam straightened up, pressing a hand against the small of her aching back, and saw Domingo's mother. It was an unusual sight, the old woman standing like a statue in her full black dress with a shawl wrapped about her shoulders and a scarf on her head. She rarely came out to the fields, because her knees were bad and it pained her to walk so far, but now she stood at the edge of the field with her back to them, staring at the sky.

"Kyra, look," Miriam said, and her sister-in-law straightened up beside her, following her eyes.

"Something is wrong," Kyra said. "She would not be out here otherwise. Domingo!"

On the far side of the field, Domingo looked around. Kyra pointed, and without another word the three of them made their way out of the field to the old woman.

"What is it?" Kyra asked, gently placing a hand on her mother's shoulder.

The *anciana* glanced at them, and there was deep worry in the lines of her eyes as she turned her face back to the sky. "A storm is coming," she said.

A little wind kicked up, rustling the sage between the bean field and the house.

Domingo glanced nervously at the gathering clouds and explained the danger to Miriam. "If rain comes after the beans are piled up for drying we will have to turn them over. It's a lot of work, but we can do it. If a second rain comes we can turn them again. A third time will ruin the whole crop." But then he shrugged it off. "One rain is not so bad."

His mother shook her head worriedly. "My bones tell me this is no ordinary storm, Domingo, and the animals are restless. The wind is strengthening from the northeast and the sky is yellow. The birds are flying low, and there are seabirds among them, hurrying inland. I have seen this once before, when I was very young. A hurricane came from the Gulf and crept into the mountains. The winds died before it reached us, but rain fell for four days and there was no way to save the crop. We went hungry that winter."

Domingo's breathing quickened, standing next to his mother, staring at the sky. "Are you sure?"

The anciana nodded. "Sí, *estoy seguro*. It is coming."

"When?"

"Tomorrow morning. Maybe before."

"Then we must gather the plants and get them inside. If we can keep them dry until the rain passes we might save the crop."

"We have no room," Kyra said. "The loft of our barn is very small and half full of hay."

He scratched his head. "You're right. It's not nearly enough. We're going to need help. Miriam, I want you to ride to your father's house and ask if we can store the vines in his loft for a few days. This must be done now, tonight."

Miriam raised an eyebrow. "I will ask, but I know my father. I don't think he will help us now."

"Try," Domingo said, and the urgency in his voice was enough to convince her. He turned his gaze to the north, where more fields lay scattered through the valley, rows of beans yellowing in the weakening light. Every peasant in San Rafael depended on the bean crop to get them through the winter. "Kyra, go and warn the others. I will hitch the cart, and the boys can help me. Go!"

Miriam saddled Domingo's horse and rode hard to her father's house. She found him in the tack room, mending harness. Caleb looked up from the workbench when she came in the door and his eyes hardened when he saw her.

"Dat, we need help," she said. No sense beating around the bush. "Domingo's mother says a hurricane is coming, that it will rain for three or four days."

His head tilted and he shrugged. "Then it will rain," he said. "You have a house with a roof. Go there."

"You don't understand. It's the beans, Dat. Our vines are pulled and laid out to dry. If it rains for three days the beans will rot and we'll go hungry this winter. Domingo wanted me to ask if we can store them in your hay loft."

"My loft is full."

"The second level, then. Or even the buggy shed—anyplace where they can stay dry for a few days. Just until the rain passes."

"I cannot help you, Miriam. It wouldn't be right. You and your husband will have to fend for yourselves."

His stare was almost blank, but she felt sure she saw a trace of sympathy in his eyes. He wanted to help. It hurt him *not* to help, but he felt pressure from the others. They would be watching to see what he would do, and he was keenly aware of his position in the community. She would not plead or shed a tear, but neither would she hold any of this against her father. The respect of his brethren was vital to him. She understood.

"All right," she said evenly, turning to go. "I'll find someone else." Climbing back up into the saddle she spurred her horse toward Emma's.

Finding her sister in the kitchen cooking supper, Miriam laid out the situation as quickly as she could. Emma didn't answer at all; she just stepped out the back door and called Levi. When he came in Emma did all the talking, explaining the emergency. Levi scratched his neck with a dirty, callused hand.

"But, Emma, she's banned," he said softly.

Emma nodded. "Jah. That's why Dat wouldn't help them. He can't do business with her."

"Neither can I," Levi said, casting a sympathetic glance at Miriam.

"But no money will change hands," Emma said. It was then that Miriam saw the little twinkle in her eye, the catlike smile. "So you wouldn't be doing business with them at all; you'd only

174

be helping a neighbor in a time of need. Besides, it's only for a few days. We're a thousand miles from the nearest bishop, Levi. It will be over before anyone can say 'Don't.'"

He scratched his chin, and Miriam saw Emma's little grin creep onto Levi's face. "Well, I guess if no money changes hands. My loft is new and almost empty—you could put a lot of vines up there. But I'm thinking the work would go a lot faster with a hay wagon."

He was right. A hay wagon was rigged with ropes. When the wagon pulled up to the barn with a load of hay the ropes were gathered from the corners and attached to a lifting hook hanging from the beam above the loft door. While that was being done, someone would unhitch the draft horses, walk them to the far end of the barn and hook them to the other end of the rope. A team of Belgians could lift an entire wagonload into the loft in a matter of minutes.

"Are you sure you want to do this?" Miriam asked, giving him an out. "There will be talk."

Levi gave Emma a little sideways smile. "Let the tongues wag," he said. "Go home. Tell Domingo I'll be there shortly."

Quickly Miriam got herself back on the horse and took off at a gallop.

Kyra caught up with her in the barn as she was putting away the horse.

"Father Noceda moved all the church benches out of the way and told the people they could bring their beans into the church—a good idea, since it sits on high ground and it was a warehouse before it was a church. You know, he really is a good man," Kyra said. "Pity he's a priest."

Levi arrived a half hour later with a team of Belgians pulling his hay wagon. The freshening wind put new strength into arms and backs that had already seen a day's work, and the hayforks flew. Dusk came and went, and they toiled on by lantern light as the wagonloads trundled out of San Rafael, around the ridge and up to Levi's farm at the other end of Paradise Valley. Men, women and children labored all through the night, filthy and utterly exhausted.

Miriam and Domingo rode on the wagon with Levi as he drove home with the last load. At the barn, his horses leaned into the hoisting rope, lifting the last of their bean vines into the loft as lightning flashed, the sky rumbled, and black night paled to a yellow gray.

A steady rain began to fall as Levi pulled his wagon into the barn and took care of his horses. Miriam and Domingo propped each other up in the doorway to watch the rain thicken in the half-light of dawn. It fell softly at first, then harder and harder. Ten minutes after the last of the beans went into the loft the rain swept through in sheets, blowing, driving, gathering into little streams that wound through fields and down the lane, growing.

"It looks like my mother was right," Domingo said, his voice raspy with fatigue. "This is no ordinary storm."

The hurricane behaved exactly as the anciana had predicted, spending its fury on the coast and then pushing inland until it came up against the mountains. By the time it reached the foothills the tired winds merely hummed about the eaves for a few hours, too weak to tear off a roof, but frustrated clouds piled themselves in against the piedmont and dumped rain for three days. Streams cut gullies through plowed fields and washed out parts of the main road in the valley. There were few places in Paradise Valley where water could stand, so the runoff streamed out of the valley and wandered to the southeast in swelling torrents. There would be terrible flooding in the lowlands, but Paradise Valley and San Rafael suffered very little damage.

Except for the bean crop. Most people didn't see the long hard rain coming, and even if they had, most of them owned no barn big enough to shelter their crop. Everywhere rows of wilted vines rotted and melted into the mud. Most of the peasants would wait a few days and then go out with long faces and slumped shoulders to turn the entire crop under. It was going to be a long winter.

But not for Domingo and Miriam. On the fourth day the sun broke through. And on the fifth day, when the ground began to dry out and firm up, they went back to Levi's farm. Kyra and her boys came with them, and together with Domingo's cousins they pitched the vines down from the loft and piled them in neat rows in Levi's pasture to finish drying.

"We probably lost a fourth of the beans from so much handling," Domingo said.

"But we saved *three* fourths," Miriam answered.

At noon Emma called everyone inside for lunch. Miriam tiptoed in tentatively, not sure what to expect, but Emma was prepared. She had pushed a small table up against the end of her long dinner table and covered both with one long cloth. She used a peso for a spacer, leaving a mere crack between the tables. On the main table sat large bowls of vegetables—creamed corn, tomatoes, butter peas and sweet potatoes—and on the little table at the end, smaller bowls of the same.

Miriam covered a little hiccup of a laugh when she saw the arrangement, and took her place at the smaller table without a word of direction, pointing for Domingo to sit opposite her. Domingo gave her a puzzled look as he sat down. Miriam said nothing; she just ran a finger down the divide between the tables, pressing the tablecloth into the void to show Domingo that the letter of the law was being preserved. Emma was bending the rules as far as she could without breaking them.

Later, when the men had gone back to work, Miriam stayed behind in the house to help Emma clean up. All three of Emma's children were napping and the kitchen was quiet; it was just the two of them. Emma was up to her elbows in a washtub full of dishes while Miriam dried.

"Thank you for that," Miriam said quietly.

"For what?"

"The table. The way you set it up. You can't know how much it meant to me. You've made the ban bearable. It was a generous gift."

"It was nothing." Emma was concentrating on her dish-washing, but now she looked up and gave Miriam that catlike smile. "Actually, it was Levi's idea. He built that little table just for you and made sure it was the same height and width as the other one."

Miriam nearly dropped a plate in shock. "Levi did that for me?"

Emma nodded. "For him to even think of such a thing is a real turning point, I think. It still makes him nervous to tread near the edge of the ordnung, but he's learning. I believe it helps that there's no bishop here."

"He's come a long way," Miriam said. "The Levi I know would never have done such a thing."

"Jah, I know. I'm so proud of him. I wasn't sure I would ever be able to open him up like that. It's just not the way he was raised."

"He's a lot like his father. And the Bible does say Gott chastises those He loves."

"Jah, but whose life is *not* full of trials? Even the righteous lose crops and loved ones. Triumph and disaster alike, it's all part of life. Our faith only helps us put it all in its place."

"That's true. I never thought about it like that."

"Neither did Levi," Emma said. "He's still divided on it, but he's trying."

"What do you mean, 'he's still divided'?" Miriam asked.

Emma shrugged. "I get the feeling he's watching me, and watching Gott, to see what happens. Helping save your bean crop, making this little table for you—it's Levi's way of testing things. I can see it in his eyes. He's testing Gott, watching to see if punishment comes from bending the rules. But Levi's mill grinds slowly, and it might be years before he makes up his mind."

Miriam chuckled, sliding another plate onto the stack. "Well, you better hope nothing terrible happens in the meantime. He'll blame you for sure."

Emma shook her head. "No, Levi never holds anything against me. He loves me, and he knows I would never do anything to harm him. That's not what worries me." Her hands stilled themselves in the washtub and she fell silent for a moment, staring out the window.

"I'm afraid he'll blame Gott."

Chapter 18

The Benders hosted their annual Thanksgiving feast in late November of 1925, their fourth since coming to Paradise Valley, and it was bigger and brighter than ever. More than a hundred Amish came to break bread together, to celebrate the fruits of their labors as only very hardworking people can.

Emma found joy in it too, and most of all, sitting at the women's table, she saw her mother had almost returned to her old self. Mamm was eating again and putting on weight. Her smile was back.

But when the meal was done, the turkey and ham and sweet potatoes and pies all ravaged, as Emma was helping clean up she saw her father standing apart from the others. Staring out over his fields he had that distant look in his eye, picking at his teeth with a wood splinter, and she could tell from the tilt of his head and the slump of his shoulders that he was troubled. A darkness had settled upon him.

There were plenty of women to help with cleaning up, so Emma left a stack of plates on a table and went to him.

"Are you all right, Dat?" she asked, touching his shoulder.

He stared blankly for a moment, shrugged and looked away. "What's bothering you?"

His chest swelled with a long sigh. "Your sister," he said quietly.

He meant Miriam. Otherwise he would have named her, or at least said My *daughter*.

"I miss them too," Emma said, the plural intentional. It was their first Thanksgiving without Miriam and Domingo, and she knew her dat missed Domingo almost as much as he missed his daughter.

"There's a hole in the family," he said. "We gather at a time like this to give thanks, and we have a lot to be thankful for, but I keep catching myself looking for Aaron and Miriam. And Domingo. It's not the same. There's a hole in my *heart*, too."

Emma knew his heart, and she watched his eyes. Looking out over the tables of food and beards and bonnets in his yard she knew that here, finally, was what he wanted, what he had set out to accomplish in the beginning. This thriving community was the very reason the whole family had worked so hard these last four years. In many ways the sight of all these transplanted Amish, living and laughing and celebrating a fruitful harvest in the wilds of Mexico, vindicated her father's heartfelt belief that people who honored Gott, worked hard and cooperated with one another, could thrive anywhere. But for her father, the achievement had come at a terrible price.

"It's not your fault," she said gently, rubbing his shoulder. "You only did what was right."

He gave a little snort, shook his head. "What I *thought* was right. My stubbornness cost me a son, and now it has cost me a daughter as well."

"What one man calls stubbornness, another might call courage and conviction," she said. "Only Gott knows what the future will bring. It was not your fault Aaron died, or that Miriam fell in love with Domingo."

"But neither would have happened if I hadn't brought us here."

"Maybe so, but we don't know what *else* might have happened. I'm pretty sure Mamm would not have lived this long if we hadn't moved to a dry climate."

"Maybe. I will not complain against what Gott has ordained, but I still wonder if I've done right."

"You did what you *believed* was right. That's all any of us can do."

Her father looked at her then, and a smile of gratitude crinkled the corners of his eyes. "I guess in the end that's all Gott asks of us."

This was one of those moments, and she knew it. Her father was a man of principle, but Emma was one of the few people who could sway him . . . if she was careful. She'd been waiting for such a moment.

"No, Dat, that's not *all* Gott asks of us," she said, and let the words hang there a moment. "He also asks those who have been forgiven of their sins to pass it on. He asks us to forgive, too."

It was a gamble, a risk she took willingly. But his eyes hardened.

"Gott asks us to forgive those who *ask* for forgiveness. Those who *repent*," he said, then turned and walked away.

Winter settled in gently, as usual. Light snows brushed Paradise Valley on occasion, but the season was never as harsh as what they'd known in Ohio. Once the winter wheat sprouted, the pace of the farm slowed. The women took to their quilting and sewing and a hundred little household improvements that had been set aside for calmer days, while the men spent their time mending fence and harness, cutting firewood, and making trips to Saltillo to market a plentiful harvest. When the weather permitted, there were wells to be dug, shops and sheds and chicken coops and smokehouses to be built, all the projects they had put off in the warmer seasons when they were in the fields from daylight to dark.

At Christmas Rachel put on the same kind of show with her school children that Miriam had always done, yet it wasn't the same. Her pupils were almost all Amish now. When Miriam left, most of the Mexican students—as well as her extraordinary gift for teaching—went with her.

Rachel did the best she could with help from Leah and Barbara, and even the new children, being Amish, behaved themselves well enough. But the eagerness, the fun of learning, the sense of discovery, was all but gone.

The week before Christmas, Emma and Levi went to visit Miriam.

"Now, we won't be exchanging any gifts with Aunt Miriam, but that doesn't matter," she told little Mose. He was in the front beside his dat, peering over the seat at her while she held the two smaller ones on her lap in the back. "Miriam says there's going to be a big party with lots of children and a *piñata!*"

Mose's tiny hat tilted and he looked up at her with eyes as serious as an adult's. "What's a piñata?"

Holding the reins, Levi looked around at Emma and frowned. "Will Miriam and Domingo provide the piñata?"

She smiled. "No, we thought of that already. Miriam said she would make sure someone else brought the piñata and everything in it. She knows the rules, Levi."

He gave her a sly grin. "Jah, and it looks like she's learning to bend them as good as you."

⁂

"It's called a *posada*," Miriam explained. There were already a bunch of people gathering in her yard, setting tables, putting out food and drink. "For each of the nine days leading up to Christmas the children march from the church to a different neighborhood in the village. Two of them dress up like Joseph and Mary, they put the girl on a burro, and all the children follow them, singing while they go door-to-door asking for shelter. Everyone refuses, except for the house that has been chosen for the day. Today is our day." Miriam beamed. "It's going to be a big fiesta."

Levi went to put the buggy away, leaving little Mose to stand by himself in the front yard, watching two old men clinging to opposite sides of a rickety wooden stepladder. They were hanging a paper-mache piñata from a cottonwood tree and arguing over how high to hang it.

Emma and Miriam carried the two younger babies to the house. "Look at him," Emma said, nodding toward Mose. "He never hears anybody argue like that at home. It scares him a little, but he can't turn away from it. Mose likes for everybody to get along."

Domingo leaned down beside the three-year-old and said, "Pay them no mind. Those two old men are the Castillo brothers. They have fought like that for sixty years, but they are only playing. They never really get angry unless someone *else* gets between them."

Emma stepped inside the front door of Miriam's house and froze, gawking. "Miriam, I guess I've never seen the inside of a Mexican house at Christmas before. This is really *something*."

185

"You mean the *nacimiento*—the nativity scene. Jah, I was a little surprised myself."

There was no Christmas tree, though in a corner stood a leafless limb from what looked like a dogwood, festooned with balls of cotton and draped with brightly colored bows and ribbons, and there were potted poinsettias scattered around the room. But the real attraction was a nativity scene that took up nearly half of the front room. The backdrop was made mostly of painted paper, sawdust pastures rising from the middle of the floor, soaring into red mountains that climbed halfway up the wall. The foothills were covered by a village of thatched huts and little houses surrounded by fences and trees, complete with hand-carved wooden people, farmers and shepherds in the fields, women haggling with a grocer, men watching a blacksmith shoe a horse, and children fishing in a blue pond beside an old man while a dog treed a hissing cat.

In the center, in a little hole of a cave, were Mary and Joseph holding Baby Jesus beside the manger. A red rooster crowed the arrival of the Christ child. There were sheep and chickens and cows, and a farm girl on a stool, milking. When Emma looked close she even saw a flock of ducks on the pond.

She stuck her head out the door. "Levi, come look! You've got to see this."

Miriam gave them a tour of the miniature town, showing off the intricately detailed figures. Even the faces were painted, each of them bearing a different expression.

"Domingo made the landscape and carved some of the figures," Miriam said proudly.

"Only a few," Domingo said. "The nacimiento has been in my family for a long time—ever since my mother was a child. My grandfather and my uncle added to it every Christmas for years. It was given to my mother when she married, and now she has given it to me." He put an arm around Miriam and smiled.

"It is our proudest possession," she said.

Domingo laughed dryly, "It is our only possession, Cuahtezqui."

There was a little uproar outside, and the singing of children drifted faintly down the street as Kyra and Domingo's mother crowded into the little house along with their aunt and uncle, Paco and Maria.

"Wait till you see the children," Miriam said. "Behind Joseph and Mary there will be wise men and shepherds and angels and a hundred other children, all dressed up."

The singing drew nearer as the throng of children paraded down the street, until from inside the house Emma could hear the thumping of shepherds' staffs in time with the music. Silence fell as the procession stopped outside the front door.

Miriam flung the door wide. Father Noceda stood between Mary and Joseph, dressed in his full cassock and holding the reins to the burro. On a signal from the priest a hundred children began singing their request, asking for shelter for the night.

From inside the house Domingo's kin sang their answer: "'Welcome, holy pilgrims, to our humble home. While it may be simple, our gift is from the heart.'"

Thus began a celebration such as Emma and Levi had never seen. A band comprised of musicians with guitars and horns and a squeeze-box played bright music while men and women danced and ate and drank, and children flocked to the piñata. Emma was surprised at first to see Miriam commanding and controlling a hundred Mexican children, but then Domingo's mother whispered to her, "See how the children love and respect their teacher? Not even Father Noceda commands their attention as Miriam does."

Three-year-old Mose got a few whacks at the piñata as all

the smaller children went first. Miriam didn't blindfold the little ones. When one of the older boys finally shattered the paper sheep, candy and little gifts flew everywhere. Miriam stepped back out of the way while the children swarmed. She ended up on the sidelines next to Emma.

"Is Levi okay?" she asked.

Emma looked around for Levi and spotted him standing alone, well clear of the festivities. "Jah, he's just a little uncomfortable around all this craziness. Leave him be. He'll get used to it after a while."

The party went on for hours, the Mexican peasants of San Rafael celebrating the coming of Baby Jesus as only peasants can. Then, in the middle of the afternoon, a squad of soldiers rode down the street and trotted their horses right up to the food-laden tables in Miriam's yard.

The band stopped playing, and complete silence fell as Domingo worked his way through the crowd and stood in the path of the captain's horse. Everyone else backed away in fear except Father Noceda, who came and stood at Domingo's shoulder. Even the children remained quiet.

The captain stayed in the saddle, his hands crossed calmly on the pommel as five armed federales fanned out in a V behind him. Ignoring Domingo, Soto fastened a hard glare on the priest. "What is the meaning of this, Padre?"

Noceda shrugged. "It is a posada, Captain. You are Mexican—surely you have seen a Christmas celebration before."

The captain rolled his eyes. "Sí, I know it is a posada, priest. It is not *my* ignorance that concerns me, but yours. Perhaps you are unaware that it is against the law to hold a religious ceremony in public."

Father Noceda's shoulders rose in a prolonged shrug as he spread his hands. "Does this look like a religious ceremony,

Captain? To me it only looks like a Christmas party for the children."

The captain didn't smile. Climbing down from his horse, he kept his eyes fastened on Father Noceda. He moved casually and gave no warning, so it came as a complete shock when he whipped his pistol from its holster and struck Father Noceda in the head with it. The priest collapsed in the dirt as if he'd been shot.

Domingo stepped between them, but before he could do anything the pistol was in his face, the barrel jammed under his nose. Domingo raised his hands very slowly, palms out.

"My quarrel is not with you," the captain said coldly, "but with this peon of the pope."

The priest shook his head and raised himself up on an elbow, touching fingertips to the blood on his forehead. Kyra rushed over and knelt at his side, holding his head.

Captain Soto kept his pistol pressed to Domingo's face as he glared down at Father Noceda. "Article 24 of our constitution expressly forbids religious ceremonies outside of the church."

Noceda winced, touching the gash on his head, and without looking up he muttered through clenched teeth, "Then perhaps you would be so kind as to give me back my church."

Soto laughed out loud, but there was a sneer in it. "Insolent to the last, I see. Perhaps, Padre, a fine will change your tone. Article 130 forbids a priest to wear his cassock in public. If I am not mistaken I have warned you about this before. The fine is five hundred pesos. Deliver it to my office. You probably already know how to find my office—it used to be your home."

Father Noceda looked up at him and started to say something, but Soto wagged a finger in warning.

"No, no, no, priest. If I were you I would not speak. The law also says that if a clergyman complains against a government official"—Soto pressed a hand against his own chest—"and I *am* a government official, you can go to prison for five years. One more word and I will have my men drag you away in chains."

No one said anything. Domingo's eyes made his contempt perfectly clear, but even Domingo would not start a fight against six armed soldiers with a hundred children in his yard.

The captain lowered his pistol slowly and stepped back, pointing a finger at Domingo to warn him to stay where he was. But he wasn't finished with Father Noceda.

"Your time is over, priest—your power broken. Superstitions like yours have left our country destitute, but our presidente is putting an end to that. You are going to find that Mexico no longer belongs to European priests and Italian popes, but to *Mexicans*." He swung up into his saddle, but before he turned the horse away he spat at Father Noceda. "You have until the end of the week to pay your fine, Padre. Don't be late."

Chapter 19

The party died instantly. As soon as the federales left, everyone gathered up their children and hurried off toward home, heads down. Kyra and Miriam helped Father Noceda into the house and sat him at the kitchen table to bandage his head. Emma and Levi stayed to clean up the mess in the yard.

By the time Emma and Levi came into the house the priest was looking better. There was blood all over his cassock, but at least his face was clean and his head bandaged.

Levi sat across the table from him. "Señor Noceda," he said, and it was no surprise to Emma that Levi would refuse to call a Catholic priest *father*, "a question is in my mind. I saw what that soldier did, how he talked to you, and it was like he was already mad at you before he got here. Why does he hate you so bad?"

Father Noceda didn't answer, but Emma saw him avert his eyes from Levi as if he were hiding something.

Domingo straightened up from stoking the little stove, for the evening was growing cold. When he turned around there was a grin on his face.

"It's a good story, Father," Domingo said, seating himself at the end of the table. "You should tell them."

Father Noceda shook his head. "Captain Soto doesn't need an excuse to pick on a priest," he said, "and at the moment I'm trying very hard not to hate my enemies."

Domingo nodded. "But you have to admit you gave him a reason to dislike you."

Father Noceda shrugged as Miriam set a cup of coffee on the table in front of him. She caught Levi's eye and raised a cup, but he shook his head. Rules.

"That wasn't me," Noceda said. "It was the hand of God. All I did was laugh at him, but Captain Soto is a little man, and I should have known it would make him crazy."

He took a sip of coffee and told the story to Levi.

"They came the morning after the long rain when I went to the church to see if there was any damage. Captain Soto rode through with his patrol at the same time, and when he saw me he decided to have a little fun."

Noceda ticked his clerical collar with a forefinger. "Soto doesn't need much of an excuse to torment a priest—the collar is fair game these days. But we were lucky. On the morning the soldiers came, the church was full of beans."

Levi's brow furrowed. "Beans?"

"Sí. Levi, you were the one who stored Domingo's beans in your loft, weren't you?"

"Sí, that was me."

"Well, a lot of the farmers in the village brought their beans to the church that same night. We cleared everything out of the church, and they worked all night, just like you did, hauling their vines into the empty building. Captain Soto and his men found me at the doors of the church the morning after the rain stopped. They surrounded me with their horses, laughing, threatening."

"Cowards," Domingo said, "threatening a priest."

Noceda raised an eyebrow. "You would be surprised, Domingo. There was a time when I would have thrashed them all, but that was another life. Now I try to live at peace with all men. Even morons. Captain Soto told me he had heard there was a new *iglesia* in San Rafael, and how very fortunate he was to find me there because he was in need of a warehouse to store all the grain he had 'bought' from the farmers in Paradise Valley.

"I said to the captain, 'I don't know what you're talking about. This is *already* a warehouse. Your godless *presidente* might be happy for you to steal the property of the church, but to confiscate a warehouse owned by a Mexican citizen might end with you in prison.'

"The captain grew very angry then, and said he would burn my church with me in it. He jumped down from his horse, knocked me out of the way and flung the bar from the big double doors."

Noceda grinned, remembering. "There were many wagon-loads of bean vines piled inside the church, and they must have shifted during the storm because when that little worm threw the doors wide a mountain of vines collapsed right on top of him. Knocked him flat in the mud and covered him from head to toe. It was like a miracle—the hand of God. Soto was cursing and screaming, his men slipping and falling in the mud while they tried to dig him out. I think perhaps it was the funniest thing I have ever seen. I laughed until my sides hurt."

"Even Soto's men were laughing about it," Domingo said. "I heard the story from soldiers who came here for beans."

Levi frowned. "They took your beans?"

"Only a hundred pounds or so," Domingo said. "We have plenty more, but I was trying to make them last because by the end of winter there will be people in the village who have none. Many of them lost their whole crop in the long rain."

"Soldiers must eat an awful lot," Emma said. "Two weeks ago they came and took Ira's prize pig."

Levi nodded. "It was the one he was fattening up for Christmas, too. Ira was spitting mad. But I still don't see why they would take your church. They already have the stone church in El Prado."

"They wanted a warehouse," Noceda said. "But the federales have to be careful who they steal from. They can take a bag of beans from a Mexican national, but not a warehouse. They can only confiscate something like that from the church."

"That's not right," Levi said. "Why doesn't somebody do something?"

Father Noceda twisted his tin cup on the table, staring at it. "They will," he said. "Rome has been too quiet in the face of this assault, and so have the cardinals. Sooner or later the people will rise up. There are already rumors among some of the village priests. But the time is not yet right, so we must not speak of these things."

Rachel kept herself busy through the winter months, doing chores, doing what she could to prepare for the wedding, and going to the post office every day. Jake wrote her at least twice a week, sometimes more, and she lived for his letters. His father knew his plans but still refused to let him return to Mexico until the day he became his own man.

"If you die down there," Jonas Weaver said, "I don't want it on *my* conscience."

More than once, when Rachel went to town in the late afternoon, she saw Atlee Hostetler or his buggy somewhere near the old church.

Harvey and Leah usually went with her, and Leah noticed,

too. "Why would he want to be around those soldiers?" she asked. "I just don't understand it."

"Mescal," Harvey said, holding the reins as they headed out of town. "Maybe tequila, too."

Leah shuddered, remembering her brush with the troops. "Well, he must want it awful bad if he's willing to spend time with *those* animals. I hate the way they leer at us."

"Jah, me too, but I won't be making this trip much longer," Rachel said. "It'll just be the two of you then."

Leah's head tilted. "Why won't you be going to town anymore?"

A shrug. "Jake comes back in six weeks—late March. When he gets here I won't have to go to town to look for his letters, will I?"

Harvey grinned mischievously. "*That's* why you've been doing so much sewing. You've got plans."

Rachel kept her eyes on the road, her expression blank. "Hush," she said.

The days dragged by, and she tried not to think about Jake more than once every minute or two because it seemed to make time stop. But in late March, when the swifts came to roost and the clover was just starting to sprout little magenta buds, the big day arrived.

Long before daylight her father hitched the Belgians to the wagon. He wouldn't be taking the buggy because Abe Detweiler was bringing a few farm implements with him and the buggy wasn't big enough.

When he got there Rachel was already in the barn, dressed and ready.

"We're late," she said. "We should already be on the road."

Dat gave her a sideways glance, straightening out the harness.

"We? Who said you were going?"

"Dat, you can't be serious."

"You have chores."

"Done," she said. She'd been at it since three.

"I don't see how three grown men are going to need your help loading Abe's planter."

She almost started to cry, but then he leaned so close to her face that his hat brim touched her forehead. His eyes widened and he said, "I'm teasing you, child. Get in the wagon."

The trip to Arteaga took forever. She'd never seen draft horses plod so, but they finally arrived.

And then they waited. The train was a half hour late. They dropped a few cars on a siding, and as her father pulled the wagon alongside, the door to a cattle car opened and there was Jake, waving.

And Abe Detweiler was with him.

Rachel could finally breathe. She hadn't even realized how fearful she'd been, how doubtful that this day would actually come, that Jake and the bishop would both arrive and all would be right with the world. The hardest thing was shaking Jake's hand. She wanted a hug, a great big, fierce welcome-home, oh-how-I-missed-you hug. She wanted to feel his arms around her, but it was broad daylight and they were in a railroad yard. Her father was there, and the bishop.

Her hand lingered in Jake's a little too long, and a quick glance from her father made her flinch and let go, but Jake's eyes spoke to her.

Wait, they said. *Our moment will come.*

She had the pleasure of riding all the way home in the back of the wagon with Jake while the bishop sat up on the bench with her father and talked.

Jake leaned close to her at the first opportunity and spoke

quietly. "If it's all right with you, we'll go talk to Bishop Detweiler after dark this Saturday, and we'll publish on Sunday. Rachel, I don't ever want to be apart from you again."

Sunday. Today was Wednesday. Four days to the announcement, fifteen to the Thursday of the wedding. A rush of excitement went through her. She smiled, entwined her fingers with his, and with a cautionary glance at the men up front, gave him a quick peck on the cheek.

"I love you," she whispered.

 ❧

"So tell me about these bandits," Bishop Detweiler said as Caleb's wagon rumbled southward on Saltillo Road. "I hear you got troops now."

"Jah, and the troops got rid of the bandits all right."

"That's good."

Caleb nodded thoughtfully. "Jah, I suppose it's a good thing. But I once said the same to a Mexican named Paco. He told me the troops had arrived and I said it was a good thing. Now, Paco had just been shot through the arm by bandits, only minutes before, but when I said it was good the troops had come, he only said, 'We will see.' Those three words have haunted me ever since."

The bishop frowned. "Is there a problem with the soldiers?"

"Several problems. First, the country is in turmoil and sometimes the troops don't get the supplies they need, so they take them from the farmers—from us. When you add it up they take much more than the bandits ever did, except they have not killed any of us. Yet."

"Like what? What do they take?"

"Horses, grain, pigs, chickens, eggs, milk, butter. They patrol the valley every day, grazing their horses in our fields, and when vegetables are in season they trample our kitchen gardens."

"They don't pay?"

Caleb shrugged. "They pay for the horses, but less than half of what they're worth. Only a few weeks ago they came and took four more horses from the valley. They said some of the ponies they captured from the bandits died over the winter, so they came to us and got good, solid standard-bred horses for the price of a broken-down old paint. But it looks like a good year for foals, so maybe we'll make do in the long run."

The bishop thought about all this for a minute and then said, "What else? You said there were other problems."

"They're violent men, Abe. Hard men who lie and steal and don't think twice about killing a man. They killed all of the bandits who fought them at El Prado. Every one of them. I watched them shoot the wounded with my own eyes, and afterwards they hung the prisoners. They took over the Catholic church in El Prado—put the priest out in the street and *laughed* about it. Their captain has no respect for Gott. No respect for anything. To my eyes, the only difference between a bandit and a soldier is the uniform."

The bishop shook his head. "Well, at least they got rid of the bandits. Jake told me they were coming there to kill."

"I think that's probably true, but we got everybody out in time. All they did was burn Levi's barn and kill his livestock. The bandits shot a few of the federales, but in the end the federales killed *all* the bandits. I guess I should be happy, but it just don't feel right, celebrating because someone *else* died, and not us."

"I see your point, Caleb, but the bandits were the killers, not you, and the troops saved you from them. Bandits live by the sword, and they die by it. Anyway, it's hard for me to feel sorry for the men who killed Aaron."

Caleb sighed. "I know. It's mighty hard to explain, but

sometimes it just feels like we got rid of coyotes by turning loose a pack of wolves."

⟡

The whole community was waiting at Caleb's place to welcome the bishop. They were glad to see Jake again too, but his return took a backseat to the long-awaited arrival of a genuine church leader. Now there would be unity. Now there would be real preaching, straight from Gott's own chosen representative.

Bishop Abe Detweiler immediately announced to the crowd gathered in Caleb's front yard that instruction classes would start the following Sunday for those who wished to be baptized, and they would also hold Communion right away because there were those there who hadn't partaken in a very long time.

"Now we will be more than just a struggling settlement," the bishop said. "We will be a church."

Chapter 20

When the day of Rachel's wedding finally arrived Mamm was so flustered she couldn't think straight, and in one respect it was a good thing. Rachel had plotted a small deception long in advance, and there was a nervous moment when her mother came to help her get dressed for the wedding. Rachel had made herself a dress for the occasion, not very different in style or color from her other dresses, but new. The seams lapped wide on the inside so the dress could grow with her if she put on weight, for she would wear it as her Sunday dress for the rest of her life, and when she died it would be her funeral dress. Rachel took great pains with it, but not because it was her wedding dress.

The fabric had to be a certain shade of dark blue and the stitching had to be just so. Mamm watched her work with pride, never knowing that all of Rachel's perfectionism served a single purpose: she wanted her wedding dress to be an exact replica of a dress that already lay folded and waiting in a drawer.

The one she was making would serve as Rachel's Sunday dress, but she never had any intention of wearing it at her wedding.

On the morning of the big day Rachel rose very early, ironed Miriam's dress, then folded her new one and put it away. It pained her to deceive her mother, but it pained her even more that Miriam would not be invited to her wedding. This way at least, Miriam was all around her. Still, Mamm had a keen eye, and Rachel was terrified she would spot some minuscule difference. But she didn't. She was too flustered.

The weather was perfect. Rachel couldn't have chosen a more beautiful spring day—all the flowers in bloom, the fields bursting with new green, the sky achingly blue, flocks of birds singing from the trees along the ridge. It was a day of opposites, of great joy and deep sorrow, a day of parting from her family and yet a day when family meant absolutely everything. A day of remembering.

She'd known from the very beginning, four years ago when Jake first kissed her, that he was the one and that this day would come. She'd been preparing for it for a long time, collecting a trunkful of dishes and flatware, a few pots and pans, sheets and pillowcases. In the two weeks prior to the wedding she'd put the finishing touches on a quilt, and last week she spent a whole day riding around to all the houses with Leah, borrowing dishes for the wedding feast.

It was also her duty to help Leah and her good friend Lovina Hershberger with their dresses, for they were to be her *navahuckers*. Harvey would escort Lovina for the day, and Rachel arranged for one of the younger Shrock boys to pair up with Leah. Bill was a handsome, quiet boy who reminded her a little of Jake. Leah hadn't said anything, but for a long time now she'd been watching Bill closely when she thought no one was looking. Leah was thrilled when Rachel told her.

The six of them sat just outside the barn door in their fine new clothes that morning, greeting each of the guests as they ambled up the lane from all over the settlement to gather in the Benders' barn. Once all the guests were inside they began singing hymns from the Ausbund, while the wedding party remained seated outside. In a little while the bishop would come out and escort Jake and Rachel to the house and into the abrode for a counseling session, but for now the wedding party remained isolated from the crowd.

Jake held Rachel's hand and said very little. They had known each other so long and so well that there was very little left to say, except "I will."

But right after the singing started Jake squeezed her hand tighter and leaned close. "Look," he whispered.

He was staring at something high up on the ridge above the barn. She followed his eyes and didn't see anything at first, but then there was a movement in a little glade between the pines. A horse took a step forward, head down, grazing. He was a standard-bred horse, hitched to an empty oxcart. Her eye drifted higher, to an outcropping of rock at the top of the clearing, where she now saw a long-haired Mexican man sitting on the rock, flanked by two lovely Mexican women in their finest clothes. From this distance she couldn't tell the two women apart, but it could only be Miriam and Kyra, with Domingo.

Her heart leaped and she could not keep her seat. With a cautious glance at the barn door she rose, stepped out into the sunlight, looked straight up at the trio on the ridge and waved an arm over her head.

They waved back.

Rachel wore a fresh white cape and apron over her dress, but now she pinched the dark skirt in her fingers and held it wide, smiling, dancing as she took a spin. When she came to a stop she clutched her hands in front of her and bowed deeply.

Thank you.

When she straightened up and looked, she knew the message had been received, and she knew which one was Miriam. Kyra and Domingo were clapping their hands above their heads, grinning broadly. Miriam would be the other one—the one who sat still and stunned, holding both hands over her mouth, leaning forward. Rachel couldn't see them, but she knew there were tears in her sister's eyes.

When Bishop Detweiler came out alone, Rachel and Jake followed him into the house for a short counseling session and prayer, and then he led the whole wedding party into the barn for the beginning of the wedding ceremony.

The bishop preached the standard wedding sermon, full of admonitions and dire warnings about divorce and the evils of marrying outside the church. She'd heard it a dozen times over the years, knew it by heart, and wasn't really listening. This particular sermon was for people with doubts. Four years she had waited, absolutely certain of her choice, assured of her future. She gazed across the aisle at Jake, and he gazed back, his eyes steady as ever.

Her father was right there behind Jake, and Harvey in his place at Jake's side, both of them listening intently to the bishop, both solid and true and dependable. Rachel was fully aware that she came from good stock. Glancing behind her she saw her mother calming Ada, keeping a tight rein with a hand on her knee. Leah, as a navahucker, sat at Rachel's side, and somewhere back behind her was Mary with her four children, Emma with her three, and Barbara. Despite her occasional flightiness, even her youngest sister was turning out to be a decent, hardworking, honorable young woman.

She ran a palm down the sleeve of her dress and thought of Miriam, who had come to the wedding after all, although forced to keep her distance. They were all here except Lizzie, who remained in Ohio. Even Lizzie had talked about making the long trek to Mexico for Rachel's wedding, though in the end she couldn't make it because it was too close to when her baby was to arrive.

But there was a hole where Amos and Aaron used to be, and now—especially now, on her wedding day—Rachel became acutely aware of just how badly she missed the twins, how deeply she wished they could have lived to see this day. Her joy was boundless and complete, and yet when she thought of her lost brothers a thin shadow fell on her like a cloud passing before the sun, and she felt a chill. Bowing her head she silently asked for peace, for acceptance. She told Gott that this was by no means a complaint, that she knew where her brothers were, knew they were happy and whole, but she missed them, that's all. She fervently wished they could have shared this day. There was a hole in her family, and in her heart.

It was only a few minutes later, when her attention had returned to Bishop Detweiler's warnings about divorce, that she heard a small noise—a very strange noise, completely out of place during a sermon, but unmistakable.

Someone had blown a tiny little note on a harmonica.

Perhaps the strangest thing was that no one else reacted at all. Abe Detweiler kept preaching without missing a beat. Not a single head turned. It had to have been Little Amos. Rachel looked over her shoulder and found Mary among the other women at the back, with her babies. Little Amos was sprawled across her lap, sound asleep.

When she turned back around she noticed an odd movement on the far side, behind the men. There were only two boys there, all by themselves on the back row. She saw them only partially between the heads of the other men and she couldn't tell who they were. Both were leaning forward, hiding their faces, their heads and shoulders shaking with laughter. Undoubtedly these were the culprits. It was a wonder one of the men in front of them hadn't turned around and smacked whichever one blew the harmonica. The two heads came close to each other for a second, a whispered message, and they giggled again in complete silence. It was very improper, and whoever they were they would be in deep trouble if the bishop spotted them.

Then they looked up. When their eyes met Rachel's her heart stopped, for she knew those faces as well as her own. Identical twins, fourteen or fifteen years old. Both of them looked straight at her, grinning, their eyes lit with mirth, their cheeks glowing, a picture of health and well-being. The one on the right wiggled his fingers in cautious greeting, and the other one winked. The rascal *winked* at her!

The vision lasted only a few seconds before the men in the nearer rows shifted and swayed and the two boys were lost from her sight. When the sight line cleared again they were gone. The back row was empty.

Rachel sat there openmouthed, motionless and staring, unsure of what was real and what was not, and yet quite sure of what she'd just been given. She took out her handkerchief and wiped away tears. Tears of joy. Whatever had just happened she gratefully accepted it as a small gift from Gott himself, an answer to a prayer. The cloud disappeared and she was filled, all over, with warm sunlight.

The time finally came for Jake and Rachel to rise and stand before the bishop, who put to them the questions common to all weddings. They promised to be faithful, to care for each other, to live together in love, forbearance and patience until they were separated by death.

The people rose, and Bishop Detweiler prayed over them. Then he placed her hand in Jake's. Jake squeezed her hand and gave her a reassuring smile, and she saw it again in his eyes—the thing he had said to her in the very beginning that had captured her heart.

"I would do a great many things for you."

When the ceremony was over the congregation remained seated while the six members of the wedding party marched out in single file. The guests would hang back for a few minutes, giving the bride and her navahuckers time to go from the barn to the house and arrange themselves at the corner table. Halfway across the yard, Jake caught Rachel's arm and stopped her.

"Look!" he said, and the others stopped as well, following his gaze up to the ridge.

Miriam, Domingo and Kyra were still there on the little bluff, but now they were standing, cheering, clapping their hands.

Rachel glanced back at the barn to make sure the guests weren't coming out yet, then took a bow. When she straightened up she blew her sister a kiss.

Chapter 21

R achel had decorated the corner table herself, the *Eck*, where the wedding party would sit. There were bouquets of flowers in mason jars, and a huge cake waited in the center of the table. Two empty tables had been arranged on either side of the front door, one for hats and the other for gifts, but only the women of Rachel's family would leave gifts. The other guests would present their gifts when the newlyweds came to visit in the coming weeks. The next few days would be very busy. Friday she and Jake would help clean up from the wedding, and that evening they would begin making the rounds.

The whole crowd filed by the Eck one at a time, offering their best wishes to the new couple and making little jokes. Levi and Emma made their way through the line and congratulated the newlyweds, but Emma left no gift. Instead, as she was about to walk away from the Eck she leaned close and whispered, "Rachel, when you can get away for a minute or two, come downstairs. I have something special for you, but I have to explain it."

The wedding dinner—the *Hochzich Middag*—was every bit as good as any Rachel remembered in Ohio except that, since they were marrying out of season, there were some things that just couldn't be had. Like celery. Back home they would have had celery standing in glasses of water on all the tables, leafed out like a decoration, but edible. It was also too early for lettuce, so there were no salads. Yet in the presence of so much food no one seemed to notice the lack. There were mashed potatoes, dressing, chicken, gravy, coleslaw, several pies for dessert, and the wedding cake itself.

After everyone had finished eating and the men were standing around rubbing swollen bellies while the women began the cleanup, Emma caught Rachel's eye and nodded toward the basement steps.

Rising, she whispered to Jake, "I'll be back in a few minutes."

By the time she worked her way across the crowded living room and down into the basement Emma was already there, standing by the bed holding a folded quilt.

Rachel reached out and ran a hand over the quilt. "Is this for me?"

Emma nodded.

"Thank you, Emma. It's beautiful!"

"Well, I'm not much of a stitcher, but Miriam is. She helped me with it. We've been working on it for a long time. But, Rachel, it's more than just a quilt. I'll have to show you. Here—help me."

They took the corners and spread the quilt on the bed. The whole thing was covered with interlocking rings the size of peach baskets, made from scraps of mostly dark blues and browns on a white background.

The sisters sat down on opposite sides of the bed, and Emma began to explain. "It's a wedding quilt. We made it from scraps of the whole family. Look"—she ran her hand over the two rings in the center—"these rings were made from your old clothes, and Jake's. This is you and Jake, you see?"

"What a wonderful idea! I love it."

"I'm not finished. These four rings, right above you and Jake, are your parents. Mamm and Dat here, Jake's parents here. I had Jake send me some of their old clothes, and while he was at it, these two rings are Lizzie and Andy."

"It's amazing."

"These down here are Miriam and Domingo. Over here, me and Levi. These two are Mary and Ezra. Here is Ada, there Harvey, and down there Leah and Barbara."

Rachel fought back tears. "I'm stunned—and honored. This is the most precious thing I've ever seen. I can't believe you would do this for me, Emma."

"I'm only happy you like it so. I wanted it to symbolize your marriage, and the family you spring from. We're all here."

"Well . . . not quite all."

"Oh, but we are. If you mean Aaron and Amos, that's the best part." Emma reached across the bed and took her hand. "I saved Aaron's shirts—that was easy. I didn't think I could get anything of Amos's, but it turned out that when he died Aaron kept his clothes. And all he did was keep them; he never had the heart to wear Amos's things. So Harvey ended up with them when Aaron got too big, but then Harvey didn't want to wear them either. He gave me everything that was left of Amos's clothes."

"So which rings are theirs?"

Emma shook her head. "I started to make rings for them, but it didn't feel right. So I finally cut up their shirts and used them for the white spaces. Some of them are a little off-white, so it's not perfect, but they're here. They're all around us."

"This is just too perfect, Emma—the whole idea of it. I'm truly overwhelmed. I will cherish this for the rest of my life." Rachel began to weep softly.

Emma came around and sat beside her, put her arms around her. "I'm sorry if I've upset you on your wedding day, child. Maybe I should have waited for another time. I know how badly you miss your brothers. It's such a shame they couldn't be here for your wedding day."

Rachel sniffed and blinked and took a great deep breath to calm herself, then looked into Emma's eyes. "But they were," she said.

When she rejoined Jake—her *husband*, she thought for the very first time—at the corner table, she found him holding a piece of paper in his hands with a look of utter shock on his face.

Rachel asked him what was wrong even before she sat down.

He shook his head and laid the paper in front of her. "Nothing is wrong. Your father . . . he has given us twenty acres of land."

Now it was her turn to be stunned. "Jake, we can build our own house!"

"And plant! He said he would pay me to work for him, and help me plant my own cash crop when we have time. We'll be able to buy more land before you know it." He lifted the paper from the table and shook it. "This is a big head start your father has given us."

She patted his hand. "We have a lot of surprises waiting, I'm sure. Wait till you see what Emma did."

They all stayed up late that evening helping clean up from the wedding, but eventually everyone else wandered off to bed and Jake went downstairs to wait for Rachel. At the last, she was alone with her mother.

"I was so proud of you today," Mamm said, wringing out a rag and hanging it on the lip of the washtub. "I think Jake is a fine young man, and he's going to make you a very good husband. He loves you so much, he would do anything for you. I can see it in his eyes."

I would do a great many things for you.

"Jah, that's true, Mamm, but I didn't know you could see it, too."

Mamm smiled, heading for the stairs. "I'm maybe not quite as blind as you think. Ach, I'm so tired, and we have to get up early tomorrow and clean. I'm going to bed."

But before she reached the stairs she turned around, came back and took Rachel's face in her hands. "You were *such* a beautiful bride," she said, then let go and walked away, muttering, "in your sister's dress."

There was no honeymoon for Rachel and Jake. They got up early the next morning to help clean up after the wedding, then spent the next few weekends visiting every house in Paradise Valley, as was the custom for a newlywed Amish couple. But even that age-old custom underwent a change. The houses in the tight settlement were all within sight of each other, and most of them were small and crowded, so instead of spending the night they went back home and slept in their own bed in the basement of Caleb's house.

It was a glorious time. Every household showered Rachel with gifts, and Jake collected a number of farm implements he would need to get started on a crop. None of them were new, for there were few new things in the valley, but a planter is a planter, new or not. He still didn't own a mule, and thanks to the deprivation of the troops at El Prado no one had a horse to spare, but John Hershberger made him a gift of a fine unbroken colt.

Rachel had collected handmade baskets, sheets, pillows, fabric, yarn, dishes, candlesticks, two crocks, some well-used candle molds and an iron kettle.

"We are truly blessed," she said one evening, eyeing the many gifts crowded into their basement abode.

Jake came to her and wrapped her in a warm embrace. "Jah," he said with a smile. "And we got a lot of fine gifts, too."

Their weekdays were harder than ever since Jake was now essentially working two jobs. He spent his days working for Caleb in the fields, and after supper every evening he would borrow a team and head down to his own fields, plowing and planting corn until it was too dark to see.

"You work too hard," Rachel said, rubbing his shoulders.

"Nonsense. I'm young and strong, and just knowing you're here waiting for me gives me the strength of a draft horse. Work is only hard when you can see no reason for it. I toil for you and me, for us, and it is pure joy. I only wish the days were longer."

It was still there in his eyes. *I would do a great many things for you.* Far and away the greatest blessing was in knowing they were meant for each other, that they had found the perfect mate who, like a matched team, would always pull in the same direction. Life could not have been sweeter.

The weeks flew by and Jake's corn came up thick and green. She brought him water in the afternoons, and they would just stand there together, looking at the corn. They saw it as the beginning of a long, healthy, beautiful life together, and they dreamed of how it would be to raise a family of their own among so many friends and family in the fertile fields of Paradise Valley.

Their bliss was perfect and complete.

Chapter 22

In the first week of June a nudge from Mamm awakened
Caleb in the middle of the night. She'd always been a light
sleeper. "Someone's at the door," she said.

He lay very still for a second, listening. He heard the bar
being lifted from the inside, the front door opening, the low
murmur of voices. Harvey, and a woman. Bunking in the living
room since Rachel and Jake took over the basement, Harvey
was a light sleeper, too. In the pitch-dark Caleb felt for the
lantern and lit it, then slipped into pants and shirt. When he
came down the stairs tucking in his shirttail, Harvey looked up
from just inside the front door.

Jemima Hostetler was there—Atlee's wife. Her eyes were
puffy and red as if she'd been crying, and the up-lighting of the
lantern she was holding made her baggy face even baggier.

"What is it? What's wrong?" Caleb asked, pulling his suspenders up onto his shoulders.

"Joe and Saloma didn't come back yet," she said, her voice
high and quavering.

At seventeen and fifteen, Joe and Saloma were the two oldest Hostetler children, but they had no business out at this hour.

"Where'd they go?"

The lantern flickered silently while she stared at the floor, clearly embarrassed.

"They went looking for their dat," she mumbled.

"Atlee's missing, too?"

She nodded, still downcast. "Jah, he almost always goes to town on Friday afternoon. He said he had to get something."

"I see." And Caleb did see. Everyone knew that what Atlee Hostetler went to the hacienda village to "get" on Friday afternoons—and often one or two other days of the week—was drunk.

"And he didn't come home when he should?"

"No." Now she looked up, pleading, apologizing. "He's almost always home by nightfall. A couple hours after dark we got worried, so Joe hitched the buggy and went looking."

"In the hacienda village?"

A meek nod. "Jah."

"And Saloma went, too?"

Another nod.

"Jemima, why would you send a fifteen-year-old girl into town after dark?"

Again she hesitated, and her voice came out small and ashamed. "Because most of the time when Atlee is late like that he's not able to manage the hack, so Saloma drives it home."

Caleb sighed heavily. Up to now he'd ignored Atlee's indiscretions because drinking wasn't expressly forbidden in their district, but now he had crossed the line. Now he had put his children at risk.

"Harvey, go hitch the buggy. I'll be right out. Jemima, you have small children at home—go look after them. We'll find Joe and Saloma." She nodded without looking up and turned toward the door. Before she opened it Caleb added, "I want you to know I plan to talk to Bishop Detweiler about Atlee. This has gone on long enough."

Jemima looked over her shoulder at him, her eyes wide. "Oh, please do . . . but don't tell Atlee I said that."

The roosters were crowing, birds chattering, and the sky had grown pink in the east when two surreys crept slowly up the main road and turned into the Hostetler lane. When Caleb drove the lead buggy up into the yard Jemima burst from the door and ran out to meet him. He stopped, and she held her lantern high, peering at the girl lying on the back seat.

Jemima screamed, and her knees almost failed her when she saw Saloma's face—a mass of yellow and purple bruises, one eye swollen nearly shut and blood smeared in wide swaths from her nose and mouth. Her kapp was missing, her hair tangled and matted.

"She'll live," Caleb said, "but she's beat up pretty bad."

Harvey pulled up beside them in the other surrey, and Caleb nodded in his direction. "Harvey's got Joe, and he's beat up worse than Saloma."

Jemima ran to look at the dark form crumpled in the back of Harvey's surrey.

"His jaw's broke," Harvey said, "and some of his fingers."

Horrified, Jemima looked back at Caleb and cried, "What *happened?*"

"We don't know." He lifted the limp girl from the back seat of the buggy and started toward the house with her. "Joe can't talk . . . and Saloma *won't*."

Jemima followed him into the house and showed him where to put her. The younger children peeked around the doorframe, and two of Saloma's sisters ran to her bedside.

217

"She drug herself a ways to get to her brother's side," Caleb said. "We found them together, but Joe was unconscious until we went to put him in the buggy. I guess we mashed his hand and the pain brought him around. With his jaw like that he's not going to be able to eat, so we're gonna have to get him to the doctor in Agua Nueva—a rough road, but it's the closest doctor."

Jemima nodded meekly. "Did you find Atlee?"

"No, we didn't see him anywhere. Nor his hack, neither."

Caleb went to put away Hostetler's horse and buggy while Harvey stayed with Joe. When he came out of the barn the sky had lightened and he could see a hack coming up the main road very slowly. Caleb squinted. The driver slumped forward as if he couldn't quite hold himself erect, and as he drew nearer Caleb could just make out a black, pointed beard.

Atlee.

Harvey's buggy horse pranced and snorted, but Caleb looked at his son and held up a finger—*wait*.

Atlee's hack crept up the lane past Harvey's buggy, finally stopping in front of Caleb.

Jemima came to the door and looked, but went no farther. "Are you all right?" she called from the doorway.

"Jah," Atlee said gruffly, and jerked his head toward Caleb. "What are *they* doing here?"

Jemima opened her mouth to answer but froze, looking back and forth between Atlee and Caleb as if she needed help answering. The fear in her eyes told Caleb all he needed to know. When a belligerent drunk asked a question there was never a right answer.

Atlee didn't wait for one. He rose from the seat and made to climb down, but he caught his toe and stumbled. Falling, he reached for Caleb's shoulder to catch himself. Caleb stepped back so the hand caught only air, and Atlee fell flat on his face in the dirt. He shook himself, then lurched awkwardly to his feet. His eyes were bloodshot, and a rancid tequila smell rolled off of him.

"I'm all right," he grunted. "I'm fine."

"No, I don't think you are. You ought to be ashamed of yourself, Atlee. Joe and Saloma were beat half to death last night, and from where I'm standing it looks like your fault."

"What are you talking about, Caleb? Why, I never even *seen* them. What happened?"

"When you didn't come home they went looking for you, and found trouble instead. Some of your federale friends, I suspect. Your children were lucky—they'll live—but Joe's jaw is broke and his hands are busted up. He can't eat like that, so somebody's got to take him to the doctor in Agua Nueva."

"Then I'll take him. He's *my* son, none of your concern." But Atlee almost lost his balance as he said it and flung his arms out to steady himself.

"You're in no shape for the trip. I'll take care of Joe—you see to Saloma. I'll send Rachel over. In Paradise Valley she's the closest thing we've got to a nurse, and I'm thinking maybe she can help."

"We don't need any help," Atlee grunted.

Caleb bristled, his patience at an end. "I'm in no mood to pay you any mind just now, Atlee. I'm the one having to take care of your children. Get some coffee in you and see to your chores." Then he turned and headed for Harvey and the waiting buggy.

He didn't look back.

"Be gentle," her father said when he asked Rachel to go tend Saloma, "but try to find out the *whole* truth about what happened."

It was odd, the way he said that. The Hostetler girl was five years younger than Rachel and they didn't know each other all that well. Anyway, it should be Saloma's family's job to take care of her unless there was some reason her mother couldn't do it. Odd. There was something her dat wasn't saying, she could see it in his eyes—some unconfirmed suspicion that Rachel couldn't begin to guess. What did he mean, the "whole truth"?

By the time Rachel got there Atlee had already gone to work in his fields as if nothing had happened. It didn't surprise her. Atlee could be alone in his fields, away from accusing eyes.

Jemima didn't want to let her in at first. She blocked the door and said, a little defensively, "We can take care of our own."

"I know you can," Rachel answered, and showed Jemima her bag. "But I've got some salves and herbal remedies Kyra showed me—stuff that'll make her feel a lot better. How's she doing?"

"I don't know—she won't talk. Hasn't said a word."

"I see. Well, you know . . . I'm only a few years older and I've been mistreated by bandits myself, so I thought maybe she'll talk to me. You never know."

Jemima pondered this for a minute, staring suspiciously, but she finally stepped aside and let Rachel in.

Saloma's mother had already cleaned her up and put a gown on her. Now the girl lay in bed with the covers pulled up to her chin, her face turned to the side. She didn't even look when Rachel sat down on the edge of her bed. Jemima eased out of the room.

"So how are you feeling?" Rachel asked softly, brushing blond hair lightly out of the girl's face.

A tiny shrug was the only acknowledgment.

"Any broken bones?"

A slight shake of the head. Saloma still wouldn't look at her. She touched a finger to the girl's chin. "Can I please just look at your face? It'll be all right, I promise. I won't hurt you at all; I just need to see."

Saloma's resistance ebbed a bit and her face turned slowly toward Rachel. The left side was one big purple-and-yellow bruise, her left eye was swollen half shut, and a thin trail of watery blood trickled from her nose. Rachel reached for the pan of water on the nightstand, squeezed out a cloth and dabbed away the blood. When her knuckles lightly brushed Saloma's upper lip she flinched.

"Is your mouth hurt?"

Saloma stared blankly, then her hand crept from under the covers. Wincing, she hooked a finger in the corner of her mouth and showed Rachel the gap where two teeth were missing.

Brutal. Whoever these men were, they were animals, and Rachel could not prevent the memory from welling up inside her—the stinking bandit manhandling her, the utter defenselessness, the sinking, hopeless feeling. Things would have gone much worse for her if Jake hadn't intervened.

But Jake *did* intervene. Rachel's attacker had come to her in the middle of the night with a specific thing in mind, and it was only Jake who stopped it from happening.

Now she looked into Saloma's eyes and saw the lingering residue of that same horror, that same disgust. Her father said they'd found Saloma's brother unconscious, which likely meant he'd tried to intervene, but failed. Suddenly she understood her father's suspicion and knew what he meant by the "whole truth."

She pulled her bag up to her lap and took out a little jar.

"This is a salve that comes from local yucca plants," she said, opening the jar. "It will ease the pain if you'll let me put some of it on you. Would that be all right?" she asked softly.

Saloma nodded.

Rachel talked to her in quiet, soothing tones while she gently dabbed salve on the girl's face with a fingertip. "I know you've heard the story about when bandits kidnapped me," she said, her eyes on her work, avoiding direct eye contact. "They treated me pretty rough, but they never beat me like this. They tied my hands and made me ride double with one of them a long way through the mountains. I slept that night tied to a tree."

While she talked, her hands worked, fingertips making light circles. She finished with the bruises on Saloma's face, wiped her hands on a cloth and kept talking as she lifted Saloma's arm.

"There was one of them who wanted to do other things to me. Terrible things," she said as she slid the sleeve of Saloma's gown up her arm. As she suspected, there were finger bruises on her wrist. Delving into memories she would rather have forgotten, she kept talking as she inched the sleeve higher. "He came to me twice, once the first night, and again the next night, in the barn. Someone stopped him, both times, or something far worse would have happened."

More finger bruises, and deeper, just above the elbow. She pulled Saloma's sleeve back down, patted her forearm reassuringly. The girl kept her eyes averted.

Rachel leaned down very close to her ear and whispered, "But Joe couldn't stop the men who attacked you, could he?"

Saloma flinched and her eyes slammed shut, squeezing out tears. "You must tell no one," she whispered, her voice quavering. They were the first words she had spoken since the assault.

"Saloma, I—"

"My mother has enough worries already, and I'm afraid of what my father will say if he finds out." Her swollen eyes opened and bored into Rachel. "Dat wasn't there. He doesn't know, and you must not tell him. Tell *no one*."

Oh, what this poor child must be going through, all alone in a house of fear, with no one to trust.

222

Rachel nodded. "All right. I will keep it to myself as far as I am able, but I know my father will ask. I can't lie to him, and if I refuse to answer he will know why. This I cannot help. I'm sorry."

"Make him *promise*," Saloma hissed through her teeth, a heartrending mixture of shame and terror.

Privacy was the poor girl's only remaining right. All others had been thrown down and trampled. Invaded.

"All right. I will make him promise. Now please, dear, tell me what happened."

Saloma turned her face away and closed her eyes. Rachel thought she had withdrawn again, but then she began to speak very softly in the high-pitched tremor of a little girl.

"Joe and me heard a noise in the dark alley and went to it with the lantern, thinking it might be Dat. It wasn't. There were two of them, in soldier uniforms, one in front of us and one behind. There was no way to run. Joe tried to tell them we were only looking for Dat, but they just laughed. And then they hit him."

She fell silent, eyes still closed, and took two or three shaky breaths. When she spoke again Rachel had to lean close to hear, for she whispered.

"The big one grabbed me and threw me down. When Joe tried to pick me up the other one hit him from behind. They both jumped on Joe and beat him and beat him and beat him. He didn't fight back or anything, and they knocked him out pretty quick, but they didn't stop hitting him. I begged them to stop, but they kicked him and stomped him with their boots. I thought he was dead."

She began to cry softly. "Then they came and . . . took me. Both of them."

Now she opened her eyes and looked at Rachel, tears

streaming. "I'm so ashamed, Rachel. I couldn't stop them. I never should have been there. It's my fault. If I hadn't been there they wouldn't have hurt Joe."

Rachel could take no more. She was crying herself as she wrapped her arms around Saloma and drew her up close in a careful hug.

"Child, you didn't do anything wrong. You only went to find your dat, and ended up in the wrong place at the wrong time. It was *not your fault*. There's a lot of evil people in the world, that's all."

Rachel whispered the words over and over while they cried into each other's shoulders.

"*So* much evil."

Chapter 23

Caleb brought the Hostetler boy home from Agua Nueva the next day, his jaw wired shut, splints on his hands and a bandage over his left eye. Rachel watched her dat drive slowly down the main road to the Hostetler place, watched him escort Joe into the house and watched him get back in his buggy and drive home. She knew what was coming and waited for her father alone in the kitchen garden with a hoe in her hands. There, no one would hear what was said.

"Tell me," her father said, "did they do to her what I think they did?"

Rachel watched her hoe mechanically chopping weeds from between the tomatoes—she couldn't meet his eyes.

"Dat, I promised I would not tell."

The lines in Caleb's face deepened. "I see. So it is true. Do Atlee and Jemima know?"

Rachel looked her father in the eye. "No. Only me. Even Joe doesn't know for sure, because he was unconscious through most of it. Please, Dat, Saloma feels bad enough. I warned her that you would ask, and that I would not lie to you. She wanted me to make you promise that you would tell no one."

He nodded slowly. "I understand. I will not speak of it to our people, but someone has to go have a talk with Captain Soto. This kind of thing can't go unnoticed, unpunished. Something has to be done or none of our women will be safe."

"It has to be *you*," she said. "Please. You must not tell the bishop, or Atlee. *You* must go and talk to the federales."

Caleb sighed. "I really don't like that little captain, and I am weary of cleaning up Atlee's messes for him. But you're right. I'm the one."

Caleb found Captain Soto in front of the church—or what used to be the church. He was watching from the portico while one of his lieutenants paraded a squad of soldiers back and forth in the open ground in front of him. Caleb climbed the steps with his hat in his hands, determined to give the captain the respect due his office, whether the *man* deserved it or not.

Soto ignored Caleb for a few minutes, shouting orders at the lieutenant, berating his men. He seemed in a foul mood until he turned to Caleb and grinned cordially.

"Good morning, Señor Bender. To what do I owe the plea-sure of this visit?"

"We have to talk," Caleb said. "About a couple of your men."

"Which ones? At present I have seventy-four in my command."

"I only know the first names, and one is a nickname. The little one was called Melky, and the big one Toro. Do you know these men?"

Soto's eyebrows went up. "Sí, of course I know them. I know all of my men—that is my business. Melquiades Chavez is a corporal, and the one they call Toro is a new recruit. Those two are always up to some kind of mischief. What have they done now?"

"They beat up two teenagers from our settlement. I took one of them myself to the doctor in Agua Nueva. His fingers are broken and his jaw had to be wired shut. He won't be able to open his mouth for weeks, and he almost lost an eye."

"Ahh, they were fighting. Señor Bender, surely you understand that soldiers need to let off a little steam now and then. Fighting is not uncommon when they are—"

"It was not a fight," Caleb said. "It was an unprovoked beating, pure and simple."

Soto's head tilted. "How can you know this? Were you there? The boy might have—"

"There was a girl, too. She was beaten nearly as bad as the boy."

The grin disappeared from Soto's face. He shouted one last order to his lieutenant, then took Caleb's arm and walked him down the steps and around the side of the barracks. "We should discuss this in private," he said, and didn't utter another word until they were inside the little house that used to be Father Noceda's rectory. The front room held a desk with a set of bookshelves behind it, but there were no books—only piles of papers and files. There were half a dozen chairs lining the walls, and a sawhorse on which rested a saddle that Caleb presumed belonged to Captain Soto because of the fine workmanship.

Soto dropped his hat on the desk and sat down, running his fingers through his hair. Caleb stood in front of the desk like a penitent, his hat still in his hands, waiting.

"They beat a girl?" Soto said.

"Sí. Very badly." Caleb shifted his feet, undecided about

bringing up the other thing. He wanted to protect Saloma's privacy if he could, but he would wait and see how things went.

"Still," Soto said with a shrug, "it is possible the boy started the fight, and the girl only wandered into the middle of it."

"No. You don't understand. Our people don't believe in fighting. This boy would never start a fight or take part in one."

Soto leaned back in his desk chair now, eyeing Caleb suspiciously, tugging at the corner of his thin little mustache.

"Your people don't fight?"

"No."

A little grin crinkled the corners of the captain's eyes. "This is what El Pantera told me the day we captured him, but I didn't believe him. And I thought the *Catholic* superstitions were strange. So this is true? You don't fight? At all?"

"Never."

"But what about that young man of yours?"

"What young man?"

"The one who was there when I hung El Pantera. He was with you—the one El Pantera said killed one of his men."

"You mean Jake Weaver."

Soto leaned forward and pointed at him, warming to a debate. "You were there, Señor Bender, in the churchyard. I remember, El Pantera said this Jake surprised his man from behind while he was unarmed and strangled him with a chain. Is this not true?"

Caleb shifted uneasily and gave a shrug. "Sí. It happened, but not without reason. The man was attacking my daughter, and Jake pulled him off of her with his chain. He never meant to kill the bandit."

"Oh, I see. He didn't *mean* to kill the bandit, but he did fight. So how do you know this boy in the alley didn't do something to provoke my men? Did he tell you how the fight started?"

"No, he still can't speak, but the girl told my daughter. She said two drunken soldiers jumped them in an alley, without provocation. The teenagers were looking for their father, Atlee Hostetler."

"Ahh, I know this Atlee. A strange little man who comes to town and drinks mescal with my men—and tequila, when they have it. It was *his* children who were beaten?"

"Sí."

Soto sat for a minute with his chin in his palm, staring out the window. Finally he turned back to Caleb with a sigh. "Well, I don't doubt that what you're saying is true, señor, but if you were not there and didn't see what happened you have only the word of these two about what really took place, and my men will undoubtedly tell a different story. Perhaps you should tell this Atlee not to let his children wander the streets at night alone."

Caleb could see how this would go. It was Saloma's word against the soldiers. Those two monsters would simply lie and walk away. Nothing would be done to control the soldiers, and then what? What would happen next time? Caleb saw that he had no choice; he was going to have to raise the stakes.

"I *have* spoken to Atlee, for what it's worth," Caleb said. Then he leaned his fists on the front of the desk and looked the little officer cold in the eyes. "But it seems to me it would be the responsibility of the officer in command to see that his men don't roam the streets at night, raping innocent girls."

Soto's head backed away and his eyebrows went up. "*Rape?* You did not tell me they raped the girl. Did she tell you this?"

"She told my daughter. No one else knows. It's not the kind of thing we talk about."

"You should have told me this from the beginning. A little fun, a little drinking, maybe a good-natured fistfight—these things are to be expected from off-duty soldiers in *any* army. But I cannot allow my men to rape civilian women. It stirs resentment among the local people, and we must live with them. You are sure about this? It is a very serious charge."

Caleb nodded. "Es verdad." *It is true.*

"Can the girl identify the men?"

Caleb took a deep breath, let it out. "I would not want to put her through that. She is very hurt, very fragile."

Soto gave this a dismissive wave. "No matter. In a case like this there are ways I can persuade Melky and Toro to tell me the truth. I will not have my men doing such things." He rose from behind his desk and straightened his tunic. "Leave the matter to me, Señor Bender. I will get to the bottom of it, and when I do I will let you know the outcome. Buenos días."

Driving home, it seemed to Caleb that Captain Soto had been extraordinarily civil, almost sympathetic. Perhaps there was a decent side to the captain after all. Maybe all it took was a little respect.

But we will see, he thought. Soto's actions would reveal far more than his words.

༄

Three days later, as a squad of federales passed through the valley on their way home to El Prado after their daily patrol, one of them split off from the others and rode up Caleb's lane. Caleb saw him coming and met him in front of the house.

The soldier looked to be about seventeen years old. A frayed secondhand uniform hung on his thin frame rather loosely so that he looked almost as ragged as the swaybacked paint he was riding.

"Señor Caleb Bender?"

"That's me. What is it?" Caleb braced himself, expecting the young recruit to pilfer some vegetables from Mamm's kitchen garden, or eggs, or a sack of oats. But he was wrong.

230

"Captain Soto wishes to see you," the boy said. "At first light, *mañana*."

Caleb nodded. "Tell him I will be there. Is this about the men who beat up the boy and girl?"

"Si, I think so. My captain said to tell you that he wishes to make a gesture of goodwill."

"Then tell him I will be bringing two other men with me. They have an interest in this matter."

The next morning Caleb hitched his buggy before daylight and picked up Bishop Detweiler from the old Coblentz place. The house was now finished, a shiny new tin roof on it. The whole settlement had pitched in to finish the house for him, perhaps devoting even more time and building materials than they normally would have. He was, after all, their bishop. They were acutely aware that he had not yet *bought* the Coblentz place and that his family had not yet joined him.

"The house looks good, and your corn is coming up thick," Caleb said as they drove down the road in the purple half-light toward Atlee's place.

"Jah, you sure told the truth about the soil here, Caleb. Paradise Valley is as fertile as any place I ever seen."

"So I guess now you'll be bringing the family down?" It was June, and though Bishop Detweiler had been in the valley since late March he still had not made any clear commitment. Both men understood that Caleb's question was a discreet way of asking for one.

"Well," the bishop said, stroking his red beard, "I don't know for sure. Maybe by harvest, if all goes well. I surely miss Sarah, and my boys are old enough now to be a big help. Be good to have them here at harvesttime."

Harvest wouldn't really begin for another three months.

Few Amishmen would willingly be separated from their family for that long, though Abe was clearly reticent about explaining why. Time to prod.

"I don't want to pry," Caleb said, "but I can't help wondering why you haven't made up your mind about staying. There haven't been any bandits at all since you got here. It's been pretty quiet."

"Jah, that's true. It looks like those troops fixed your bandit problem, that's for sure." Then his ruddy face twisted in a doubtful grimace and he added, "But it's the troops I worry about. All these men with guns riding back and forth through the valley every day, they make me nervous. Now they went and beat up Atlee's young ones. I don't know, Caleb. I keep hearing things about this Presidente Calles, and how bad he hates the church. If the Mexican government persecutes the Catholics, how long will it be before they persecute the Amish? It just feels like there's something in the air—like we're waiting for a storm."

Caleb chuckled. "Well, I expect this meeting with the commander of the federales will put your mind at ease. He was pretty friendly when I talked to him the other day, and when he sent for us he said he wanted to make a gesture of goodwill."

Abe nodded, staring at the fingers of deep red crawling across the eastern sky as Caleb tugged on the reins and turned the buggy into Atlee's lane.

"Maybe so," he said. "Maybe everything will be all right."

Chapter 24

Captain Soto was waiting for them in his office, wearing his dress uniform as if he was expecting important dignitaries, a half-dozen medals pinned to his chest and a cavalry saber hanging at his side. He clearly recognized Atlee, but Caleb introduced him anyway, stating mostly for Atlee's benefit that he was the father of the boy and girl who had been beaten. The captain shook his hand and even bowed a little, oddly obsequious.

Abe Detweiler didn't understand anything they said. He'd only picked up a few words of Spanish so far, and he kept glancing back and forth between them, unable to follow the conversation.

When Caleb introduced Detweiler to Captain Soto, the grin, and all traces of obsequiousness, disappeared.

Soto shook Abe's hand, but he was glaring at Caleb as he did it. "Did you say this man is your priest?"

"*Mi obispo*," Caleb repeated. My *bishop*.

The captain's eyes shifted back and forth between them, and Caleb saw an unmistakable trace of indignation in the glance.

"Correct me if I am wrong, but is not a bishop a high-ranking priest?"

Bishop Detweiler may not have understood the words, but it was clear from the expression on his face that he'd read the anger.

"He wants to know if you're a priest," Caleb said.

Detweiler hesitated for a second, then shrugged. "Sí."

"We would not use that word," Caleb said, "but I suppose he is the same as a priest."

Soto's eyes narrowed. A trace of a smile came back to his lips, but there was a sneer in it. "I suppose it makes no difference. As I told my courier, I have brought you here today to set things right." He paused while Caleb translated for Detweiler. "I am aware," the captain continued, "that my men have sometimes been a bit of a burden on the farmers in your valley, and you have been very generous in selling us your horses at a discount."

Translating this, Caleb was tempted to say *stealing* the horses, but he didn't.

"My lieutenants and I have thoroughly investigated the incident involving your two children, Señor Hostetler. We have apprehended the men responsible, questioned them at length and extracted the truth from them."

Translating for the bishop, Caleb almost used the word *tortured*, but again he refrained. Still, the captain's words, and his tone, left Caleb with an ominous feeling.

"These men have confessed their crimes in a fair and open court-martial, and they will now face justice. You will see I am a man of my word, Señor Bender. As I told you before, I will not tolerate men in my command who rape innocent girls."

Caleb froze. Atlee, who had learned Spanish very quickly, probably from the federales, understood every word. His mouth fell open and he stared at Caleb in horror.

"Rape? Caleb, my Saloma wasn't *raped*, was she?" He said this in Dutch, so now the bishop knew as well.

"Caleb?" the bishop said. "Answer him."

Soto had sense enough to wait, though he understood not a word

Caleb looked Atlee in the eye. "Jah, it's true. Saloma didn't want it told, and I didn't mean for it to come out this way, but that's what happened. She told Rachel. That's why they beat Joe so bad, because he tried to stop them."

Atlee's face twisted into a mask of horror. His knees buckled, but Bishop Detweiler caught him by the shoulders and steadied him.

"Señor Bender, is there a problem?" Soto asked.

"They didn't know about the rape," he said bluntly. "I was the only one who knew, and I was trying to keep it secret—for the girl's sake."

Soto's head tilted, his brow furrowed. "My apologies. You are a very strange people," he said quietly. There was a curiously insidious smile on his face. The smile of a predator.

It reminded Caleb of El Pantera

It was then that he heard faint marching noises from out-side—the side of the rectory facing the high stone wall of the hacienda thirty yards away. But the curtains were drawn and he couldn't see what was happening.

The captain must have heard the marching too, because he went to the big double window and drew back the curtains.

Outside, Caleb could see the backs of six soldiers, side by side at parade rest, the butts of their rifles standing on the ground by their feet. Beyond them, with their backs to the stone wall of the hacienda in the shade of a live oak tree, stood two soldiers, one much larger than the other. Their hats were gone, the stripes and insignia stripped from their uniforms, their hands tied behind their backs, and a look of hopeless despair on their bruised faces.

Suddenly it all came together. He knew why Soto had called them here and why he was wearing his fancy uniform with all the medals, the polished sword and scabbard hanging from his belt. He now understood the smug grin on the captain's face and knew what was about to happen. The soldiers outside waited only for their captain's signal.

"Captain, I *beg* you," Caleb said. "Please. You must not do this thing."

"*Justicia*," the captain said slowly, dragging the word into a sibilant whisper, enunciating every letter.

Caleb shook his head. "Do not do this. None of us want it, nor would we call it justice. All we ever wanted was to make the streets safe for our daughters."

Soto's eyebrows rose. "Sí, I will show you how that is accomplished, señor."

"What's going on?" Detweiler asked, clutching Caleb's shoulder. "What is he saying?" Caleb ignored him.

"This is a hard country," Soto said, "and we have gone through hard times. It is the duty of a leader to meet serious crimes with swift and harsh punishment, or else he will be perceived as weak. In hard times, Señor Bender, the weak perish."

"What is *happening?*" Bishop Detweiler asked again, and this time he raised his voice.

"He's going to execute them," Caleb said softly, and Detweiler's ruddy face went ghostly pale.

The bishop's eyes grew wide. "No! You must not do this!" he said, imploring with every fiber, the veins bulging in his neck. "Captain, I assure you, the boy and girl—the *victims* of this crime—if they were here, they would beg you not to do this thing. Please, have mercy!"

Caleb translated his words.

Soto stepped closer to the bishop and gave him his best El Pantera smile. Their faces only inches apart, he stared hard into the bishop's eyes, seething hatred on full display as he spoke through Caleb. "Señor Bender, tell your *priest* that in my investigation of these crimes I learned of the punishment given to your own murdering kin—this Jake Weaver—the young man who admitted attacking an unarmed man from behind and choking him to death. He freely admitted this! His punishment was to be thrown out of the church. For TWO WEEKS!"

Soto screamed this last from his tiptoes, purple with rage. And then, just as suddenly, he calmed himself and that sinister smile returned.

"Tell your priest he is no longer in America. This is *Mexico*. I have told you before, Señor Bender—mercy is a luxury I cannot afford."

The little captain turned his back on the bishop and went to the window.

"This is why I brought you here today," he said. "To show you what real justice looks like when it is meted out by real men."

Soto nodded to his lieutenant, who stood outside watching him, waiting.

The lieutenant barked an order.

The six riflemen snapped to attention.

The lieutenant barked again. Instantly the riflemen brought their weapons up to their shoulders and took aim at the two prisoners.

"No!" Caleb whispered. "Please, NO!"

Soto snorted derisively, his back to the three Amishmen, his hands clasped behind him.

They heard the beginning of a third order barked by the lieutenant outside, but it was drowned in the roar of rifles.

Caleb drove in silence, in shock, the same as the bishop who sat stone-faced on the bench beside him. Atlee Hostetler hunkered in the back seat, brooding.

Finally, when they were well clear of the hacienda village and halfway home, Atlee leaned forward.

"I can't believe you kept this from me, Caleb. I thought you were my friend."

Caleb's jaw clenched. He had done only what he believed was right.

"I *am* your friend," he said, with more conviction than he felt, "but your daughter wanted me to promise I would not tell anyone what I knew, including you. A promise is a promise, and I think your daughter's wishes are more important than your own—this once."

"But she is *my* daughter, not yours. It is my right to know. Anyway, I don't know what you're so upset about. Those heathens got what they deserved."

Bishop Detweiler turned halfway and looked back at Atlee.

"Only Gott has the right to judge a man's soul and decide whether he should live or die, Atlee. For us to do that is arrogance. I wouldn't want to be the cause of any man's death, for any reason. I would rather see him forgiven, that he may turn from his ways and find peace with Gott."

But the bishop's rebuke only fueled Atlee's anger.

"It's this country," Atlee growled. "None of this would have happened if we weren't living in this godforsaken uncivilized country."

His words were aimed at Caleb, and they found their mark. For a long time now Caleb had lived with deep doubts, especially since Aaron's death. He wasn't sure of anything anymore, but his doubts were his own, certainly not subject to the challenge of an angry man seeking to justify his own failures. Atlee was only trying to shift the blame, point a finger anywhere other than himself.

Without looking around, Caleb answered very calmly. "None of this would have *happened*, Atlee, if you didn't spend your evenings in town drinking tequila with the federales."

He actually felt the buggy lurch a little from the force with which Atlee flung himself back in the seat. But Atlee would say no more; he had no answer.

The bishop was quiet for a while, his eyes on the road ahead, his ruddy face closed, thinking. Caleb found Detweiler's silence more disquieting than Atlee's rage. The bishop was the one man whose thoughts could grow into an edict that affected them all. When he finally spoke, Caleb's worst fears were confirmed.

"There's truth in your words—both of you," Abe Detweiler said. "Atlee, there is no escaping your part in this. You should be home taking care of your family, not out spending hard-earned money on drink and carousing. This is the truth, and if I hear of it again you will answer to the church."

Then Abe's voice softened and he turned to Caleb.

"But Atlee's right about one thing—and that little federale captain too, in his way. It causes me great pain and sorrow to say it, Caleb, for I know how you have toiled—and the price you have paid—but none of this would have happened if we weren't living in Mexico. Life is cheap here, and unforgiving. Our children have been beaten and raped, and murdered, our crops and horses taken, and the men who came to save us from bandits are no better than the bandits themselves." The bishop shook his head wearily. "I could never bring my family to this land. Mexico is no place for us."

For Caleb, the words rang like a death knell, the entire future of the Paradise Valley settlement decided, nullified in one brief sentence. Abe Detweiler would not stay without his family, and once he got back to Ohio and spread the word, no other bishop would ever come down. Without church leadership it was only a matter of time until everyone packed up and went back home.

It was over. Just like that.

Chapter 25

The following Sunday they held services in Yutzy's barn, and at the end of the service Bishop Detweiler gave them the bad news.

Caleb noted that Detweiler said nothing about what he had seen and heard that morning in Captain Soto's quarters, but he did make it clear that he would not be staying.

A great moan went up from the people, and some of the women started crying. They all knew, as surely as Caleb, what this meant. It was the beginning of the end.

"I won't be leaving right away," the bishop said, "because three of our youth are taking instruction classes for baptism and I won't quit on them. But the classes will be done in the middle of August. Come early September we'll have Communion, and after that I'll be going back to Ohio."

After lunch the men reconvened in Yutzy's barn to discuss the situation. They pulled four benches into a square and sat in silence for a bit, heads in hands, saying nothing. Abe Detweiler sat in with them, and it was he who finally broke the silence.

"I want you all to know I'm sorry to have to leave," he said, "but after what I've witnessed here I just can't make myself bring my wife and children to Mexico. And I guess you're all thinking no other bishop will come."

"They won't," Caleb said. "Everyone knows it."

There were nods and murmurs of agreement. Even Abe Detweiler nodded solemnly.

"So what will you do?" the bishop asked. It was up to each individual man to decide what was best for his family.

They all looked to Caleb, waiting.

He sighed. "Well, it's midsummer and we all got crops in the ground. It don't make sense to leave before harvest and let it all go to waste. I'm thinking we'll get the crops in, take the produce to Saltillo and get what we can for it. We can still be back in the States before Christmas, and maybe get settled someplace else in time to plant in the spring."

Again there were nods of approval, from everyone except Atlee Hostetler, whose eyes burned. He glared at each of them in turn, but none would look at him because they all held him responsible, in some measure, for what had happened. In a close community there were few secrets. The story had spread so that by now everyone knew, more or less, that if Atlee hadn't gotten drunk, his children wouldn't have gone looking for him, they wouldn't have been attacked, those two soldiers would still be alive and the bishop wouldn't be leaving. Life would have gone on. If it weren't for Atlee they wouldn't be losing their homes.

They wouldn't say it out loud, but they wouldn't look at him, either. Atlee stood it for as long as he could before their silent censure pushed him over the brink. He jerked himself to his feet and jabbed a finger in Caleb's direction.

"You can stay here till Christmas if you want, but I won't," he said. "I won't stay a minute longer than I have to. Me and mine will be on a northbound train within the week. I know the gossip that's going around, and I won't stand for it."

John Hershberger looked up at him and said with a calculated and irritating sweetness, "Where will you go, Atlee?"

"North Carolina," Atlee spat. "I heard about a place there where some Amish bought a reclaimed swamp. Good black dirt, and cheap. They're making a pile of money growing peppermint. You can harvest my crops and *keep* the money for all I care. I'm leaving *now*. The sooner the better."

With one last hard look at Caleb, he jammed his hat on his head and stomped out. No one said a word. They didn't even watch him go.

There was silence again for a long time. Finally, John Hershberger pulled out his corncob pipe, thumped it against his bootheel, packed it, lit it, took a draw on it and said, "What will we do with our farms, Caleb? You think we can sell them?"

"We can try, but you won't find a lot of buyers in Mexico. Most people don't have that kind of money, and the ones who do are selling."

"What about the haciendado? Is there any chance he'll buy the land back? We made a lot of improvements."

Caleb shook his head. "I don't think so, John. He's who I meant when I said the people with money are selling."

John drew on his pipe and blew a smoke ring. "There has to be somebody. We put a lot of work into this valley, and it would be a real bargain for anybody with eyes to see. Trouble is, nobody knows about it. Maybe we can put up posters in Saltillo where lots of people will see it. You never know."

"That's a good idea. And if we don't sell our farms before Christmas maybe one of us could stay on down here to keep trying."

243

John shrugged, drew on his pipe. "I could do that for you if you want me to."

"What about your family?"

"No. I might have to travel a bit and I wouldn't want to leave them alone. It would be better if they go stay at my brother's in Fredericksburg till I get there."

Caleb spent the remainder of the afternoon halfway up the ridge behind his house, sitting on his rock, the little outcropping at the tree line where he went when he wanted to be alone with his thoughts, and with Gott. It was a black day, a day for mourning the impending loss of his farm—all those months and years of toil, wasted. But Caleb Bender understood that toil was a man's lot in life, that he would always work from dawn to dusk no matter where he was, and deep down he felt a far more disturbing loss.

It was Gott himself. Where was Gott now? In the beginning Caleb felt sure it was Gott who'd led him to Mexico. He was so convinced that he'd persuaded a hundred others to follow him, and now they would suffer for his foolishness. He had paid for his convictions with the life of his son, and now he would lose a daughter as well. Aaron would remain in Mexico, forever separated from his twin, and so would Miriam.

Truth be told, the loss of Miriam now hit Caleb even harder than the death of Aaron because she had *chosen* her path. Gott allowed Aaron's passing; Miriam left on her own. Now his beloved daughter would face not only shunning but complete exile. She might as well be dead.

I wonder how she will feel about her choice now? he thought, and the thought was tinged with bitterness. He tried very hard, but in his anguish he could not banish the anger from his mind.

Sitting alone on his rock with his face in his hands, Caleb

pondered his fate until he could stand it no longer. He raised his head, and his red eyes looked to the heavens.

"Why, Gott? Have I not been your faithful servant? Tell me where I have sinned! Why do you hide your face from me and treat me like an enemy?"

⟡

Rachel went home after lunch and waited for Jake alone in the basement of her father's house. Now that he was married, Jake was considered the head of his household, allowed to sit in on the meeting of the men.

His steps were ponderous on the stairs, as if he carried a great weight. He came down and sat beside Rachel on the edge of the bed, on the double-wedding-ring quilt Emma had given them, put an arm around his wife, and sighed.

"We're going home," he said. "It was as your dat feared. Bishop Detweiler says he will stay until September, but then he's leaving. There won't be another bishop coming."

Rachel nodded grimly. "So that will be the end of things."

"Jah. We'll leave after harvest." He shrugged. "I guess it's not so bad for me and you. We haven't built a house yet, nor a barn, and if I can sell my corn we'll leave with a little money in our pocket. We'll lose less than anyone else."

She shook her head sadly, staring at the floor. "No, I'm thinking I'll lose *more* than anyone else. It grieves me to think of leaving Miriam behind."

Jake sighed deeply. "I hadn't even thought of that until now, but you're right. This is indeed a dark day."

In a little while there came a knock at the head of the stairs. Rachel looked up with eyes red and swollen. "Jah?"

"It's me—Emma. May I come down?"

"Surely. Come."

Emma came only partway down the stairs and leaned on the rail. "Rachel, we're going to visit Miriam. Someone has to tell her what has happened. Do you want to come?"

"Jah. We'll be right there."

Levi was helping Emma down from the surrey at Miriam's house in San Rafael when Domingo and Father Noceda walked over from Kyra's.

"Why the long faces?" Domingo asked. "Has something happened?"

"Not yet," Levi said, "but it will. That's why we came. Miriam's sisters need to see her, to break the news."

Domingo stepped aside, pointing vaguely to the back of the house. "She's in her garden, gathering for supper."

Rachel and Emma hurried around back while Levi and Jake stayed with the men.

"What's going on?" Father Noceda asked.

"We're leaving," Levi said, his tone nearly as downcast as the women. "All of us. The whole settlement, after harvest."

"But *why?*" Domingo asked, visibly shaken. He knew what this would mean to his wife.

"We're losing our bishop," Levi answered, "and there won't be another. Our people won't stay if there can be no church."

Levi explained to them about the beating of Atlee's children and the execution of the two soldiers, but left out the part about the girl, so he was caught off guard by Domingo's first question.

"Will the girl be all right?"

Levi stared. From the depth of concern on Domingo's face it was clear that he knew.

"Someone told you about the girl?"

"No one had to tell me. Soto would never execute two of

his own men for anything less than murder or rape, and there was no murder."

Levi nodded. "Rachel was with the girl, right after. She said Saloma will get over the beating, but not the other. It's a shame. Her family is leaving right away, going back to the States."

"We will pray for her," Father Noceda said as he crossed himself.

Levi looked over his shoulder. The three sisters could be seen on the edge of the garden, huddled together, crying.

"I don't know what they'll do without each other," he said.

Domingo's eyes grew hard and cold. "It's those stinking federales. They make life miserable for all of us."

"We were just talking about that when you drove up," Father Noceda said. "Two days ago Captain Soto posted a public notice on the bulletin board in the post office. Presidente Calles has added a whole new list of laws to the constitution—rules he wrote himself. They're calling it *Calles' Law*. A priest is now a second-class citizen, no longer allowed to vote. We can be imprisoned for the slightest offense, even for holding an opinion."

"Our new presidente is out to destroy the church," Domingo said, "and he will stop at nothing. Things are going to get much worse. Already there are rumblings among the people. They will not stand for this."

Levi raised an eyebrow, for he had heard what Domingo did not say. "You think there will be another war?"

"Sí. It is coming, mark my words."

The three sisters clung to each other at the edge of the garden as if they were sinking, permanent separation looming over them like the threat of hell.

"What did Dat say?" Miriam asked, choking back tears.

Emma shook her head. "He didn't say much of anything. I asked him if he wanted to come and talk to you and he said no. Then he went up to the ridge to be alone. He was pretty upset."

"With me?"

Emma shrugged. "With everything, I think, but you're a big part of it. All he can see right now is he's losing a daughter."

Miriam's voice came out small and lost. "I don't think he sees me as a daughter anymore."

Emma took Miriam's face in her hands and tried to smile. "Of course he does, Miriam. Dat can't see you any *other* way. Why do you think he's so upset? He knows that when we leave he may never see you again, and in the front of his mind he blames you for that. But you know how he is. Deep down he blames *himself* for bringing us to Mexico in the first place. That's where his anger really comes from."

"Do you think he will ever be able to forgive me?"

"Oh, child," Emma said, folding Miriam into a gentle hug. "Of course he will. In time."

Chapter 26

As soon as he could get up a load of produce Caleb made a run to the market in Saltillo, fifty miles to the north, and while he was there he nailed up leaflets on telegraph poles and bulletin boards around town, advertising farms for sale in Paradise Valley. Every nail pierced a dream. Every blow of the hammer reverberated in his heart.

But he did it anyway, for the same reason he did everything else: it needed doing. He went through the motions that day and for the rest of that summer, working his fields, feeding his cows and horses, mending fences as if nothing had changed. As if he weren't leaving. He came out of his cornfield one afternoon and ran into Emma, who was watering the trees she had planted along his lane.

He just stood there and watched her for a moment, standing very still until she straightened up and saw him. He pointed casually. "Seems a little silly, watering trees when you know you won't be here to see them grown."

But Emma only smiled and went for another bucket of water. As she was pouring it at the base of the next tree she said quietly,

"A wise man once told me, 'Do what today calls you to do, right up until the day you can't do it anymore.'"

Caleb chuckled, staring at his feet, remembering. By the time Emma turned around he was carrying a bucket of water to the next tree.

She smiled, blushing. "Thank you, Dat."

"I guess it's true," he said as he walked past. "The apple doesn't fall far from the tree."

Often in the course of a day's work Caleb found himself stopping and staring, gazing out over his land, up at the red ridges or the purple mountains in the west, and in those moments he was surprised to discover in himself a subtle but familiar sense of grief—the same one he had felt before leaving the family farm in Salt Creek Township. For all its faults, Paradise Valley had become his home.

On a Sunday in the latter part of August the bishop baptized the three young people who had finished their instruction classes. Two weeks later, in early September, the church gathered for council meeting and Communion—their second, and last, in Paradise Valley.

The members of the church met in Caleb's barn on a Friday, men on one side and women on the other. Bishop Detweiler preached for two hours, a heartfelt sermon in that singsong rhythm of his, about humility and self-sacrifice, the attitude of Jesus. As the sermon drew to a close, Caleb and John Hershberger went out to bring in the bread and the wine, since there was no deacon.

It was a beautiful service, emblematic of all they believed, but on this day it was especially poignant because they knew it would be the last time they would meet together as an official church. Throughout the serving of the bread and wine, and the washing of one another's feet, a deep and reverent silence held, broken only by the occasional sound of a woman sniffling, fighting back tears. As sweet and lovely and profoundly meaningful as it was, their last Communion in Paradise Valley had the inescapable feel of a funeral. It was, in a way. They were all mourning the death of a dream.

The next morning, before daylight, Caleb hitched his buggy and went to pick up Abe Detweiler. As he started down his lane he saw in the darkness across the valley what must have been twenty-five kerosene lanterns glittering like stars in front of the old Coblentz place. Everyone had set aside their chores and gathered to see their bishop off and to wish him well.

&

All that was left to the Amish of Paradise Valley was one last harvest, and they went about it with their customary zeal. The only difference this time was that they didn't cut hay. There was no point. They would not be wintering here.

"Leave it for the troops to graze their horses," Caleb said, a little bitterly. "At least this time they can't steal it after we do all the work."

Wagons came and went every day, making trips to Saltillo, mostly hauling corn to sell in the market. Here, too, Caleb saw reason for complaint.

"When we bought this place they promised us a rail line. 'To market and back in one day,' the man said. So where is the railroad now? A day late, like everything else in this country."

No one came to make offers on the land. Not a single one. When the haciendado arrived on his estate to supervise his own harvest Caleb went to see him in his office.

"We're leaving," he said bluntly, standing before the haciendado's desk in the grand mahogany and marble library. "Going back to Ohio. We had a bishop for a little while, but after the way your troops behaved he couldn't see his way to bring his family down here."

"My troops," the dapper Don Louis Alejandro Hidalgo replied. "As I recall, it was *you* who wanted them so desperately—I only wrote the cheque. And I would also point out that while the federales have protected your people from the bandits, they have been precious little benefit to me."

Caleb stood there, hat in hand, with no answer. The man was right. "One mistake among the many I have made," he finally said, "but perhaps, in the end, the biggest one."

"A pity. We hate to see you give up after all your hard work. Your farms are thriving. I can scarcely believe how my old pastureland has blossomed in your care. Are you sure there is no way you can stay?"

Caleb shook his head. "Our church is the center of our lives. If we have no bishop, we have no church, and if we have no church we cannot stay."

"Well," Hidalgo said with a shrug, "I suppose you must do what you must do, though I can't say I understand it. Is there anything I can do to help?"

Caleb fidgeted for a moment, trying to find just the right words. "We were wondering if you might be interested in buying back your land."

"I see. So *that's* why you have come to me. Señor Bender, I wish I could help, but in the current political climate my financial advisers are all telling me to divest myself of agricultural holdings and reinvest in oil and industry. Oil is the future of our country, if those fools running the government don't nationalize all of it."

Caleb tried one more time. "I'm not sure I speak for all of them, but I know that some of us would be willing to sell it back for ten dollars an acre—the same price we paid for it. And like you said yourself, we've improved it quite a bit."

Hidalgo studied him for a minute, and Caleb could tell by the sideways expression that the battle was already lost.

"I'm sorry," Hidalgo said, "but my assets are tied up. I am in no position to buy back your land, even if I wanted to. But I wish you well. We will miss you and your people."

⌒⌒

One morning in early October Emma was feeding her children while Levi devoured a plateful of eggs and biscuits. She straightened up for a moment and stared out the window at the sun, just now peeking over the horizon in the east, the low adobe houses of the Amish silhouetted in the valley between.

She was spooning a bit of scrambled egg into Will's gaping mouth when Levi said, "Domingo told me he was going to start pulling his beans today. It looks like a good crop."

"I hope they'll be all right," she said. "I worry about Miriam, with us gone."

"Why don't we go help? The harvest is going good. I think I can spare a day."

Her father had made a tradition of it, every October going to Domingo's fields with a spring-toothed harrow and a team of Belgians, which made short work of pulling the bean vines out of the ground. But Dat hadn't been back to Miriam's at all since the ban. Now Domingo and his cousins had to do all the work by hand.

"You wouldn't mind?" she asked. "People will talk."

Levi gave her a mischievous grin. "Let them. Anyway, what does it matter? The bishop's gone, and pretty soon we will be, too. What will they do, ban me?"

She smiled warmly. Her husband really had come a long way.

253

Right after breakfast Levi hitched the harrow to his Belgians and left. Emma followed along a little later in the buggy with the children. She also brought lunch, as was her custom when visiting Miriam. That way nobody had to fret over the rules about eating food Miriam had raised or prepared. Miriam just pushed two tables close together in the yard and served herself from separate bowls. It didn't take long to get used to the arrangement.

Since Levi's Belgians freed Miriam from having to work in the bean field, the sisters spent the day with each other working around the house.

Emma chuckled as she hung laundry on the line. "I've never done laundry on a Wednesday before."

"I know, isn't it fun? I teach the children on Mondays, so I wash on Wednesdays now. Some of the old habits die really hard, but some things I do different just because I can."

She paused for a second, watching the men work in the field. "It's good of Levi to help with the beans. Those draft horses will save us three days' work."

Emma peered across the fields at Levi and his team. "You know, it didn't cross my mind this morning but I bet this wasn't about the beans at all. I think it's just Levi's way of letting me spend time with you—while I still can."

"He's changed so much lately," Miriam said quietly as she shook out a painted skirt and hung it on the line. "He's so much more relaxed. You've been the best thing in the world for him." She hesitated for a second, then said, "It's a shame my niño won't get a chance to meet his aunt Emma."

"Your *niño*? Miriam, you're going to have a baby?"

A bashful smile. "Jah, I'm pretty sure."

Grinning from ear to ear, Emma gave her a spontaneous hug, then leaned back and looked down. "I'll let you in on a secret. I'm pretty sure our family's going to be growing soon, too."

"No! Emma, *really*? That's wonderful! I pray it goes better this time."

Emma had miscarried twice since Will was born. "It will," she said. "I have a good feeling about this one."

"Have you told Levi?"

"No, I don't want him to worry. It took me forever to convince him the miscarriages were not Gott's judgment against us. This baby is fine, and Levi will be, too."

"Life is good," Miriam said, "but it's never easy."

It was an unseasonably warm day, and the children were still outside playing after supper when Emma and Miriam went to load the dishes in the buggy.

"Did you ever find that other bowl?" Miriam asked.

"No, I can't imagine what happened—"

But then she saw it. The bowl. Her eldest child, Mose, was sitting spraddle-legged in the dirt near Kyra's barn with the bowl on the ground between his legs. His younger sister, Clara, stood stock-still, not ten feet from him, staring.

Emma squinted, not sure exactly what she was seeing at first. There were two dark shapes, one beside each of Mose's legs, and in the tricky, slanting evening sunlight the two shapes appeared for all the world to be coiled snakes. Then one of them moved, and a slender head inched toward Mose's leg.

Emma ran wailing to rescue her child, but before she could reach him she heard footsteps and Domingo caught up with her. He grabbed her by the arms and stopped her in her tracks.

"Wait!" he said.

Emma struggled to break free, single-mindedly fighting to save her baby from danger.

"WAIT!" Domingo repeated, holding tight. "They're not poisonous. It's all right."

"But—"

"Trust me. Just watch."

Levi appeared at her elbow, and Miriam peeked around Domingo, holding Will. They all watched in silent, breathless amazement.

The bowl between Mose's legs was half full of soup, left over from supper. Oblivious to the adults standing right there watching him, Mose dipped a spoon into the soup and held it out to the snake on his right. The snake's head moved closer, and it appeared to Emma that his tongue actually flicked at the spoon. Shivering with fright, she started again to bolt after her child, but this time it was Levi who stopped her.

"Shhh," he said. "It's okay. Domingo's right—they're not poisonous."

Above the pounding of her own heart Emma could hear Mose's little voice.

"One for you," he said, holding the spoon out slowly, carefully, to the snake on his left. The snake's head moved almost imperceptibly toward the spoon, and his tongue flickered. It looked for all the world as if the snake was eating from the spoon, neither child nor snake showing the slightest sign of apprehension. Mose dipped the spoon again, holding it out to the other one. "And one for you." This one, too, appeared to crane his neck and sip.

Mose returned the spoon to the bowl, but the snake he had just fed followed it, his head poised above the boy's leg in anticipation.

"It's not your turn," Mose said, and gave the snake a casual bop on top of his head with the spoon.

Unfazed, the snake retreated, suitably admonished, and waited his turn while Mose fed the other one.

Miriam's mouth hung open. In a soft voice tinged with awe she said, "I have never in my life seen anything like that."

"Neither have I," Domingo said, "but I have heard stories."

Emma glanced up at Domingo. "You've *heard* of something like this?"

"Only in old people's tales. There's an ancient Nahua myth about a boy who charmed snakes. *Remember* this," he said. "Remember it well. If there's anything to the old legends, this one will grow into a very wise man someday—a man others will listen to and respect."

There was a riveting gravity in Domingo's words. His voice dropped almost to a whisper as he looked Emma in the eyes and added, "He will be a *peacemaker*."

Chapter 27

A deepening gloom hung over all the Amish as harvest drew to an end. November was normally a time of feasting and celebration, a time when all the sweat and toil and uncertainty was behind them for the year, the means for surviving another winter safely stored away in barns and cribs. Late fall was a time when farmers could finally relax and smile and enjoy the fruits of their labor.

But not this year. As soon as harvest was done they hauled entire crops to Saltillo and sold them for whatever they could get, sometimes selling by the wagonload. This year the end of harvest meant loss and defeat, the end of their community and the abandonment of all they had built. It meant parting, and a long journey to a whole new set of problems.

Ira Shrock led the first caravan. The Yutzys and Yoders went with him, after long and tearful goodbyes. Caleb stood in his yard, a terrible sadness settling on him as he watched the odd procession of heavily laden wagons and buggies ferrying children and farm implements and furniture slowly down the road and out of sight around the end of the ridge. The Bylers and Roman J. Millers parted the next day, leaving only the Benders and the Hershbergers.

Miriam and Domingo went to mass that Sunday morning dressed in their wedding clothes, the only fancy clothes they owned. Miriam pinned a small black scarf to her head because Catholic rules said her head had to be covered in church. It often struck her that the Catholics had nearly as many rules as the Amish—they just drew the lines in different places. She lit three candles when she came in: one for safe passage for the Amish who had already left, one for her family, and one for her unborn child.

The old warehouse where they worshiped had dirt floors and crudely made benches. Parishioners brought little rugs and towels for kneeling, to keep their knees out of the dust. Miriam was used to it. She had worshiped in barns all her life, though the services had always been held on the second level, the rough wooden floor scrubbed spotless. Nevertheless, the old warehouse made her a little homesick. Especially the light.

There were no windows. The only daylight came through the peak vents way up high. Father Noceda had nailed up shelves for lanterns and oil lamps, lending a comforting golden glow to mass. When Miriam was teaching school she found the lack of windows actually helped. A window, particularly on a bright fall day, was an irresistible distraction for most school-age boys.

But on this particular Sunday the absence of windows kept them from seeing the federales coming until it was too late. Miriam and Domingo only heard the hoofbeats at the last second, right before the barn doors burst open and Captain Soto trotted a standard-bred gelding right up the center aisle.

Father Noceda was standing up front, delivering his liturgy when Soto barged in. The sight of the federale captain trotting his horse up the center aisle sent everyone into a panic. Women screamed, and men herded their families toward the walls, knocking over benches and tripping over one another.

Father Noceda stood his ground behind the Communion table, hands clasped in front of him. He didn't move an inch, drawing himself perfectly erect and stoic, a commanding presence in his full cassock. His eyes remained on the captain, fierce and searing, as the horse trotted right up to the Communion table.

Another wail went up from the people as the captain's horse pranced sideways and Soto's booted foot shot out, kicking over the Communion table. Bread scattered, and wine splashed as high as Father Noceda's face when the table slammed down at his feet.

He never flinched.

"What is the meaning of this?" Noceda said, his fiery eyes conveying much more than his tone of voice. Red wine trickled down his forehead.

Domingo, who up to now had been shielding Miriam, turned to her and whispered, "Get to the door and get out. Hurry!"

"Where are you going?"

"I can't let him kill himself," he said, turning away.

Miriam started toward the open door, pushing people in front of her and relaying Domingo's words—"Get out! Get to the door!"

Behind her, Domingo scrambled over upturned benches, against the tide of the fleeing crowd, heading toward the priest. In front of her she saw a dozen armed federales file quickly in and spread themselves across the back. But the people ignored them, surging into the open center aisle and running for the exit.

She paused in the aisle near the door, watching the scene up front as frightened parishioners shoved their way past her.

Captain Soto leaned down from his saddle, glaring at the priest. "Article twenty-four of our constitution expressly forbids worship anywhere except in the confines of a church building," he said, and she knew from his voice that he was wearing that little evil grin.

"This IS a church!" Noceda roared, on the verge of losing control.

Soto's horse pranced in a full circle while the captain's eyes scanned the upper reaches of the old wooden structure. He turned back to Noceda.

"No, Padre. You told me yourself, it is a *warehouse*. You cannot have it both ways."

Most of the people had made it outside. Only a few elderly people now hobbled past Miriam. The federales fanned out around the walls and watched their captain, clearly waiting for some kind of signal.

Soto turned his back to the priest, and his grinning lips calmly uttered one short command to his men. "*Quemarla.*" *Burn it.*

Even from the back of the warehouse Miriam saw Father Noceda's smoldering rage burst into flame. He planted a foot on the edge of the overturned Communion table and hurled himself through the air. He would have speared Soto flush in the back had it not been for her husband.

Domingo saw it coming. With a running start he flashed through the air and intercepted Noceda, tackling him to the floor.

The captain's back was turned and he didn't see what happened. He was watching his men snatch the lanterns and oil lamps from the shelves and smash them against the walls.

Kerosene and lamp oil exploded into great rolling clouds of flame, instantly engulfing the dry wooden timbers.

Before Domingo could right himself the captain was gone, charging down the center aisle on his horse, nearly trampling Miriam as he galloped out the back door. His men bolted out right behind him, arms up, shielding themselves from the intense heat.

Flames climbed the walls, licked at the rafters. Black smoke rolled across the floor, blocking Miriam's view.

Over the rumble of the flames Miriam screamed, "DOMINGO!" Before she could draw breath to scream again, Domingo burst through the wall of smoke, running, stumbling, coughing, with Father Noceda slung limp over his shoulder.

It felt as though the three of them were shoved out the door by a roaring gust of smoke and heat, the dry old warehouse going up like paper.

Outside, in the bright sunlight, the scene was pure bedlam. Some people were running away as fast as they could, herding their children from harm, while others attacked the soldiers as they tried to get to their horses, flailing at them with whatever they could find, cursing and shouting.

Captain Soto, the only one already mounted, drew his pistol and fired several shots into the air, scattering the angry mob. Taking advantage of the smoke and chaos, Domingo mingled with the escaping crowd, whisking the priest away before the federales spotted him.

When Miriam looked back she saw black smoke pouring from the roof vents and flames lapping around the eaves.

Twenty minutes later Father Noceda sat at Miriam's kitchen table with a cup of coffee in front of him, rubbing his jaw and glaring at Domingo.

"It is a sin to strike a priest," he grumbled.

Domingo shrugged, suppressing a grin. "I chose the lesser of two evils, preventing a greater sin."

Miriam hadn't seen any punching. "Domingo, did you hit him?"

A cheerful nod. "Sí. He tried to get up and go after Captain Soto. It seems our gentle padre has a fire in his belly."

"I would have beaten that little . . . *What* greater sin?" Noceda demanded.

"Suicide. He would have shot you."

Miriam gave a nod, eyebrows raised. "He's right, Father. The soldiers would have killed you."

"Or, if you were lucky, put you in jail for the rest of your life," Domingo added.

"Maybe it would have been for the best," the priest said. "I cannot live like this."

Miriam sat next to him, rubbed his shoulder. "It was only a building, Father."

"Sí, but the only one we had. And you have lost your school, too."

"But I didn't lose the children. A building can be replaced."

"This *was* the replacement. Something must be done. If this Calles and his minions are allowed to rule much longer, there will be no church at all in this country."

"What *is* the church doing?" Domingo asked.

"Nothing! The archbishop does not support insurrection, but it is coming whether he likes it or not. It is time for me to choose between the church and my conscience."

Noceda sat up straight, and Miriam saw a new and terrible resolve in his eyes.

"I have seen enough," he said. "There is no longer any choice to make."

"What are you going to do?" Domingo asked.

"Fight."

"Fight? By yourself, with no weapons?"

"They are raising a rebel army in Jalisco, in the hills south of Guadalajara—even *without* the support of Rome. They call themselves the *Cristeros*. The commander's name is Vega— Father José Reyes Vega."

"I have heard of him," Domingo said. "They say he is a born general, a brilliant tactician."

"A genius," Noceda said, nodding.

"*Father* Vega?" Miriam said. "You mean he's a priest?"

"Sí. There are many ways to defend the faith, child. Father Vega will put the fear of God into the federales, and teach them humility."

"But you know nothing of fighting," Miriam said. "You're a priest."

"I wasn't always. I was a soldier once, and now it looks like I will be again. I'm tired of being persecuted by the federales. Sooner or later someone has to take a stand against this madness. If Vega will have me in his rebel army, I will fight."

"Then so will I," Domingo said quietly. "Someone has to watch your back."

"Domingo, you can't be serious!" Miriam cried, and her hand dropped almost unconsciously to her belly. "War is *never* the answer! Your father died fighting, and your sister's husband. Don't you think there are enough fatherless children in this family?"

He reached across the table, laid his hand on hers and looked her in the eye. "Miriam, from the very first I have never made a secret of the fact that I am a warrior. It is in my blood. You did not complain when I fought bandits to save your sister, or when I fought them to save *you*. Father Noceda is right—it is time to take a stand against these people. There is a time for every purpose, Miriam. A time for peace and a time for war, and if there has ever been a time for war, this is it. It is coming. It is inevitable. Good men are going to fight and die to free us from these monsters. How will I live with myself if I hide from the fight and let others die in my place?"

She couldn't look at him, because in her heart she knew he was right. He'd told her he was a warrior from the very beginning. On top of that she'd been taught from birth that a woman must obey her husband, and this was her husband. Her pacifist upbringing railed and cried and screamed warnings from the deepest corner of her soul, but she couldn't let herself listen to them.

This was her husband.

She pressed a knuckle hard against her upper lip for a long moment, willing herself not to cry. When she finally looked up her eyes were clear. She took a deep breath, let it out.

"When will you go?"

There would be no school the next day, nor any day until Miriam could find another place to meet. After breakfast Domingo went off with Father Noceda to "talk to some men about where to find this rebel army."

He was really going to do this. She had tried her best when they were alone in the night, but she couldn't persuade him and she would never ever try to force him. Now, more than ever, Miriam missed her family. She'd lived her whole life in the close company of a bevy of sisters, and times like this—times of deep personal crisis—showed her just how badly she needed them.

As soon as the men left, Miriam wrapped a serape about her against the chill of the November morning and went out to saddle Domingo's horse.

Riding down the main road through the middle of Paradise

Valley she saw the men of her family—her father and Harvey, her brothers-in-law Ezra and Levi and Jake—up near the barn, loading a planter on the hay wagon. Her mother and sisters would be in the house, packing.

She rode on for another quarter mile and turned into Emma's lane. Emma was outside in the bright morning light, hanging laundry on the line.

"You're washing clothes on the day before you are to leave?" Miriam asked as she swung down from the horse.

Emma shrugged, took clothespins from her mouth. "It's Monday. Anyway, we'll need clean clothes for the trip." But when she saw Miriam's face she dropped the clothespins into the basket and came to her. "What's wrong?"

Miriam broke down and cried in Emma's arms. She had not cried in front of Domingo. Not once.

"Domingo is going off to fight," she wailed.

"Oh, child. I'm so sorry."

Amish never fought, so all their experience of such a thing was secondhand. Back home, English men from Millersburg and Berlin and Walnut Creek had gone off to fight in the Great War, and it seemed the only news of them that ever circulated into Amish circles after that was when one of them was killed. Amish children grew up with the matter-of-fact conviction that men who went off to war always came home in a box.

In the deepest part of Miriam's mind it was a foregone conclusion, no matter what Domingo said. He was going to die.

"There is a war?" Emma asked.

"Not yet. It is coming."

"Maybe it won't happen," Emma offered. "Or maybe he will live! Domingo knows how to take care of himself."

"So did his father. So did Kyra's husband. So did Elliot Burgess."

Burgess was an Englisher from Fredericksburg—the only man the Benders had known personally who went off to fight in the Great War. He came home in a box.

Emma touched her fingertips to Miriam's belly and her voice dropped. "Did you tell him you are with child?"

Miriam nodded. "'All the more reason,' he said."

The sisters talked for an hour while they hung laundry and packed dishes into a wooden crate, wrapping them with towels and rags. It helped a lot, talking to Emma. Nothing she said would change the fact that Domingo was going off to war, but in times of frustration and grief it always helped to share the burden with a sister. It was as if Emma lifted part of it from her and carried it herself.

"We will pray for him," Emma said as Miriam mounted her horse to go home.

Right after Miriam left, Emma loaded Clara and Will into a little wagon, and Mose came alongside to help pull the wagon as she walked over to her father's house. Emma's instinctive reaction to this kind of news was the same as Miriam's—she had to talk to a sister.

Rachel was in the kitchen with the others, packing up. Emma hung back in the living room and made Rachel come to her so the others wouldn't hear, but it did no good. When she told Rachel the news, she recoiled in horror.

"Domingo is going to *war?*" Rachel said, too loudly.

Leah dropped a plate. Mamm and the others looked up in shock as a deathly silence fell.

Rachel's lip quivered. "But he'll be *killed.*"

It got worse. Now she saw Dat, standing in the kitchen doorway. She hadn't heard him come in.

"Is this true?" her father asked. "Domingo is going off to fight?"

Emma nodded.

"Against who? The federales?"

"Jah. The priest is going, too. Captain Soto and his men came to San Rafael yesterday and burned their church. Noceda was outraged. He said there's going to be an uprising, and he wants to be part of it. Domingo decided to go with him."

"They'll be killed," her father said, without emotion. "Who lives by the sword, dies by the sword."

Then he turned and went back out without doing whatever it was he had come in for in the first place.

Chapter 28

"We leave in three weeks," Domingo told her when he came home that evening. "I don't know how long we will be gone, but I'll write when I can. You can stay with Kyra and my mother if you wish—in fact I would prefer it. You will be safer there."

"Perhaps they can teach me how to be a widow," she said angrily, her back to him, flipping tortillas.

He came and put his arms around her. "I will be fine," he said. "I'm not some child who can't keep his head in the heat of battle."

"There was talk among the women in the market today. They say the federales are invincible. They say this peasant army is ill-prepared, that it will be a slaughter—shopkeepers with clubs and farmers with hay scythes against battle-hardened troops with guns."

He took her by the shoulders and turned her around so he could look into her eyes. "You must not listen to the women in the market," he said. "They know only of fear and waiting. In their need to shelter their children they sometimes forget the honor of their men and the fire inside them. Miriam, these *are* honorable men, fighting for a just cause—the freedom to worship as they please. Is this not why you came to Mexico in the first place?"

"Jah," she said, "but we would never have gone to war over it. There is always a better way."

"Is there? If no one resists them, how far will they go? If the federales persecute the Catholics, how long will it be before they come after the Protestants? The Amish?"

"After tomorrow there will be no Amish to persecute," she said.

He looked down at her belly. "This godless regime must be stopped, Miriam, at whatever cost. Would you have our child grow up without knowing God?"

"Would you have him grow up without knowing his *father?*"

Domingo chuckled, squeezed her. "I will be there for him, Miriam. And I will tell him how his mother's cheeks grow red when she is angry." His voice softened as he reached up to touch her face. "And how lovely she was when she came to me in the evening with a moonflower in her hair."

That evening Miriam cleaned her little house until it shined and then stood by the front window, waiting, watching. Her family would be leaving in the morning, all of them, and there was a very good chance she would never see any of them again. Ban or no ban, surely they would come tonight to say goodbye.

But no one came. She stood by the window until long after dark, until she knew it was far too late for a family who had to rise early the next morning and start the long trek to Arteaga.

Domingo came and put his hands on her shoulders, spoke gently into her ear. "Let's go to bed, Miriam. They aren't coming tonight. Tomorrow morning they will have to pass right by San Rafael on their way north. I will go with you, and we will be waiting for them on Saltillo Road."

Dejected, she moaned, "What if they don't stop?"

"Then we will wave to them as they pass by. Miriam, we can only decide what *we* will do. What your family chooses is up to them. It has always been so."

⸰

Caleb tossed and turned all night and finally gave up long before the rooster crowed. He got up and dressed himself, lit a lantern and wandered across the dark valley to the little grave-yard at the foot of the opposite ridge, where four small crosses stood next to a larger one under a cottonwood tree.

The air was still and cold, a full moon hanging over the mountains, so bright the stars faded and the trees left shadows. Never in his life had he felt such confusion. Nothing seemed right. He wanted to talk to Gott, but for the first time in his life he could not feel Gott's presence, even in the silence.

So he talked to Aaron.

"I guess this is the last time I'll be here," he said. "But I want you to know how bad I miss you—you and your brother both. I hope you found one another. I like to think so."

He sat silent for a long time, then with a great shuddering sigh he looked up to the heavens and cried, "I do not want to leave this place!"

But when he looked across the valley and saw lantern light in the windows of his house he forced his feelings back down into their proper place, got up, dusted the back of his breeches and ambled down the hill on aching knees. There was work to be done, and it would be a long drive to Arteaga.

John Hershberger took the lead in the caravan of wagons and buggies and hacks trundling out of Paradise Valley. He'd decided to abandon the farm, now that harvest was done, and take an apartment in Saltillo, where he might have better luck finding buyers. He would put his family and all their earthly goods—furniture and farm implements and buggies and wagons and cows and horses—on the train in Arteaga and then go on to Saltillo alone.

It was full daylight when they passed by the edge of San Rafael, and Caleb sensed the tension in Mamm, sitting beside him on the bench of the heavily laden wagon behind a team of Belgians. Up ahead he saw a trio of people standing on the side of the road as if they were waiting for a ride, and he knew who it was even before he drew close enough to recognize them.

Miriam, come to say goodbye.

Mamm touched his shoulder. "We must stop," she said. "It's not right to leave without speaking to her."

He didn't answer. Inside he was dying a little, unsure if his heart could take the strain of looking into Miriam's eyes, knowing it was the last time he would ever see her. He steeled himself, hunched forward, keeping a tight grip on the reins and his eyes straight ahead. He didn't plan to stop, no matter what Mamm said, but John Hershberger was in the lead. Up ahead, John waited until Caleb's wagon was about to pass Miriam and Domingo and Kyra, then halted his wagon, blocking the road. The whole caravan ground to a stop for no apparent reason.

Caleb's wagon sat ten feet from Miriam.

She was right there, looking up at him. Caleb refused to even look. He kept his eyes ahead, the reins in his hands. Mamm took one look at him and climbed out the other side.

The others came too—Miriam's sisters and Harvey, Levi and Emma, Mary and Ezra, Jake and Rachel. They poured out of their wagons and buggies and came running to Miriam, gathering around her while Caleb sat stone-faced, refusing to budge. His breathing quickened, listening to their tearful goodbyes and seeing all the desperate clutching and hand-holding from the corner of his eye. It was killing him.

Finally, unable to stand it, he climbed down and walked away, up toward the front, to ask John why he was holding them up.

John sat calmly in his wagon, smoking his pipe. He nodded when Caleb walked up, tipped his hat.

"What did we stop for?" Caleb demanded.

John suppressed a wry grin as he held up the corncob pipe. "I had to light my pipe," he said.

Busybody. A child would know he didn't have to stop a whole caravan just to light a pipe.

"Well, we need to get going again," Caleb said, his jaw working. "We have a long way to go yet."

Without another word he stalked back toward his wagon, but John turned around and called to him.

Caleb stopped, glared over his shoulder.

"She's your daughter," John said gently. "Do what's right."

But in that moment Caleb's anger burned, and he was in no mood to be told what was right. If John Hershberger hadn't been such an old and good friend, Caleb would have given him a tongue-lashing right there in front of everybody and told him to mind his own business. But he didn't. In his rage he headed for the little crowd gathered by his wagon, a single thought in mind.

I'll show you what's right.

His family parted for him, and he walked straight up to Miriam and Domingo. A hush fell. Miriam's hair was down and loose, and she was dressed like Kyra in a printed skirt and

275

peasant blouse, a shawl wrapped about her shoulders. It hurt Caleb to see her that way; it insulted him.

He didn't reach for his daughter or speak to her. He fastened a hard glare on Domingo instead.

"I heard you were going away to fight in a war," Caleb said.

Domingo nodded. "Sí, es verdad. We leave in a fortnight."

Caleb drew a deep breath. "May Gott have mercy on you. When the day comes that you lie bleeding to death on the battlefield, perhaps you will see the folly of your ways. I want you to know that when you are dead your wife need not suffer hunger or deprivation."

When you are dead, he said—not *if*.

"If Miriam can find her way back to us, and if she repents, we will forgive her and take her in. She will be welcomed. She will always have a roof over her head and food to eat. Perhaps in your last hours this will bring you some measure of peace."

Miriam hung her head and wept.

"Now let's get moving!" Caleb shouted, and turned away without another word. His daughters ran crying, and as he helped Mamm up into the wagon he could hear Miriam above the others, weeping as she turned toward home.

It's her own fault, he thought as he tugged the reins and the big draft horses lunged against the traces. *I did not ask for this. She brought it on herself.*

It took all day to get to the station in Arteaga, and it was nightfall before everything was loaded into cattle cars. The train pulled out the next morning, leaving only John Hershberger waving from the platform.

They were silent, all of them. The family was torn apart, even from each other. Morose and dispirited, they had all merely gone through the motions while they loaded what was left of their lives on the train, none of them speaking unless they had to. Though the gloom was common to them all, they kept it to themselves, refusing to share it, each of them lost in his or her own dark thoughts.

Even Emma was confused and disoriented. This was a new thing, as if Satan himself had ripped the family apart and built walls between them, and it frightened her. Emma spent the first day alone in a corner of the cattle car, comforted by the rhythmic clacking of the steel wheels, thinking.

They had all suffered grievous losses, Emma not least among them. She'd left behind the farm she and Levi built, their first home, where she'd planted a thousand trees, and where all three of her children were born. A great many dreams died when they pulled out. She understood loss.

But Emma knew that wasn't the source of this new darkness. An eternal optimist, she knew from countless stories in the Bible that dreams swept away by the hand of Gott would soon be replaced by new dreams, and brighter. Houses could crumble to dust and barns could burn, but her faith was not in temporal things. Gott was Gott. Life would go on.

They had lost a brother, yet Emma understood that even death was part of life, part of Gott's plan. The words spoken at a funeral always comforted her and brought her peace: the Lord gives and the Lord takes away; blessed be the name of the Lord. That wasn't the problem either.

It was her father. She'd never seen him like this. Caleb Bender had always been as dependable as the dawn, faithful and wise. Whenever the family suffered storms he had always been their anchor—even-tempered, patient and farsighted. It was Caleb Bender's vision that held them together. The Bender family could weather any storm so long as their anchor held.

But now Dat was not himself. Full of wrath and regret, his anger and impatience drove wedges between them all. Perhaps somehow Satan had found a crack, a way to reach even her father. Since leaving Miriam in tears by Saltillo Road he had barely spoken a word, and his dark fury was contagious.

Emma sat up late into the night talking to Gott, and the second day on the train she went to talk to her father. She found him sitting on a nail keg, staring out through the slats at a countryside painted in brilliant reds and golds as they traveled north into the hills of Tennessee. He didn't even look at her as she sat down on the floor and leaned back against the slats next to him. She reached out and touched his knee.

"Dat," she said, "it's not your fault."

He didn't react at all, and was silent for so long she was afraid he hadn't heard. But then he spoke, softly.

"I led them down there."

"You only did what you believed Gott wanted. There's no wrong in that."

He shook his head sadly. "Then it must not have been Gott's voice I was listening to. There's plenty of wrong in *that*."

"Why would you even think such a thing?"

"Because I *failed*. Because we probably won't be able to sell our farms, and everyone who followed me failed. Because the friends who listened to me lost everything—even children. Half of them left a child in the ground in Paradise Valley, as I did."

"There was an epidemic, Dat, just like the one in Ohio that took Amos. It's not for us to decide who lives and dies, or when, or where."

Still, he refused to look at her. "I was wrong. I led people astray. Gott didn't really want us in Mexico."

She fell silent for a moment, pondering this. "So the test of Gott's will is that we succeed at whatever we do?"

He looked at her now, but his eyes narrowed. "What do you mean? What are you saying?"

A shrug. "I'm saying maybe it *was* Gott's will—all of it. Maybe we weren't meant to succeed."

He turned away again. "Why would Gott do that?"

"I don't know. To test us? To teach us something? Why did He send Moses into the wilderness for forty years? Good things only teach us to be grateful. It's from failure, loss and hardship that we learn what we really believe. Like you—now."

He shook his head. "What am I to learn from this disaster, Emma? I'm going home beaten and embarrassed, poor as Job. What am I to learn from that?"

"I don't know, Dat, because Gott's questions are personal and I'm not you. But I know that somewhere inside you lies a question, a choice that must be made, and only you can make it. I'm thinking maybe the rest of your life hangs on which way you choose."

Chapter 29

There was a crowd waiting for the Bender clan when they arrived at the train station in Fredericksburg, mostly relatives and church members. John's brother met the Hershberger family at the station and took them home with him. Even so, the caravan up to Salt Creek Township ended up being far longer and more boisterous than the one that left Paradise Valley.

Looking around him, Caleb saw that the world had changed since he left. On the slow procession out of Fredericksburg he noticed more buildings, more people and far more automobiles than five years ago—and every one of them in a hurry. The pace of life seemed to have quickened in his absence, the rush and crush of the 1920s now roaring past the plodding Amish.

He hadn't forgotten a thing. Every pebble and pothole in the road, every fence post, every front porch and every barn lot was as familiar to him as his hat, as if he had never left. When they turned the corner and the old saltbox house came in sight at the top of the hill it brought a lump to his throat. He was home. Whatever hardships lay ahead, his family would be able to handle them.

What was *left* of his family.

Jake and Rachel retired to the Weaver farm two miles down the road, where they would live until they got on their feet. Everyone else went straight to the old Bender place. The Bender house was packed to the rafters that first night, but Ezra and Mary and their five children left for Millersburg first thing in the morning. Ezra had made arrangements to work for a cousin, making furniture. They would rent a house in town.

The following day Levi took Emma, who was now noticeably pregnant, along with their three children and all their household goods and farm implements, to a farmhouse up in Apple Creek. Levi's brother had decided to move to another church district and agreed to let Levi tenant-farm his old place until he could raise the money to pay for it.

Even Harvey would be gone within a month. He had come of age almost two years ago and started drawing pay from Caleb, saving every penny. The first Sunday back in Salt Creek Township the bishop shocked everyone by announcing that Harvey and Lovina Hershberger were going to be married.

Harvey, Caleb's last son, was *leaving*. Still in his fifties, every passing day left Caleb feeling more and more like a broken old man. His heart cried out to Gott, but Gott was not there. He felt no warming presence, thought no reassuring thought. Gott had turned away from him, disappointed.

It got worse. That afternoon he went for a long walk, alone, then came home to a house that was no longer his and sat down to a supper cooked by his daughter from food provided by his son-in-law. There were fourteen people around the long table—Lizzie and Andy with their six children, and Caleb and

Martha with Harvey, Ada, Leah and Barbara. On top of that, Lizzie was pregnant again.

Gnawing a chicken leg in the middle of dinner, Andy said, "We have a surprise for you, Dat. It's been a good year and the house is getting a little crowded, so we decided to build you a *dawdi haus*—across the lane by the buggy shed."

Caleb sat back, staring at him. "That wasn't part of our deal, Andy. I never said anything about a dawdi haus when I sold you the farm."

"I know," Andy said with a shrug, "but that was because you didn't know you'd be needing it. You were going to Mexico and not planning on coming back. But when a man sells his farm to his son-in-law that's usually how it goes—he gets a dawdi haus out of it. It's only right."

"But what about my girls?" A dawdi haus was always small, a retirement home for an older couple. There would not be room for Ada, Leah and Barb.

It was Lizzie who answered. "Dat, Ada will fall to us sooner or later anyway, and there's plenty of room here for Leah and Barb." She cast a mischievous grin in the direction of the two teenage girls and added, "At least until they get married."

Mamm blustered at this. "You shush, Lizzie. They're children yet."

"Mamm," Leah said, with marked indignation, "I'm eighteen, and Barb is sixteen now."

"Oh my," Mamm said quietly, gazing in shock at her two youngest. "You're right."

"Anyways," Andy said, "they're a big help to Lizzie. So what do you think, Dat?"

Charity. Andy was being charitable. It was hard for Caleb to take, but he was in no position to argue. If the farm in Mexico didn't sell he could not afford to buy his own place. Andy was master of this house now, and if Andy wanted to build him a dawdi haus he had no right to object. Caleb was no longer the man of the house.

"Thank you, Andy. That's very kind of you," he said. He tried to smile, but there was no joy in him. He felt old and useless, a grandpa being put out to pasture.

Harvey and Lovina were married in early December. He'd saved enough to buy a small farm a few miles to the west—just an old house on a marginal piece of farmland, but no one doubted that Harvey could make it work.

The whole family gathered at Lizzie's for Christmas. The entire Bender clan was there, and it felt just like old times. Even then, Caleb felt alienated and estranged. His heart ached, for he saw only the holes in his family.

Amos and Aaron were missing.

And Miriam.

And Gott.

Domingo had been gone for a month and Miriam still hadn't heard from him. She sat at the kitchen table in Kyra's house beside her mother-in-law, anxiously poring over the newspaper Kyra had just brought from town. The date was January 3, 1927, and the headline froze her blood.

UPRISING IN JALISCO!

"Domingo is in Jalisco," she gasped.

Kyra nodded, pushing a chair up next to her. "And Raul."

"Raul?"

"Father Noceda."

Miriam gave her a sideways look, then turned back to the column on the front page. "It says here they're calling it the Cristero Rebellion. On the first day of the new year a man named Garza issued some kind of proclamation saying, 'The time of battle is here, and the victory will belong to God.' It goes on to say that 'campesinos and peasants armed with pitchforks and clubs have overrun villages in Jalisco, but the cities remain well defended.' The government is sending in federales. They're saying this disorganized rabble will be hunted down and slaughtered when the real army gets there."

Slaughtered.

Domingo!

"Does it say anything about Domingo?" his mother asked.

Miriam shook her head, choking back her fears for the sake of Kyra and her mother.

"No, Mother, there is no mention of Domingo . . . or Raul," she added, with a purposeful glance at Kyra. "There is nothing about organized rebel armies at all, only of peasants conquering little outposts, but it's happening all over Jalisco. I have a feeling this is only the beginning. Maybe we will hear from Domingo soon. In the meantime, all we can do is pray."

"I will light a candle," the anciana said.

⟨⟩

Two hundred miles to the southwest, Domingo was bandaging a wound on Father Noceda's head.

"That went well," the priest said, grinning proudly despite the gash at his hairline. He was sitting on a stump, a rifle propped across his knees while he cleaned and oiled it.

"You were lucky." Domingo leaned over him, dabbing at the head wound with a bit of rag. "One inch to the right and

I'd be burying you now. Do you *have* to wear your collar and skullcap when we fight?"

"Oh, sí! They protect me."

"No. I keep telling you, Father, your eyes and your wits protect you. Your compadres protect you, and your rifle protects you. Wearing your skullcap and collar is the same as painting a bull's-eye on your chest. If you must wear them, at least cover them up. Hold still."

Noceda ignored him. "Father Vega knew exactly what he was doing, attacking that garrison. His tactics are impressive."

Domingo nodded. "A well-coordinated attack. It was over before they knew what hit them. But these were only *agraristas*—we will find out what our general is made of when we face real troops for the first time."

Noceda's eyes glowed with admiration. "Vega is a native, like you, and a priest, like me. Who would have thought he would make such a fine commander?"

The noise of drunken laughter drifted across the encampment, and they looked up to see Father José Reyes Vega himself heading for his tent, a giggling girl under one arm and a half-empty bottle of tequila swinging from the other. He threw back the flap of his tent and staggered inside.

"The girl from the cantina," Domingo said. "Father Vega may be a good general, but he's not much of a priest."

❧

More than a thousand miles to the north, Caleb spent most of that winter working on the dawdi haus, with help from Andy and a steady stream of neighbors and friends. The people of the church couldn't seem to do enough to help the "Mexican Amish," as they came to be known. People knew they had not been able to sell their farms, that they had left everything and come home virtually penniless after years of toil. Their undis-guised pity was a matter of some annoyance to Caleb. Nearly everything these days was cause for annoyance.

Worse, the Mexican Amish were treated like celebrities. Everyone wanted to hear tales of a foreign land, especially the part about the bandits. Some people were happy to oblige them, but Caleb never said much, and when asked about it would usually just mutter something like, "Farming is farming. It's all the same, except Mexicans don't eat cabbage."

People finally stopped asking him about Mexico, which he didn't mind at all, but he also noticed that no one ever asked him about Miriam. They offered condolences for Aaron yet never mentioned Miriam. Perhaps it was just as well. Already sometimes he had trouble remembering her face.

Chapter 30

Noceda was difficult to convince, but after the third close call Domingo finally got him to wear a slouch hat over his skullcap and button his jacket up over the clerical collar.

The Cristeros were becoming seasoned fighters, and Domingo's reputation as a fierce warrior was growing. They won skirmish after skirmish, but only against local militia, mostly farmers themselves. They didn't face the battle-hardened federales until late February.

In his first real test, at the battle of San Francisco del Rincón, Father Vega did in fact prove to be a genius. His Cristeros anticipated every move of the federal troops, countering and out-flanking with astonishing prescience.

By nightfall the battle was over, the federales utterly routed. Noceda and Domingo sat by a campfire, eating tortillas and beans from tin plates.

Noceda gloated. "I told you, didn't I? Father Vega will teach these federales humility."

A volley of rifle fire echoed from a nearby ravine before Domingo could answer, and both men looked up.

"What was that?" Noceda asked.

Domingo turned back to his beans. "Your warrior priest is executing prisoners."

Another volley echoed from the ravine as the campfire crackled and sparks shot skyward. The grin disappeared from Noceda's face. "Well, I suppose he has no choice. We can't spare men to guard prisoners, and if we release them we will have to fight the same men again tomorrow."

Domingo stared at the priest, but didn't answer. His doubts were his own. Noceda was an educated man, and anyway his logic was sound. Released prisoners would be armed again tomorrow, and Cristeros would die at their hands. It was war, and difficult choices had to be made.

A week later the Cristeros won another decisive battle against regular army troops. Four days later, in desperation, the federales hurled a company of crack cavalry against them. It should have been a mismatch—seasoned soldiers on horseback against an army of peasants on foot—but again Vega outsmarted them. He sacrificed a squad to draw the cavalry into a narrow rocky valley, where his men held the high ground on both sides, then cut off their escape route. The Cristeros suffered heavy losses, while the cavalry was annihilated.

Domingo and Noceda distinguished themselves fighting shoulder to shoulder in the battle, and as a result were awarded two of the captured horses.

They spent the evening grooming their horses in a stable at the edge of a newly conquered town. Noceda was ecstatic.

"The Cristeros are undefeated, Domingo, and Father Vega is becoming something of a legend. What do you think of him now?"

Domingo stroked the side of the fine bay horse with a brush. "My opinion of him has not changed," he said without looking up. "He still goes to his tent every night with women and tequila."

"But our cause is just," Noceda said, "and the general fights like a madman! We are winning the war because of him, ridding our country of these atheist dogs. Is it not enough for you that he serves God's cause?"

Domingo shrugged. "How does a priest serve God's cause and trample his vows at the same time?"

Noceda's eyes narrowed. "Do you not think the end justifies the means? Do you not think religious freedom is bigger than the petty indiscretions of one libertine cleric?"

Domingo lowered his currying brush and turned to face Noceda. "Petty? Raul, do you remember what happened after our last 'victory' over the federales? We didn't hear the shooting of the prisoners that night, and you said you thought perhaps Vega had grown a conscience."

"Sí. He didn't execute the prisoners."

"But he *did*. Martinez was there, assigned to the detail. He said our supply train was ambushed and we were running low on ammunition, so Vega ordered them to slit the prisoners' throats. *That* was why we heard no gunshots."

Noceda was quiet for a moment, then asked, "Are you sure about this?"

"Sí."

Some of the zeal went out of the priest's eyes then, and he spoke quietly. "But in the end, Domingo, what is the difference? Guns or knives, dead is dead."

"The difference is *honor*," Domingo snapped. "There is no honor in dying like a butcher's pig, and there is no honor in Vega. I was not always a Christian, and I remember well what people thought and said about the church. In Vega I see everything people have hated, for centuries, about the church. I'm sorry, Raul, but I'm starting to wonder about that collar you wear."

"That's unfair. Not all priests are like him."

"No, they are not. You're as upright as any man I have ever met, but Vega is the one whose name everyone knows, the one who is becoming a legend. He is our *champion*. And he is evil."

On a Sunday afternoon in March, right before planting time, Abe Detweiler and his family came to visit the Benders. Caleb and Martha had just moved into the dawdi haus. Caleb took Abe out to show him around the farm while Sarah and the children ate cookies in the dawdi haus with Mamm.

The bishop trailed a hand along the top edge of a fence, walking out the back lane as they made small talk about the weather and about Caleb's children. After a while there was a long pause, having exhausted all the news, and Abe Detweiler said, "People are worried about you, Caleb."

Caleb's eyebrows went up. "About me? Why?"

"They say you're not the same. You don't hardly talk, and they say you're . . . grouchy."

"Pfff. Grouchy. Have I been grouchy with you?"

"No, but to be honest you don't seem like you're at peace with yourself. Or with Gott. Is everything all right?"

They were walking along the edge of a field, angling down toward the pond. Caleb sighed. "I just don't understand, that's all." And then he told Abe Detweiler about the discussion he'd had with Emma on the train, about Emma's suggestion that Gott had sent them to Mexico to fail, to learn something. "But I've pondered these things all winter and I can't come up with it," Caleb said. "In the beginning I knew for sure that Gott wanted me to go to Mexico, but look what happened. I failed. I lost everything, and I drug others down with me. Tell me, Bishop, what am I supposed to learn from humiliation and defeat, from losing my children and ruining the lives of my friends?"

Detweiler thought about it for a minute and said, "Well, maybe it's all in how you look at it. Why did you go to Mexico in the first place?"

"So our children wouldn't have to go all the time to the consolidated school."

"Because of the new law—the government. And what did you find?"

"You already know. In the beginning bandits robbed us and there were no police to protect us. When we finally got troops, why, we found out they're worse than bandits."

"Jah," Abe said thoughtfully. "So maybe that's what Gott was trying to tell you. That one government is as bad as another."

Caleb crossed his arms on his chest and stared out across the pond, his eyes hard. "I know that now, but what does it profit me?"

Abe shrugged. "Caleb, Anabaptists have always been persecuted and we always will be, one way or another, because we are different. It was the government who chased our forefathers out of Europe in the first place. The trouble with government is that it is always run by men who seek power and fortune. A government has the power to take away a man's money, or even his life."

Caleb nodded, remembering the look of horror on Abe Detweiler's face when the rifles roared.

"But short of making a man angry and discontent," Abe said, "or putting him in prison, or killing him, they cannot change him. They can make a man a little safer maybe, but they can't change his heart or show him the right way to live. Only Gott can do that. Maybe Gott took you down there to teach you to put your faith in *Him*. 'We live, not by power or might—' "

" 'But by the spirit of the Lord of hosts.' I know. I didn't have to go all the way to Mexico to learn that, Abe."

They talked on through the afternoon, yet as he watched the bishop's buggy driving away that evening Caleb knew nothing had been resolved. Everything Abe Detweiler said was true, some of it even insightful, but none of it was new to Caleb. He had already thought through these things. He had searched his own heart and satisfied himself that he had *never* really put his faith in government.

Nor did he now.

Whatever Gott was trying to tell him was still beyond his grasp. Even the bishop couldn't put his finger on it.

Emma's words still rang in his head. *"Gott's questions are personal . . . somewhere inside you lies a question, a choice only you can make, and the rest of your life hangs on which way you choose."*

But how could he choose when he didn't even know Gott's question? And Gott these days was eerily silent.

Caleb's darkness remained.

Miriam grew heavy with child. By early April her daily walk to the post office in San Rafael became something of a struggle, and Kyra started going with her. Emma and Rachel wrote her regularly, and since the first of the year she'd gotten a letter from Domingo at least once a week. Emma's baby was due sometime in early May, the same as her own. Rachel planned on being Emma's midwife, which made Miriam a little jealous, but what really bothered her was her dat. Though she never talked about it, when she picked up the mail she always flipped through it immediately, looking for her father's familiar handwriting. It was never there, but she couldn't keep herself from looking, from hoping.

Coming back home one afternoon Miriam opened a letter from Domingo and read it as she walked.

"What does he say?" Kyra asked, trying to sneak a peek.

Miriam pressed the letter against her chest. "He says the things a husband says to his wife when he is away. Things meant only for my eyes."

"All right," Kyra said, backing away. "But what *else* does he say? Surely he sends news of how the war is going."

"You mean news of how *Raul* is doing. He says Father Noceda is well and he misses us all, that so far they have been lucky and only gotten a scratch now and then. But I wouldn't be too optimistic, Kyra. What Domingo calls a 'scratch' might be a mangled arm or leg."

Miriam stopped suddenly and pressed a hand against her swollen belly. "My niño is kicking," she said. "He'll want out soon."

She folded the letter and slid it into the pocket of her skirt as she started walking again.

"There is something about Domingo's writing that bothers me, Kyra. He has always been honest about the fighting and how things are going, but I sense a change in him. He's not himself. He seems dark and angry. Something is not right."

"Read it to me—the part you're talking about."

Miriam opened the letter again and read the last half out loud.

Kyra nodded. "You're right. He doesn't say it, but he is deeply troubled. Something is wrong."

⌁

Near the end of April word came down through the ranks that the Cristeros were going on a different kind of mission, and something about it filled Domingo with a dark sense of foreboding.

"We're pulling out in the morning," he told Father Noceda. "There are rumors about a train, a shipment of gold. Now I suppose we're going to be train robbers for God."

Noceda shrugged. "It takes money to finance a rebellion. All for the cause," he said.

Not everyone went, but Domingo and Noceda were among the handpicked company Father Vega led out in the gray light of dawn, a hundred of his best warriors on horseback. They rode north for four hours, and Vega himself chose the place for the ambush, a mountain pass where the railroad tracks made a climbing curve with plenty of trees and rocks on both sides of the tracks. His men used dynamite to blow a section of track, leaving a crater under disjointed rails.

Vega knew the schedule, and the Cristeros were hiding on the flanks when the train came along right on time. The curve of the tracks prevented the engineer from seeing the trap until it was too late, and sparks flew from steel wheels thrown desperately in reverse. Couplings clanked as the engine braked and cars jammed against one another, but the engine was still grinding forward when it nosed over into the crater and canted to one side belching black smoke.

The Cristeros swarmed out of the woods on horseback and on foot, shouting their battle cries. Yet before they could cross the fifty yards of open ground the doors slid open on two freight cars. Vega had warned his men there would be an army escort, but they didn't expect to be met with machine guns.

The Cristeros eventually secured the train, after a brutal firefight and heavy casualties. Horses and men lay writhing and dying all across the killing ground while the unscathed poured into the freight cars to finish off what remained of the soldiers.

Domingo was down, shot through the thigh. He took cover behind his dead horse while he cinched a bandanna around the wound. It was all over in minutes, and as the gunfire trailed off he struggled to his feet and went looking for Noceda. He found the priest not far away, unhurt except for a twisted leg trapped under his dead horse. Domingo freed the leg and they limped away to the shade of the trees, holding each other up.

Noceda was cinching a proper bandage around Domingo's thigh in the edge of the woods when a bone-chilling wail ripped the air. They glanced up at the train in the distance, where a squad of Cristeros heaved small, heavy crates from a freight car onto a wagon, but that wasn't where the wail came from.

In the middle ground they saw a group of officers huddled together. Father Vega staggered out from among them clutching his head, then fell to his knees, his face a twisted mask of anguish. Curiously he didn't appear to be wounded.

A bleeding Cristero came from that direction and hobbled into the woods near them.

Noceda stopped him. "*Qué pasa?*"

The soldier glanced over his shoulder. "The general's brother is dead. Shot through the head."

They stood together, watching as Father Vega leaped to his feet and waved his arms about, screaming orders at his officers.

Men with kerosene cans rushed toward the train, and for the first time Domingo noticed the passenger cars—two of them, full of civilians. Men, women and children hunkered in their seats, peering out the bottoms of the windows.

Noceda shook his head. "Father Vega would never do that. Surely he wouldn't do that."

But he did.

A chorus of terrified shrieks rose up from the passenger cars as the troops doused them with kerosene and then tossed the empty cans under the cars as they ran.

Vega shook a fist, shouting in an incoherent rage, leaping for joy when someone struck a match and the two passenger cars burst into flames.

Noceda didn't blink, nor turn away from the scene. He

made himself watch it all, made himself listen to the screams, his back straight and his jaw tight. Domingo understood. It was a kind of penance.

He leaned close to Raul. "Have you seen enough *now*, Padre?"

Father Noceda didn't say a word, didn't look at him. Slowly he pinched the crown of his slouch hat, lifting it enough to pull the skullcap from underneath, then dropped the cap on the ground beside his rifle. Unbuttoning the collar of his jacket he reached inside and tore out the white clerical collar. It fell to the ground beside the skullcap. There was a dead, lost look in his eyes as he turned his back and limped away, unarmed, into the woods.

Domingo took a long look around to see if anybody was watching, but all eyes were riveted to the burning passenger cars.

He left his rifle and limped after Raul.

Chapter 31

On May Day the Benders' church held Sunday services at the Weaver farm. Rachel was waiting by the barn when Emma and Levi rolled up. Helping her sister down from the buggy Rachel took one glance at Emma's swollen belly and said, "That baby will be born this week. I'm coming home with you today."

Emma smiled. "I was hoping you'd say that. As long as you're there I know everything will be all right."

"Are you worried? Is something wrong?"

Emma beamed. "No. Finally, for once, everything has gone perfectly. I guess that's what worries me."

Rachel carried Will while Mose and little Clara followed them toward the barn where services would be held. She leaned close and whispered to Emma, "It's going to be a boy."

Emma studied her face. "How do you know?"

"You're glowing. A girl baby steals your beauty for herself, but you're not missing one ounce of yours. This one is a boy."

"Thank you," Emma said, blushing.

"I got a letter from Miriam this week," Rachel said. "Her little one is due, too. Wouldn't it be wonderful if your babies were born on the same day?"

"Jah, it would." But a darkness passed over Emma at the mention of Miriam. "I only hope she'll be all right—without you there to take care of her."

"Kyra is there," Rachel said. "And her mother."

In the late afternoon when Levi and Emma were ready to go home, Rachel went to pack a few things. "I don't know how long I'll be gone," she told Jake.

"I do," he said. "You'll be gone until after Emma's baby is born and she's back on her feet. I'm proud of you, Red." He only called her that in private, and it made her blush. "Be safe. Do good."

That was the very thing she so loved about Jake. He always understood, always supported her. She kissed him then, without even looking to see if anybody was watching.

In Kyra's front room in San Rafael, Mexico, Miriam sat in a rocker, knitting constantly, mainly because it was the only thing Kyra would allow her to do. No more walking to the post office or anywhere else. Her time was too close.

Her needles came to rest in her lap as she stared wistfully out the window. "I'm worried about Domingo," she said. "There hasn't been a letter for ten days. I wish he was here. His last letter sounded so depressed, and then nothing."

"Domingo can take care of himself," Kyra said as she stirred a pot of beans.

"That's exactly what worries me. In his last letter he said it's different in a battle—unpredictable, men and bullets flying every which way. He said every man's life is in the hands of his compadres." Her needles went back to their clicking. "It's his *compadres* I don't trust."

Kyra glanced over her shoulder. "You can trust Raul. Anyway, you're in no condition to go looking for him again, and I wouldn't know where to start."

The needles clicked, the pot of beans bubbled.

"What's it like?" Miriam asked.

"What?"

"Having a baby. What's it like?"

Kyra laid aside the big spoon and wiped her hands on her apron. She squatted beside Miriam's rocker and took her arm. "It's the very heart of life, sister. Unbearable pain and unbearable joy all rolled into the same tortilla, and you cannot refuse a bite of it. Never in your life will you feel more alive than the day your first child is born. When it is over you forget the pain and keep only the joy."

"Oh, I hope so." But she sighed heavily. Just now there was very little joy in her.

"What's wrong?" Kyra said gently.

Miriam shook her head. "I don't know. Please don't think I don't trust you, Kyra. I do. You're the most capable woman I've ever met and I trust you with my life, but I have had a dark feeling about the coming days. A shadow lies over them, and I am afraid. I wish Rachel was here."

Kyra squeezed her arm. "You *have* a sister here, Miriam. I may not have Rachel's gift, but I love you, and I swear to you I will let nothing bad happen."

༄

Long after midnight on Tuesday night Miriam awoke in pain, profoundly surprised to hear her own voice crying out in the pitch-black silence. She tried to sit up, but the pains intensified.

Kyra came running in her nightgown, the golden halo of an oil lamp lighting her way. She knelt by the cot, the very one where Domingo slept before he was married.

"Miriam, is it happening?"

She nodded, clutching her belly. "I think so."

Another halo of light floated from the back bedroom. Kyra's mother.

"What do I do?" Miriam asked, breathless and panicked.

"Nothing," her mother-in-law said, smiling. "Try to relax. The niño will tell you when he is ready. Make yourself comfortable if you can. This is your first. He will not be in any hurry."

Kyra put on a pot of coffee. They lit the lanterns and fired the stove, then made themselves a small breakfast, though Miriam wanted none of it.

The pains gripped her like an iron fist when they came, but her mother-in-law assured her she was not yet ready. "Be patient. Rest. You're going to need your strength."

Three hours passed, and the window faded from black to pearly gray. The sun rose, yet Kyra and her mother seemed unconcerned. Kyra boiled water, ironed rags and blankets. Her mother knelt several times before the little corner shrine, lit candles and prayed to her crucifix. Several times between spasms they came and rubbed the aching muscles in Miriam's back, but they did nothing to make the baby come. Miriam's patience was wearing thin.

"The pains are still too far apart," her mother-in-law said. "Wait. Save your strength."

⁂

That same morning in a two-story, white frame farmhouse in Apple Creek, Ohio, Emma doubled over suddenly at the breakfast table, a look of shock on her face. It took her a few seconds to regain her composure, but then she said calmly, "I think it's time."

Levi panicked, spilling lukewarm coffee on Mose as he jumped up from the table.

Rachel gripped his shoulders to get his attention. "Calm down, Levi. I want you out of here, but I'm going to need some help. Take the children next door and tell Ida Mae to come when she can. Then go to work. We'll take care of Emma, and I'll let you know when it's time for you to come in. It'll be a while yet. Shoo!"

Levi's fearful eyes lingered on Emma, but after a moment he gathered up the children and left.

The Miller farmhouse was a quarter mile away. By the time Ida Mae let herself in, Emma was already in bed and Rachel was standing by the stove, ironing. A big pot of water was just beginning to boil. An Old Order Amish woman in her mid-thirties, Ida Mae Miller had seven children of her own, the youngest only six months.

"Are you sure the children will be okay by themselves?" Rachel asked as Ida took over the ironing.

"Oh, jah. My Mary is fifteen—good as grown. She'll look after the young ones while the boys see to their chores."

It was a good thing Ida Mae was there. Childbirth had never gone quickly for Emma, but this time it did. It all went smoothly, and two hours later she held a brand-new baby boy in her arms.

Rachel sat beside her, wiping Emma's flushed face with a freshly ironed rag.

"Big sister, I think you finally got it figured out. I told you this one was a boy, didn't I? Do you have a name?"

Emma grinned broadly. "Tobe. It was Levi's pick, and it suits him, don't you think?"

Rachel smiled, gently stroking the infant's face. "Perfectly.

He looks like a Tobe. As soon as we get everything cleaned up I'll call Levi in to meet his new son."

⸙

Finally, after the sun had risen and the oil lamps were snuffed out, Kyra and her mother sat down beside Miriam and timed the interval.

Kyra's mother nodded. "It is time."

The next hour was the most intense of Miriam's life—unbearable pain and exquisite joy mingled, exactly as Kyra had described it, and she could not refuse a single bite.

Then, at the very peak of her endurance, came relief. She lay back, exhausted, too tired to raise her head even when she heard the squeals of delight from Kyra and her mother. But her heart shivered when she heard that rusty little cry, and her strength came rushing back.

"You have a son!" Kyra said, her smile as full of sunlight as the kitchen window.

They cleaned him up and laid him against her, raw. For the first time Miriam felt the flesh of her own son warm against her, felt the pounding of his tiny heart, smelled that unique infant smell.

His eyes cracked open for the barest instant, and she grinned up at Kyra. "He has his father's dark eyes," she said.

Kyra nodded proudly. "And his cheekbones. He will grow into a handsome young man."

"What will you name him?" Kyra's mother asked.

Miriam's eyes went to the window, to the sunlight streaming in on a house devoid of a man. She was silent for a moment, but her heart poured out a desperate plea. She shook her head. "I will wait and let his father name him."

It was an act of faith, a hope that her prayer would be answered.

Kyra came and knelt by her cot, took her hand. "How do you feel now, sister?"

"Oh my. I feel like a woman who just gave birth. It was as you said. Already the memory of the pain is fading, but I hold the joy in my arms."

"But the other thing," Kyra said. "Now that the birth is behind you, what of the darkness that has plagued you? Is the shadow gone now?"

Miriam looked into Kyra's eyes and saw fear. She looked into her mother-in-law's eyes and saw the same. Both of them were waiting for an answer, and it suddenly became clear to her. They were worried that her premonition, this shadow of impending doom that had clouded her mind the last few days, was not about the baby at all, but about Domingo. They were terrified that some deep place in Miriam had sensed the unspeakable.

Miriam smiled. "The shadow is gone," she said.

It was a compassionate lie, but a lie nonetheless. Still, she was confused, because in her bones she knew—absolutely *knew*, without reservation—that Domingo was alive.

And yet the shadow remained.

She fed her nameless child and held him close, kept him warm—her little piece of Domingo. After a while she was able to eat something herself and then, completely spent, fell sound asleep.

When she awoke, he was there.

Domingo. Sitting quietly at her side, holding their son.

❧

"Rachel?"

Rachel glanced over her shoulder, and the worried look on Ida Mae's face made her heart skip.

"It hasn't stopped," Ida said.

305

A chill ran up Rachel's spine. For the first time in all her experience as a midwife she didn't know what to do. In a shaky voice she said to Ida, "Go find Levi. Tell him to get to the nearest Englisher house where they have a phone and call Dr. Beachy in Mount Eaton."

Emma chuckled. "Don't worry, child, I'll be fine. I just always have to do something to make things complicated."

"Ida," Rachel said, stopping the older woman in the doorway, "tell him to *hurry*."

Rachel fought valiantly, using every trick she knew and even inventing a few new ones, but nothing worked. Twenty minutes later she could see the color draining from Emma's cheeks, and she seemed tired and listless. Rachel's own breath came quicker, for the situation was getting desperate. If things didn't change very soon she knew how this could end.

The door hinges squeaked and Ida Mae crept back into the room. Emma lay quiet, her eyes closed.

"I found Levi," Ida Mae said, putting a hand on Rachel's shoulder. "He jumped on a horse, bareback, and rode away like a crazy man. Has it gotten any better?"

Rachel shook her head, said nothing. She would not voice her deepest fears in front of Emma.

"Is there nothing we can do?"

"Pray," Rachel said. And they did.

"I'm cold," Emma mumbled, "and so tired." The arm holding Tobe slipped a notch. She didn't object when Ida reached out and took the baby from her.

Emma lay still for a long time. It seemed like an hour passed before her eyes drifted halfway open and she caught Rachel in an unguarded moment of profound fear, staring at her.

Her eyes locked on Rachel's, her face ash gray, her voice high and raspy. "Am I going to die?"

Tears came to Rachel's eyes. "No, Emma, no. The doctor will be here any minute. You just hang on!"

But Emma shook her head weakly. She even tried to smile. "It's all right, child. I trust Gott. He knows what He's doing."

"Rest, Emma. Please don't talk. Don't use up your strength. The doctor will be here soon."

Emma's chest heaved, her breathing becoming labored. "Oh my. Levi's not going to understand this at all. Rachel . . . you must help him."

Rachel fought back tears as she pressed a hand to her sister's chest and felt the rapid heartbeat. "Emma, please," she moaned, her voice breaking. "*Please* don't go."

Emma closed her eyes and rested for a time. Rachel feared the worst until her eyes opened halfway and stared at the ceiling, at nothing. Her breathing came fast and shallow. "I can't see," she whispered.

Emma said nothing else, and in a while there began to be spaces between breaths. As Rachel sat up she heard the crunch of gravel in the drive, and the sound of a car engine. Ida rushed out and brought back the doctor, a plump man in his mid-fifties with glasses and a receding hairline.

"How is she?" the doctor asked as he set his leather bag on the bedside table and wiggled his stethoscope into his ears.

"Not good." Rachel gave him the bare facts, then took the baby and left the room.

She found Levi in the living room, bent over with his hands on his knees, trying to catch his breath. His hat was gone, his shirttail half out and his chest damp with sweat.

"What's wrong?" he asked, between gasps. He didn't even seem to notice the baby she was carrying, so great was his fear.

"You have a son," she said, holding the infant out to him. "A fine, strong baby boy."

He made no move to take the child. "Emma?" he croaked, his eyes full of anguish. "Oh, please tell me it's not Emma."

"The doctor is with her," Rachel said softly. It came out almost like an apology, for she was wracked with guilt. Midwife. She was no midwife and wasn't sure she ever had been. When it came down to it there wasn't a single thing she could do to save her own dear sister.

Levi grabbed her by the arms and gripped so tightly it was a struggle to keep from dropping the baby. Forgetting his own strength he drew Rachel up onto her tiptoes, and his eyes bored into hers.

"Rachel, do something! You get in there and do something right now! Don't you let my Emma die!"

Terror and grief and rage all ran together in his eyes, dredging up the unwelcome memory of Jake's face in a flash of match light that night in Diablo Canyon. Levi's whole world was spinning out of his grasp and there was nothing he—or Rachel—could do about it.

"Levi, please . . . you're hurting me."

Slowly his arms relaxed. He lowered her and then let go.

"Levi, I'm sorry," she wailed, openly weeping now. "I'm so sorry. There's nothing any of us can do now but pray. Come, sit on the stoop with me and hold your new son."

She finally talked him into going outside, where he held the child as if it were a stick of firewood, paying little attention. He reminded her of Ada, rocking himself back and forth exactly the way Ada did when she was frightened, staring across the road with eyes drowning in horror, chanting a brief prayer over and over.

"Please, Gott, please . . ."

They couldn't have been out there more than five minutes when the front door opened and Dr. Beachy stepped out onto the porch, holding his leather bag. Rachel didn't wait for him to speak. She saw it in his eyes. Gently she reached over and took the baby from Levi.

The doctor stood there for a moment, his kind face sagging as he mustered his courage, and then asked Levi, "Was she your wife?"

Levi rose on wobbly legs, shaking his head and murmuring, "No, no, no . . ."

"I'm sorry," the doctor said. "There was nothing I could do."

Levi stumbled past him into the house, moaning. Rachel stayed where she was and held little Tobe close, huddling over him as if she could shield his ears from the terrible wailing that rose up from the bedroom. In a moment she heard heavy feet clomping, running, staggering, and the slamming of the back door.

"The baby will need a wet nurse for a while," the doctor said.

Rachel nodded. "Ida Mae can see to that."

"Good. Rachel, I'm so sorry. I'd like to think things would have gone differently if I'd gotten here sooner, but it's just not true. Once she hemorrhaged I'm afraid the outcome was a foregone conclusion."

Rachel looked up, in tears. "There must have been *something* I could have done, *someway* I could have saved her."

He shook his head. "No, there wasn't, and you can put that thought right out of your mind. There's not one thing you, or even I, could have done. Not here. She might have had a fighting chance if she'd been in a hospital when it happened, but even then she might not have made it. This is a terrible tragedy and I'm deeply sorry for your loss, Rachel, but let me assure you—it wasn't your fault."

She nodded. He was a doctor, so he was probably right, but it was small consolation just now. Her mind was spinning, her whole world coming apart at the seams.

Emma was no more.

The reality settled on her like a blanket of snow and brought with it the first cold wave of grief.

Oh my sweet Lord, Emma is gone! What will we do without Emma?

Chapter 32

News of Emma's passing spread like a grass fire, and a shock wave of grief swept through the entire Amish community. It was a thunderbolt that stopped people in their tracks, knocked some of them to their knees, wrung gasps of disbelief and involuntary wails from others.

Caleb kept himself together for the sake of his family, though on the inside he felt hollow as a gourd. In small private moments his heart cried out to Gott, but his pleas only echoed and faded like a cry in a canyon. Amos, Aaron, Miriam, and now Emma. Where would it end?

Mamm collapsed when he told her. The girls put her to bed in the dawdi haus and stayed by her side while Caleb attended to chores. He kept his hands busy because when he tried to sit still the emptiness caught up with him and froze his heart. Now and then, puttering around in the yard, he heard an isolated wail, but he was never sure whether it was Mamm or Ada.

The women of the church swarmed to Levi's farm, and within a few hours there were six of them cleaning up the house and readying Emma. In the evening there were men who took over the chores as well, leaving the family to their grief. Later, a group of friends from the church would keep vigil all night, talking in hushed tones so as not to disturb the family.

Late in the afternoon Jake's buggy pulled into Levi's lot. Rachel saw him through the window and ran to meet him in the barn.

She was surprised to find she had any tears left, but when Jake folded her into his arms she wept all over again, instantly rediscovering her need for him.

"I've never in my life been so glad to see anyone as I am right this minute," she said.

Jake nodded, cradling her head under his chin. "I'm here. I'll always be here."

"I failed, Jake. I did everything I could, but nothing helped. The one time Emma really needed me, I failed her." She wept bitterly, her face buried in his chest.

"Hush, Red," he said, gently stroking her back. "This was not your doing. Gott's will is sometimes a mystery. If it had been His will for her to live, surely He would have shown you how to save her."

Jake held her tightly for a long time, letting her cry herself out. Finally she backed away, red-eyed. "Jake, you didn't happen to see Levi anywhere on your way in, did you?"

"He's not here?"

She shook her head. "He hasn't returned. No one knows where he is."

"I saw someone walking by the woods on the way in, but it was a long way off so I'm not sure. I'll go look for him."

It was full dark by the time the back door opened and Jake guided Levi through the house by his shoulders as if he were blind. Levi's eyes were vacant, his steps wooden. Jake took him upstairs and put him to bed, then tiptoed out and closed the door.

"Frightening," Rachel said. "Is he all right?"

Jake shrugged. "I don't know. I found him like that—sitting in the middle of the wheat field, staring at nothing. He never said a word. I don't think he's right in the head."

It was a long and sleepless night, a night of impossible paradox—Jake warm against her back while Emma lay cold and lifeless downstairs.

Jake's dat brought the church wagon early the next morning, and he and Jake set up the benches. Levi didn't get out of bed, and no one had the heart to force him. When they were done with the benches, Jake and his father went in and found him wide awake, staring at the ceiling. Levi was compliant enough, but he never said a word as they got him up and washed him and dressed him.

An endless parade of buggies trotted into the lane all day long, parking beside one another in a line that stretched down the service road for a hundred yards past the barn. They filed in one by one to glimpse Emma as she lay in the other room on a high narrow table with a white sheet draped across her from the waist down, pale lifeless hands clasped over her chest. Then they filed back out to spend an hour or two on the church benches with their friends and kin, reminiscing.

Levi remained in the room with Emma the whole time, but it was as if he didn't see her. He would shake a hand if it was offered, nodding grimly at the somber condolences, but he showed little emotion and said nothing.

Rachel glanced at him once, through the bedroom doorway, and whispered to Jake, "Where *is* he?"

A front roared through during the night, and the day of Emma's funeral dawned unseasonably cold with a blustery wind rippling fields of new grain under a cloudless sky. Trees swayed angrily, and even the birds lay low.

The weather seemed fitting in a way, for the same cold wind blew through every heart. For Rachel—for all the Bender clan and anyone who ever knew Emma—any kind of day would be chilled and diminished by the business of putting Emma in the ground.

She lay serenely in her box and listened politely to three sermons. Rachel sat where she could see Emma's face and tried not to take her eyes away the whole time, dreading the end of the last prayer because she knew what would come next. Throughout the morning her mind was filled with memories of Miriam and Emma. So much of her life was intertwined with the two of them—so many moments full of laughter and tears, shared secrets and desperate longings. So many words whispered in the night. And love. Apart from Jake, there had never been anyone so close to her heart as Miriam and Emma. In the naive optimism of youth they saw themselves together forever.

A picture bubbled to the surface of her mind, like a gift, a crystalline memory of the night she spent with Emma when she was laid up in Paradise Valley, a thousand years ago. Emma's voice came to her whole and clear, every word ringing with silver laughter.

"Someday, when we're just two old biddies rocking in the shade with a hundred grandchildren doting on us and bringing us cookies, we'll look back on this and say, 'Remember the night the Hershbergers came to Mexico, and we were piled up in bed like queens?'"

Forever, they thought, only yesterday. Now she was separated from Miriam by a thousand miles, and from Emma by even more.

Rachel wept when they closed the lid and tightened the screws, for she would never see Emma's face again in this world.

Caleb was numb. All of it went by in a surreal blur as he stood close enough to see the boards they laid in place over Emma's coffin and hear the dirt whumping softly on them while four hatless men sang the ancient funeral song, the wind tossing their hair into their eyes. Only Levi stood closer, and he never moved, never flinched, never shed a tear.

When it was over, and all that remained of Emma was an oblong mound of loose soil, the men put their hats on their heads, collected their families and filed silently out of the graveyard.

"The Lord gave, and the Lord hath taken away; blessed be the name of the Lord."

Later in the afternoon the Benders all gathered at Levi's house and the women began preparing the evening meal.

Rachel went out back to dump out a dishpan, and when she looked up she saw a lone figure walking away, passing under the oak tree out by Levi's cornfield, where the land sloped up to the woods at the far end of his property. His back was to her, walking slowly with his head down and his collar turned up against the wind. Even at that distance she knew the shape of her father and felt the bottomless grief in that bowed head, those slumped shoulders. She hurried back inside. In a moment she came out again, empty-handed, buttoning her coat. Trotting down the lane with her hands in her coat pockets she caught up with him at the edge of the trees.

She pulled up a few paces short and called out, "Dat? Are you all right?"

He turned when he heard her voice, came back to her and gently squeezed her shoulder. "No, I'm not. A man shouldn't have to bury his children—it's supposed to be the other way around. I don't know if I will ever get over this. I thought maybe it would help if I could get away for a bit by myself."

Rachel understood. She felt the same way.

"Would you like me to walk with you? Or I can go back if you'd rather be alone. I just thought—"

"It's all right. It was the crowd I needed to get away from. Anyway, today of all days, how could I refuse the company of a daughter?"

They walked in comfortable silence up the gentle slope, following a beaten footpath through the trees. The wood was only a few hundred yards deep, and they came out at the endless clearing where the railroad tracks passed through on the way to Fredericksburg.

Dat went straight up onto the tracks and began stepping from crosstie to crosstie like a child, hands clasped behind his back. Rachel kept pace on even ground, letting him have his space. He kept going for nearly a mile, his head down watching his step, his hat brim covering his eyes, so he was nearly upon the workmen before he noticed them. A clank of metal caused him to stop and look up.

There were two of them, next to a small handcar with their backs to him. One of the workmen bounced his full weight on a claw-foot pry bar, trying to break loose a stubborn spike. The pry bar slipped off and he fell down, busting a knuckle.

Dat moved a step closer, watching. The two workmen eyed him suspiciously, but they didn't speak.

"Try it from the other side," Dat said, pointing at the spike.

The one with the pry bar ignored him, cinching his coat tighter about him and peering up at the sky. Now that Rachel could see them clearly she thought the two men looked Mexican, but she didn't seriously entertain the notion until the man her father had addressed turned to his partner and spoke in Spanish.

"I want to go home," he said wearily. "I wish I was back in San Luis Potosi, where the weather doesn't crack my bones and we don't have to put up with these ignorant yanquis."

Her dat stared blankly for a moment, as if he hadn't understood, but Rachel saw the narrowing of his eyes. Suddenly his anger boiled over and he said, in flawless Spanish, "In San Luis Potosi you would live at the mercy of a rich hacendado. You would work all day in the scorching heat for a few pesos while bandidos steal your burro and federales take your women. The *jefes* politicos would burn your church and throw your priest in jail, and you would have to live in a mud house with scorpions and snakes. If life is so terrible here, why don't you go home?"

Both of the Mexicans froze, staring at him. "*Su español es muy bueno,*" the other one said in a hushed tone. *Your Spanish is very good.*

"Sí," Caleb spat. "Most of the ignorant yanquis around here speak Spanish very well. Perhaps you should choose your words more carefully." Before they could answer he turned his back to them and stalked away, back toward Levi's house.

As he brushed past Rachel, she heard him mutter, "Even here, I can't get away from it."

He kept up an angry pace, coiled fists swinging at his sides. Rachel had to trot to catch up.

"Dat, I think maybe you were too hard on those men. They meant no harm."

His face was red, his eyes like stones. "I'm sorry, it just offended me. Anyway, it don't seem right for people to be working on the day we put Emma in the ground."

She waited a while before she answered, letting him walk off some of the venom. But something had to be done. The whole world was out of kilter when Caleb Bender became irrational.

She finally touched his arm, gently, and said, "Dat, it's a weekday, a regular workday for those men. They were only doing their job. They didn't even know Emma—there's no reason to be angry at them."

No answer. Instead he kept walking.

She took his arm to slow him down and pleaded, "Listen to me. You haven't been right since we came back to Ohio. You never talk, you never laugh, and you're always angry. Everyone tiptoes around you, praying for the day you'll be yourself again. Please talk to me. What's wrong?"

"*Everything*, Rachel. Nothing has been right since we left Paradise Valley. I still don't know what Gott expects from me, and I grow weary of asking. Nothing ever changes. No matter what I do I'm still a broken old man who's lost everything . . . and now Emma. I've searched and prayed, and still I don't know Gott's question. How can I answer if I don't know the question?"

"What question? What are you talking about, Dat?"

His voice softened perceptibly, but he wouldn't look at her. "Something Emma said to me on the train, on the way home from Mexico—that we don't always understand Gott's purposes, that He uses our failures to teach us, to help us grow. Emma believed Gott was asking me a question, and she said the rest of my life would depend on my answer. Rachel, I still don't know what she meant . . . and her voice haunts me. I can hear her like it was yesterday."

"So can I. I miss her so."

"There will never be another Emma, that's for sure. I don't see how anybody can be so like me and yet so different."

He had calmed down a little and slowed to a more leisurely pace as they approached the woods where the trail led back to Levi's. It was easier to talk now.

"She *was* a lot like you, Dat. Emma was wise."

A faint smile came to his face, the residue of fond memory. "Sometimes a good deal wiser than I am, I'm thinking."

Rachel shrugged. "She just saw things different. It's like she could see inside people and know what they needed."

"You mean like Levi."

"Exactly. Emma was always so good with him. She said no one had ever shown him gentleness or patience, so she was gentle and patient with him. I'll never forget the day Miriam and Domingo drove up to help with the barn raising at Levi's. It was right after they got married. Miriam had on her Mexican clothes, and her hair was down in a braid. Levi wasn't sure what to do, so Emma took him off to the side and talked to him. She didn't think anyone was listening, but I can still hear her voice to this day. She said, 'Who has been forgiven much, loves much. Gott is love, and love forgives. Who are we if we don't do the same?' I saw the change come over him then. From that day on Levi treated Miriam and Domingo like family. Emma always knew how to talk to him."

A memory washed over her as they came out of the woods by Levi's cornfield, and she couldn't resist a chuckle. "Dat, you never saw that little table, did you?"

"What table?"

"In Emma's kitchen, in Mexico. After Miriam was banned Emma got Levi to build a smaller table the same height as their kitchen table, and whenever Miriam would visit, Emma would push it up to the end of the big table so Miriam could sit right beside her. She used to put a peso between the tables for a spacer. I'll never forget what she told Miriam. 'I'll give the width of a peso to the ban,' she said, 'and everything else to love.' Like I said . . . Emma had your wisdom."

She went on a few paces before she realized her father was no longer walking next to her. He had stopped several paces back and was just standing there, staring across the fields to the east, breathing through his mouth.

"Dat, are you all right?"

As she drew closer she noticed the faint line of silver at the bottoms of his eyes.

He spoke softly, with a kind of reverence in his voice. "Emma didn't get that bit of wisdom from me. It came from her mother."

"What do you mean?"

"When Mose was born, right after we moved to Mexico. We knew the timing wasn't right, and I wanted to—"

"Dat, you *knew*?"

"Jah, Rachel, we can count. It was your mother who talked me into letting it go—not saying anything to the church. Mamm's exact words were, 'Is not love greater than the law?' Sometimes, when somebody speaks the truth in just the right words it fits into you like a key in a lock, and you know it like an old friend. It seems to me, now, the best of Emma's wisdom came from her mother."

His voice broke with this last. He turned away from Rachel, and his eyes focused on the hill a mile away where Emma now rested. A relentless wind tugged at his hat brim.

"Rachel, you go on back to the house now, and tell them don't hold supper for me. I got some more walking to do. Tell Mamm I'll be back by dark."

☙

Caleb stood alone in the slanting light, in almost the same spot where he had stood among a host of others at noon. He held his hat loosely at his side and rubbed his bald head as he looked down on the mounded grave.

"Even now," he said softly, "my children teach me. Emma, I don't know if it came from Gott or out of your own true heart, but what you said was right.

"These last few months I been searching high and low, trying so hard to see what Gott wanted me to learn from failure, from losing my farm—a house that will one day crumble to dust and land that won't remember me. And all the while the real question was right there in front of me. I know now what made me bitter. I know why Gott turned His face from me. His Word is plain. I know you tried to tell me, Emma, but some people are so close, so like a man's own mind that he doesn't really hear them until they're gone."

He took a deep, shuddering breath, wiped his eyes on a sleeve and whispered, "But I hear you *now*, child. I see the truth, finally. I want you to rest easy, and know it'll be all right. I'll make everything right."

It was dark by the time Caleb got back to Levi's. The windows glowed with the soft yellow light of lanterns, and as he came through the back door he was met with the familiar acrid smell of kerosene.

Mamm looked up at him from a hickory rocker, and he gently prodded her shoulder.

"We have to get on home," he said. "I need to get an early start in the morning."

Chapter 33

Rachel stayed on at Levi's after the funeral to take care of the children until other arrangements could be made. Ida Mae kept Tobe. He would most likely stay with her until he was weaned.

Levi barely touched his breakfast. He said nothing, even to his children, his only expression an empty, stony glare. He ate a few bites and shoved the plate away, then stuffed a hat on his head and went out without a word.

Clara and little Will stood on a chair and helped Rachel with the dishes while Mose went to help his dat with the chores. Mose was almost five now and already a willing worker. When the housecleaning was done Rachel walked Clara and Will over to Ida Mae's to check up on their new brother.

"He's fine," Ida said, handing over the swaddled bundle. "No trouble at all. A sweet boy, and I'm thinking he's going to be a handsome little woodcutter."

Rachel pulled back a corner of the blanket and peered at the sleeping face. "He looks just like his mother," she said, and it brought a lump to her throat. "Oh, Ida, I miss her so. I can't imagine a world without Emma in it. To think of her now, up there on that bald hill . . ."

She could see it through the window, that naked green dome a mile away, wearing a white picket fence like a lopsided crown, and a thought came to her. It was a wonderful idea, and she didn't know why she hadn't thought of it before.

"Ida," she said, "can you keep the little ones for a while? There's something I need to do."

Ida Mae gave Rachel a dismissive wave, laughing. "Jah, what's a couple more? Go!"

Rachel ran back to Levi's, hitched a mule to the hack, tossed a shovel in the back and drove to the nearest woods. Walking the edge of the woods, the shovel on her shoulder, she soon found what she was looking for: an oak sapling, a little taller than she was, symmetrical with a good straight trunk the thickness of the shovel handle.

She smiled. "How about this one, Emma?"

It took her nearly an hour to dig it up, saving as large a root ball as possible, and then her ambition caught up with her when she tried to lift it. By the time she got it loaded on the hack she was filthy from head to toe, and smiling with deep satisfaction. It was perfect.

Driving the hack up the hill toward the picket fence she saw the lone figure of a man standing in the graveyard with his hat in his hands, head down. She hadn't expected to meet anybody, and after a quick, embarrassed inventory of her grimy hands, muddy feet and filthy sweat-stained dress she thought seriously about turning around. But when she looked up again she was close enough to recognize him, and she felt a little foolish.

It was just Levi.

The graveyard sloped gently down from the crest of the grassy hill. Rachel pulled up to the fence and set the brake. Levi stood silent beside the fresh mound, never once looking up at Rachel. Little Mose stepped out from behind him, a miniature copy of his dat in his wide-brimmed hat and bowl haircut. He smiled when he saw his aunt Rachel, and came running.

Rachel marked a spot at the highest point of the graveyard and pried off the turf with her shovel, setting it aside, then started digging the hole. Mose couldn't stand it. He begged for the shovel until she finally paused. Every time she looked at Levi she heard Emma's voice echoing in her head.

"Levi's not going to understand. Rachel . . . help him."

"Here." Rachel handed Mose the shovel, which was taller than the boy. "Dig me a nice deep hole, this big around, okay?"

He grinned from ear to ear and rolled up his shirtsleeves, just the way his dat always did. Mose wasn't heavy enough to sink the shovel all the way but he chipped away at it, undaunted, a little man.

She opened the gate in the picket fence and walked quietly over to Levi. His eyes were red, his face wet, and when he finally saw her coming he turned away at first.

But then he spun around to face her, wiping a shirtsleeve across his eyes, angry and defiant.

"I don't *care*. I won't hide *anything* anymore," he hissed, knifing a hand sideways, palm down. "No more secrets. Gott is not mocked. I sowed deceit, and look what I have reaped!" He choked on tears, even as he raged.

Rachel moved a step closer and reached out to touch him, but he jerked his arm away. Her heart broke for him, and tears left tracks in her own dirt-stained face.

Gently, with utmost compassion, she said, "Levi, Emma would not want you to feel this way. She never once blamed

Gott for any of it—she always just said she was not good at hav-ing babies. Emma would never have blamed anyone, least of all Gott. Levi, this is the darkest day of my life—and yours—and I don't see how any of us can live without her. But it was an accident. An awful, unbearable, tragic accident, *not* the hand of Gott. Emma was heaven-bound and she knew it."

"She couldn't know that," he seethed. "She could hope, but she couldn't know, and neither can you. That's just arrogant." Then his voice softened, staring at the grave, and he said mourn-fully, "You don't understand. We sinned, me and Emma . . . and we hid it."

"I know. I've known about it from the very beginning. There are few secrets between sisters."

A hard glare. "Well, it was a secret from the *church*. We never repented, and where there is no repentance, there is no forgiveness."

"Emma repented in her heart, and before Gott."

"But not before the church! And just like *you*, Emma thought that didn't matter." He jabbed a forefinger at her, and his voice rose in anger. "You're *wrong!*" he cried. "*Emma* was wrong! Adam and Eve sinned and hid it, and they were cast out. David sinned and hid it, and Gott took his son. Ananias sinned, and when he tried to hide it from the church he fell dead on the spot. If you sin and hide it, you *pay!* She was wrong, Rachel!"

He waved his arms, shouting now. "Emma was wrong about everything, *all* of it. We should have obeyed the church when they banned Miriam, but we didn't. We did things we never should have done."

Rachel shook her head, her eyes pleading. "You helped Miriam and Domingo out of *love*, Levi. How is that wrong?"

"It was disobedient. It was *willful!*" He screamed this last in rage, but then he broke down and crumpled to his knees. "And now I have paid with my Emma's life. I wish Gott would have taken *me*, but that's not punishment enough. I will live with this grief for the rest of my days."

He wiped his eyes on his sleeve again, and quieted. She thought maybe he had gotten it all out, but in a moment he stood up and turned on her with a new and frightening fire in his eyes.

"I will tell you this," he rasped, shaking a finger, "and it is a promise before you and Gott both. I will *never again* defy Gott's church! Sin will *never again* hide in my house! I will root it out."

His head tilted back, and his red eyes looked up to the heavens. "Hear me, Gott . . . as I have heard you. No sin will go unconfessed, no sinner unrepentant in Levi Mullet's house. Never again!"

Without another word he clapped his hat on his head and stalked away, leaving Rachel stunned. He vaulted over the little picket fence and broke into a run, toward home.

She wanted desperately to run after him, to plead and beg and argue—for Emma—but she couldn't abandon Mose. A breeze tugged at the stray tufts of red hair escaping from her kapp as she looked down at Emma's grave.

"Levi will take this mighty hard . . . help him."

Emma's words rang in her head. She had failed. Standing there, filthy and sweaty and bedraggled at the foot of Emma's grave, she felt as small and helpless as a child. Once again she had failed Emma.

But she had seen the iron resolve in Levi's eyes and knew. He was a man; he needed to be alone. Maybe in a few days, or months, or years, his anger would fade. Maybe in time he would begin to see the light—*Gott's* light—reflected from Emma's life. Heavyhearted, Rachel turned about and trudged back up the hill.

Mose had stopped his digging. Now he was sitting spraddle-legged on top of the dirt pile, waiting patiently for her to return, playing in the dirt. She watched him scoop a handful and hold out his little fist, letting the dirt sift through his fingers and fall next to his left knee, play-talking to himself as he did it. As Rachel came through the gate he scooped dirt with his other fist, held it out and let it rain down beside his right knee.

"And some for you," he said cheerfully.

Good, she thought. Either he hadn't heard his father or didn't understand. Either way, he seemed perfectly at peace, unperturbed by the storm around him.

Children, she thought, shaking her head. *They are the most amazing creatures.*

She picked up the shovel and went back to work.

Chapter 34

In the late afternoon, after being cooped up with the baby all day, Miriam laid him down and pressed a hand against the small of her aching back. "I need to get out for a bit and stretch my legs," she told him, smiling. Wiggling his hands and feet, he smiled back. There had been no word from Rachel or Emma in almost two weeks, so she left the infant with Kyra and walked briskly to the little adobe post office on the main street at the other end of San Rafael.

They were about to close up for the day, but the postman handed her a letter and then locked the door behind her. She turned toward home, her attention on the envelope in her hands—a letter from Rachel—but before she could open it she heard the distant sound of heavy hooves in the dirt street and glanced over her shoulder.

What she saw was impossible, like something out of a dream—a pair of Belgian draft horses pulling a farm wagon. Her heart stuttered, her fingers flew to cover her mouth and she took an involuntary step backward, for she knew the horses, the shape of the wagon. Even at a distance she knew the sil-houette of the solitary driver, the cut of his hat and the slope of his shoulders.

Dat.

He was the very last person on earth she expected to see in San Rafael, well over a thousand miles from Salt Creek Town-ship, unannounced.

She waited, hardly daring to breathe, clutching the envelope too tightly in her hands.

When he came abreast of her he pulled up on the reins and the horses came to a shuddering stop. In that moment, when she first looked into his eyes, she knew something had changed.

There was a palpable sadness in him, but something else, too. He looked at her in a way she hadn't seen since she mar-ried Domingo. The anger was gone, and he looked at her as if she was his daughter.

He patted the seat beside him, and she climbed up.

"That letter," he said, nodding at the unopened envelope in her hands. "Is that Rachel's handwriting?"

She glanced down at it. "Jah."

"Don't open it yet. Better you hear it from me." He took a deep breath and hung his head. "I have terrible news."

Miriam wept bitterly, sitting beside her father, his arm around her, consoling. In a little while, when she could speak, she looked up at him with swollen eyes.

"You came all this way just to tell me this?" she asked.

He thought for a second and said, "No, not *just* to tell you, but partly because of it. In a way it was Emma who sent me here. She was the one who opened my eyes. We have her to thank when we see her again."

We, he said, as if he thought Miriam might still one day find herself in heaven. Emma had indeed wrought a miracle.

"You've changed," she said.

He nodded. Then, as if he needed someplace to focus his attention while he talked, he clucked at the horses and tugged on the reins. They surged ahead at a slow walk.

"You are my daughter, Miriam, and I love you as I love all my children. I think maybe only a powerful love can fire so great an anger, so great a disappointment. But anger is sin, and disappointment is only selfish.

"I am bound by the rules of the church to uphold the ban against you—I made a vow, and I will not break it. But I am also bound by love, as Emma was.

"The church says I cannot eat your food, or accept a gift from you, or give one, or do business with you. Simple rules, really. But Gott has taught me that I cannot be whole myself unless I forgive, so in my heart I forgive you, Miriam. Completely and forever. You are my child."

The wagon rattled slowly on. Only now, when he had said his piece, did he turn his face to her. It was a sad smile, but a smile nonetheless.

The shadows were stretching across the main street, though it was still daylight. Daylight or not, public place or not, Miriam leaned close, kissed her father gently on the cheek and wrapped her arms around him.

A few minutes later he started to pull in beside her little house when she stopped him.

"Go on up to Kyra's barn," she said. "You can put the horses away there while I go in and break the news to Kyra and her mother."

"Kyra and her mother," he repeated softly, a note of concern in his voice. "What about Domingo?"

"Oh jah, I forgot to tell you! He came home safe and sound . . . almost. He was wounded—*again*—but not too bad this time. He's out limping around in the bean field."

Caleb unhitched the team and put them away, pitching a little hay in their stalls and making sure they had food and water. Then he gave them a quick brushing, for they had put in a long hard day without complaint. When he turned to go, Domingo was standing in the doorway of the barn, backlit by the setting sun.

Neither man moved. Domingo just stood there with his hands at his sides, his eyes full of suspicion, watching. He nodded slowly.

"Señor Bender."

"So the war is over?"

A shrug. "For me."

"It's good to see you again. I was afraid I would not."

Domingo's head tilted. "Afraid? The last time we met it sounded like you would be *happy* for me to die in battle so you could have your daughter back."

Caleb's eyes wandered. "The last time we met that might have been true, but I am not the same man I was then. Riding down here alone on the train I have had plenty of time to think about these things—about the laws of Gott and the laws of man, whether it's right for a girl to follow her heart or for a man to take up arms to defend those he loves. Mexico is a different world, with different rules—a world where, as you said, a man must fight or die—and in this world I have only seen you act with honor and courage. You have always treated me with respect and done what you believed was right. Countless times I used you and your guns to protect my family, and several times you have risked your life to save my daughters from a terrible fate, so how is it right for me to judge you now? Judgment is for Gott alone. It is not my place. I was wrong and I ask your forgiveness."

Domingo still had not moved. He stood ten feet away, staring. "You would ask forgiveness from the man who took your daughter from you?"

Caleb closed the gap between them. Stopping an arm's length away he looked Domingo in the eye and said, "The man who marries my daughter is my *son*. I would ask forgiveness from my son."

He held out his hand, but Domingo ignored it and wrapped him in a fierce hug.

"In Mexico we are not afraid to embrace," Domingo said, and kissed his cheek. "Welcome to Mexico, my father."

Walking from the barn to the house Caleb told Domingo about Emma's passing, and they shared a private moment of grief.

"It just doesn't seem possible," Domingo said. "Emma, gone. She was a wonderful woman and a good friend. The world will miss her badly. And Levi! How will Levi ever live without her?"

Caleb shook his head. "I don't know. I fear for him."

◦◦

Miriam was huddled in the living room with Kyra and her mother when she heard the back door open and saw her father and Domingo coming in from the barn. Rising, she dried her eyes and went to her husband.

"*Él me ha perdonado,*" she said with a proud glance at her father. *He has forgiven me.*

A rusty cry came from the bedroom. Miriam hurried out and came back carrying her baby. "Dat," she said, holding the infant out to him, "we want you to meet your new grandson."

Caleb held the baby timidly in his work-roughened hands

as if the child were made of glass, yet she noticed he was careful to support the head. He'd learned that much from Mamm.

"He's a *beautiful* boy," Caleb said, beaming. "What is his name?"

Miriam glanced at Domingo, who nodded slightly, a trace of a smile wrinkling the corners of his eyes.

"Caleb, Father. His name is Caleb."

Kyra went back and forth from the kitchen, cooking supper while Miriam sat with her dat in the living room, catching up. Miriam felt a little ashamed at first because any other time she would have been helping Kyra, but not today. Her father was allowed to eat Kyra's cooking, not hers. There was only one table in the kitchen, so when everything was ready she had Kyra serve up separate bowls and leave hers on the counter. Miriam remained standing by the rough-plank counter as the others seated themselves around the table. All things considered, it seemed a trivial price to pay for having her father back.

Kyra asked Caleb if he would like to give thanks, but as he was about to bow his head he looked up at Miriam. A sadness came over him and he shook his head.

"I cannot do this," he said quietly, pushing his chair back. Miriam had no idea what he was up to until he went across the living room to the little shrine in the corner underneath the hanging crucifix and began to remove the candles from the table. There was a small shelf fastened to the wall, and as he started to place the candles on it he looked over his shoulder at Kyra.

"Lo siento, Kyra," he said. "I should ask your permission. Is it all right for me to do this?"

There were tears in Kyra's eyes. "If you're doing what I think you're doing, Señor Bender, it is *more* than all right. Christ is smiling."

Caleb lifted the little table and carried it to the kitchen. He fished a peso from his pocket and used it for a spacer as he pushed the two tables together, then brought Miriam's plate and placed it on the smaller one.

"Here, daughter," he said. "You sit here, next to me."

They were halfway through the meal when Father Noceda came in, fixed himself a plate and sat down beside Kyra.

"You're not wearing your collar," Caleb said. "And you look like you've been working."

"Sí, I have left the priesthood," Noceda answered, shoveling beans into his mouth and chasing them with a bite of corn bread. Hard work had apparently given him an appetite.

"What happened? Did the troops finally get to be too much of a problem for you?"

Noceda shook his head, swallowing. "No, the troops pulled out a month ago, reassigned to the fighting in the west. It was the Cristeros who changed my mind." He fairly spat the word *Cristeros* as if it were distasteful to him. He cast a warm glance in Domingo's direction and added, "A wise friend has taught me that the kingdom of God is not to be found in buildings, or gold, or armies, or presidential *palacios*. It is in the hearts of peaceful men, trying to feed their families."

Caleb's eyebrows went up. "You learned this from fighting? Perhaps there is wisdom in war after all."

Noceda grinned. "Perhaps. So, Señor Bender, how long will you be staying?"

"Only a few days. I'm afraid I will have to get someone to take me to Arteaga, though. I think my mare is coming up lame, and the stallion won't be able to pull the wagon by himself."

Miriam turned, stared at him. "Dat, there's nothing wrong with that mare. She walks fine."

335

"I been working horses for forty years, child. I think I know when one of them needs a rest. Anyway, Kyra, I was wondering if I could leave them here with you. And the wagon too, I guess."

His request hung in the air for a silent, awkward moment. It was Domingo who finally said what they were all thinking.

"Señor Bender, we only have a tiny little pasture, and it is poor. It is barely enough for our own animals. How will we feed a pair of draft horses?"

Miriam held her tongue, waiting. She knew her father well enough to know he would never make such an imposition. He was up to something.

Caleb wiped his mouth on a napkin. "What you need is more pasture. Perhaps a bigger place. I happen to have a farm for sale."

Kyra's face darkened. "We cannot afford your place, Señor Bender. You know this."

"But I've been trying to sell it for months and no one has made an offer. Not one. Rich Mexicans are selling, not buying, and the poor can't afford it. The Amish won't come because there is no church, and Englishers won't come because of all the fighting. I can't keep paying taxes on a place that produces nothing, so I'm thinking the best thing I can do is sell it to you at a discount."

"How much?" Kyra asked, clearly skeptical.

"A hundred pesos," he said.

"No, I don't mean the discount. I mean what is your price?"

"A hundred pesos." He didn't blink.

Dead silence. Kyra's mouth fell open. "Señor Bender, you are loco. You have completely lost your—"

Caleb raised a palm to interrupt her, then said rather gruffly, "There's no use trying to talk me down, Kyra. That's my final price and I won't take a peso less. Take it or leave it."

Miriam cleared her throat. "Kyra," she said very softly, "give him the hundred pesos."

Kyra frowned at her, openmouthed. "But, Miriam, the *out-house* is worth more than that. It's a two-hundred-acre farm with an irrigation system, a big house, a barn—"

Miriam cut her off. "Kyra, do you not see what my father is doing? He can't do business with me or my husband. Give him the money, por favor."

Caleb pulled the deed from his coat pocket, unfolded it and laid it on the table.

"I got this from Hershberger, in Saltillo," he said, and shot the tiniest little grin at Miriam.

She understood then. This was no sudden impulse. He'd been planning it the whole time.

Kyra got up, went to her bedroom and came back with a stack of coins. She set them on the deed. "Thirty-two pesos. It's all I have."

Kyra's mother went out for a moment and brought back seventeen more pesos to add to the pile.

"Miriam, how much do we have?" Domingo asked.

Miriam pulled a leather pouch from her dress pocket and emptied it onto the table. Four coins, ten pesos each.

"A loan," Domingo said to Kyra. "That makes it *your* money."

"A total of eighty-nine pesos, if I'm counting right," Raul Noceda said. Then he emptied his own pockets and dropped ten more pesos on the pile. "This is everything I have. My job doesn't pay very well, and my widow's mite still leaves you a peso short."

"A hundred pesos," Caleb said flatly. "My price is my price."

They all stared at Caleb, who didn't budge. Again it was Domingo who broke the silence.

"What do we do now, Dat? There is no more."

"It's only one peso," Caleb said. "Look around—you can find a peso anywhere. People drop coins all the time. Maybe there's one on the floor."

Kyra frowned indignantly. "Señor Bender, I assure you I sweep my floor every—"

She was interrupted by the rattling of dishes, followed by a small *clink* as Caleb quickly withdrew his hand from the edge of Miriam's table. Raul Noceda chuckled as he reached under the table, picked up the peso from the floor and dropped it onto the pile.

Without a word Caleb raked the money and put it in his pocket. Then he signed over the deed and reached out to shake Kyra's hand.

"There. Now you should be able to feed my horses until I come back for them . . . in a year. Maybe two," he said with a wry grin. "They're very good horses, a breeding pair in their prime. If I were you—"

"I think we get the idea," Domingo said.

"You know, Domingo, that reminds me. If nobody stole it yet, there's a broken plow the Yutzys left behind in their barn. With a little elbow grease, maybe you could mend it."

After dinner Caleb went out back to stretch his legs. Propping a foot on the fence behind the garden he stopped to admire the sunset. The sun had sunk into the mountains, leaving streaks of blood red and royal purple smeared across the whole wide horizon, and jagged mountains silhouetted black in the foreground. Behind him there were already a few stars winking against black velvet.

He heard soft footsteps. Miriam came to him quietly, taking his arm and watching with him in silence for a while.

Finally she said, "Dat, I can't thank you enough for what you've done. You can't even begin to imagine how much this means to me."

338

His eyes stayed on the horizon, content. He was whole now, perfectly at peace.

"It was nothing," he said. "I would have lost it anyway. This way at least I got something out of it."

She glanced up at him, her brow furrowed in confusion. "You mean the farm? Jah, thank you for that, too."

His head tilted down, grinning at his feet as he laughed at himself, but also at the daughter he thought he had lost—a daughter whose mind was so like his.

"Domingo was right," he said softly. "The kingdom of Gott is in the heart. It's not important *where* we live, but *how*."

She tightened her grip on his arm. Her touch was warm, his daughter.

"I need to borrow your oxcart in the morning," he said. "Would you like to go with me?"

"Where?"

"Paradise Valley. I want to tend Aaron's grave. And Kyra's garden tells me there hasn't been much rain lately," he said, glancing over his shoulder. "We'll need to water Emma's trees."

Acknowledgments

THE DAUGHTERS OF CALEB BENDER is my first series fiction, as all my previous efforts have been stand-alone novels. It's also my first historical, the first time I've written extensively from a female point of view, and the first time I (or likely anyone else) has set an Amish series in Mexico. The process has stretched and challenged me, and without the help of a lot of people I'm certain such a massive undertaking would have been entirely impossible. I could not have done it without the following people:

My wife, Pam, who, besides being an extra pair of eyes, has given me the ability to create believable women. For me, a woman's mind is a terrifying landscape, where I would never dare to venture alone and unescorted.

My father, Howard Cramer, whose Amish upbringing has supplied me with a wealth of authentic details and priceless anecdotes.

My cousin Katie Shetler, who tried very patiently to help me understand the Amish mind-set, and sometimes even succeeded. Any glaring blunders are entirely my own.

Marian Shearer, a local writer born and raised in Mexico, who corrected my Spanish and graciously shared her encyclopedic knowledge of Mexican life, culture and geography.

My old friend Larry McDonald, who has been and continues to be a constant source of support and encouragement.

Lori Patrick, a freelance editor who not only gave me honest feedback and some insights on midwifery but also wrote the back cover copy.

A host of other friends too numerous to list (but you know who you are), who helped me shape early drafts through brainstorming sessions and fireside chats.

My editor, Luke Hinrichs, both cheerleader and coach, who brings all the various aspects of writing, editing, cover art and marketing together into a cohesive whole.

My agent, Janet Kobobel Grant, a keen-eyed editor and wise counselor.

Last, but certainly not least, this work owes a great deal to a book by David Luthy titled *The Amish in America: Settlements That Failed, 1840–1960*. To my knowledge, it is the only comprehensive written record of the Paradise Valley settlement, and it was instrumental in creating the backdrop for this novel.

About the Author

Dale Cramer is the author of the bestselling and critically acclaimed novel *Levi's Will*, based on the story of Dale's father, a runaway Amishman. Dale's series, THE DAUGHTERS OF CALEB BENDER, is based on an Amish colony in the mountains of Mexico, where three generations of his family lived in the 1920s. Dale lives in Georgia with his wife of thirty-seven years, two sons and a Bernese Mountain Dog named Rupert.

For more information about the author and his books, visit his website at DaleCramer.com. Or readers may correspond with Dale by writing to P.O. Box 25, Hampton, GA 30228.

More Amish Fiction From Dale Cramer

For more on Dale and his books, visit dalecramer.com.

As his son's life hangs in the balance, Will is forced to return to his father's Amish farm—a place he fled many years ago. Can he reconcile three generations of past events before it's too late?

Levi's Will

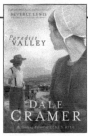

When new laws take away their freedom, one Amish community seeks religious sanctuary in Mexico. But is the road ahead more dangerous than what they left behind?

Paradise Valley
THE DAUGHTERS OF CALEB BENDER #1

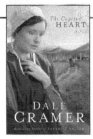

With the constant threat of danger looming over her beloved, displaced Amish community, is she willing to sacrifice everything for a man she's forbidden to love?

The Captive Heart
THE DAUGHTERS OF CALEB BENDER #2